I am Nicki Chim, a forensic blood expert like no other . . .
I do not test blood. I taste it.
I do not collect samples. I drink them.
For I am a vampire.

The study of blood is my life, or unlife, if you prefer. Contrary to all the legends and myths about hematomans, we're sensitive creatures, able to taste disease, chemical influences, and even mark blood type. We share a symbiosis with humans in that regard. I can tell the exact bouquet of the individual on whom I feed. In my own clan of bloodletters, I can usually figure out immediately whose been abusing himself by the flavor of the drink. Spectral array analysis can't be faster than me in determining what is in a person's bloodstream.

I smoothed back my long, straight hair with one hand as I made a small incision at the victim's ankle. A bubble of blood trickled out and I caught it on my forefinger.

Glancing around, I saw that no one paid me any attention, so I tasted it. . . .

The Winter Man
The stunning, brilliantly original thriller
from newcomer
Denise Vitola

The Winter Man

DENISE VITOLA

BERKLEY BOOKS, NEW YORK

THE WINTER MAN

A Berkley Book / published by arrangement with
the author

PRINTING HISTORY
Berkley edition / November 1995

ISBN: 0-425-15055-0

BERKLEY®
Berkley Books are published by The Berkley Publishing Group,
200 Madison Avenue, New York, New York 10016.
BERKLEY and the "B" design
are trademarks belonging to Berkley Publishing Corporation.

PRINTED IN THE UNITED STATES OF AMERICA

10 9 8 7 6 5 4 3 2 1

1

Friday, November 13

HER BREATH RATTLED. She had swollen winter sinuses, and it was a labor to draw air through her nose. A nasal drip skimmed down the back of her throat to further clog the passageway to her lungs. The towel he had jammed into her mouth prevented her from uttering a sound or taking a breath.

She had been careful to screen her clients, just so something like this wouldn't happen. With Maggie's death, her pimp had been on his best behavior; he had not let his greed overcome his common sense. He'd spent hours doing background checks on customers, trying to avoid losing any more of his girls to this killer. The *Washington Post* was full of stories and warnings about the Winter Man working the District of Columbia.

Working. Wasn't that a strange way for the papers to put it?

He was killing. Her.

She watched him pause at the bedroom window, pulling back the mauve drape to stare out over the street. Looking beyond him, she saw that it was snowing. It would be her last time to see such beauty. She squinted hard at the feathery flakes, committing them to a memory that would no longer serve her. The huge gargoyles molded into stone lintels on the theater across the street glared back at her with mocking smiles.

He was a big man, powerfully built. He had come with

good credentials and a letter of recommendation, and so what did she do? Let him tie her to the bedposts with her own stockings.

Did it matter that she thought he was a healer, a person to be trusted?

He turned back to watch her squirm against the bindings. He noticed her flushed face. The blood was rushing to her head, and it was going to be a mess afterward. His scalpels and ivory handle saws would be slick in his hands.

The instruments were neatly arranged on her nightstand.

He moved from the window, dropping the curtain upon her final, precious view. Stepping to the wrought iron floor lamp, he adjusted the lighting to a softer tone. Turning her stereo on, he filled the room with Gregorian chant. It was his recording. He'd thought to bring it over the last time they had met.

With slow deliberation, he padded to the chest of drawers and poured out two glasses of champagne, raising one to salute her. Slugging off the wine, he turned to carefully mound caviar onto a soda cracker. She could hear the crunch of the wafer when he bit down into it.

There was a time at the beginning of this ordeal when she thought he might have let her go. He had sat naked in the middle of the room on her soft, pink shag carpet to meditate on her fate, but she'd kept whining and begging through his reconsideration, and he had finally stuffed her mouth.

He lingered over the food, drinking from both glasses before dipping his fingers into each to trace the champagne over his forehead, face, and then down to his heart.

Grunting, he took a deep breath and turned to remove a cotton ball and a bottle from his tool bag. He sat on the bed and began to wipe at her hairline with mineral oil. His touch was gentle and warm, and the red hair dye she wore for that day smudged off onto his hands.

He had bald fingers. No print would remain, and he would never be found out. His victim would leave this life with no hope of ever reincarnating. She would never be able to avenge her death. She would be deader than dead.

A bit of the hair color ran into her right eye and glitter from candles placed in each corner of the room made her blink rapidly. He paused to tenderly dab it clear and then stretched back her lid painfully far to have a close look inside. Tears squirted from her other eye.

"I'm the universe's last survivor's policy," he said.

He retreated into silence and finished his swabbing until he reached the crown of her head. It was only a brief second before he turned back to his tools to choose a wide-bladed scraper. Hair dye stained his thumbnail.

Leaning close, he smiled, putting the blade to her head and carefully shaving her skull.

The music crescendoed, and she could hear the wind serenade her. Without a soul, even the Devil wouldn't have her.

Since my body temperature is lower than most of the corpses that come into the Medical Examiner's Office, I didn't mind when Chief Anthony called me in the middle of the night to fight a blizzard for him.

Entering the crime scene, I shook some of the snow off my black overcoat and walked up to Lieutenant Joe Walsh, touching the back of my hand against his cheek and making him jump. I always did this when I met him, because I liked to see him flinch. His pen stuttered across his notebook page. He shivered and glanced at me. "Nicki Chim," he muttered. Then louder, "Don't you ever use your pockets?"

I smiled slightly and looked toward the crime scene activity. "The Winter Man?"

"Yeah. Third snowstorm, third murder. It's him. Where's Anthony?"

"Stuck in some bar in Georgetown. He asked me to do the examination. Shall we take the tour?"

"I suppose. I think I've got my nose acclimated by now." The policeman led the way through the apartment and the party of chattering investigators.

It was a fashionable, pink and beige place of plush carpets and overstuffed chairs, but the softness was cut by the sharp lines of what I call harsh art; those pieces bought simply for their decayed condition. Some decorators and architects think it adds texture to the walls and furnishings. Personally, I think it looks like shit, but as Gale tells me over and over, all my taste is in my mouth.

The living room sank from the entrance hall and rose again when it reached the corridor leading to the kitchen, dining area, and the bedroom. A uniformed officer sat on the ledge, checking badges and talking on his radio. Two paramedics lounged on the couch, waiting for me to give them the nod to deliver the body to the morgue.

"Who was the victim?" I asked Walsh.

"Her name was Gitana O'Quinn. She was one of Jow Lord's pricey girls. She did business out of her suite here."

"Wasn't the last one a hooker, too?"

"The first murder was. On his second date, he cored a janitor. A man with grandkids, for Christ's sake."

"I came in on the tail-end of that one. I didn't do much work on it. There has been a flurry of murder cases keeping me busy these last few weeks."

We stepped up to the bedroom door and Walsh halted, pulling out a handkerchief to plug his nostrils. I chuckled at him, shaking my head.

I've been an independent consultant for the District of Columbia for twenty years, serving as a hematologist.

Before that I worked in Bern, Switzerland, and before that I did runs in London and Geneva. In all that time, I must have entered hundreds of crime scenes and never once minded the smell of death.

Well, hell, why should I? When I was unfortunate enough to run into a hematoman during the Bolshevik Revolution of 1917, I stank just like that. Hematoma is a medical term, and it means to swell with blood. I stuck an extra letter on the end and came up with my own name to describe us folks who are vampires.

The word vampire has such a coarse sound. Besides, it has a lot of vile associations that I just don't agree with. For instance, since joining the ranks of the hematomans, I've never once been able to turn into a bat or a wolf, and I thank God I don't have to sleep in a coffin of dirt from my homeland, which by the way, is Pittsburgh, Pennsylvania. In fact, thinking on it, I've never been able to turn into anything other than what I am: an undead American of Russian and Mongolian descent who was visiting the old country when she shouldn't have been.

Walsh spoke, his face rag muffling his words. "You first, Nicki."

I stepped into the room and was nearly knocked flat by a fleeing detective bent on drawing some fresh air in another part of the apartment.

You would think it was a real experience for some of these guys. They go rushing into the evidence room and come rushing right back out, holding on to their noses and their puke. They all start whispering when I walk onto a crime scene, and I love it. Iron Gut Chim, that's me.

The victim was tied with panty hose to the posts of a king-sized brass bed. She was naked and shapely, and her feet were neatly covered with a brightly patterned quilt. I moved closer, sidestepping the police photographer. The smell of blood overpowered my salivary glands, and I swallowed hard to keep my fangs from popping out my upper lip.

Walsh provided the play-by-play. "I figure she's been dead about six hours, just enough time to start ripening up, but then, you can tell better. We found the apartment's thermostat on max, too. Maybe the perp wanted her to stink sooner than later. There was a tape in the player over on the shelf caught in a continuous loop when we arrived." He checked his notebook. "Gregorian chants from Hungary." He squinted some more, adjusting his handkerchief. "There were white candles placed in the four corners of the room, burned down to the level of the holders, and champagne and caviar. Good Russian stuff." He pointed. "There, sitting on the dresser."

The prostitute's head had been shaved and a hole had been bored through the top of her skull. I stared at it, realizing how neatly he had done the job. From years of hunting and killing on the streets, I could see there was no hurry here.

Walsh continued. "Her murder was accomplished by using a trephining saw to open her head. The killer left his instruments all nicely arranged in a canvas satchel on the kitchen table." He coughed.

I sniffed hard, picking up another scent besides that of blood. "What is that?" I murmured.

"What?"

"I smell something else."

"Are you crazy? How can you smell anything but blood and shit?"

I took a moment to scan the room and noticed over on the bureau an arrangement of purple flowers wilting in a crystal vase. They were probably the source of the odor.

I shook my head, dismissing the scent, and leaned close to the corpse, pulling back the covers. I scanned for postmortem lividity, the dark blue discoloration that came from the blood settling with gravity. Her lower extremities showed signs of tarnishing. I checked her torso, but found her upper body to be clean. She had died where she was tied, then. "When was she found?"

"Approximately eleven P.M. by another hooker."

"When did it start snowing?"

"It got going good about three o'clock this afternoon. Where were you?"

"Asleep. I work nights, remember?"

I gently touched the victim's neck to test the rigidity of the muscles there. Rigor mortis affects the jaw and neck first and then flows into the whole body. She was good and stiff, but it was a dicey call, considering how hot the apartment was. Proteins coagulate faster in the heat, and considering the nature of the wound, she had severe injury to the nervous system. Everything would tighten up after that. Checking, I saw that Gitana's hands were squeezed into little balls.

I examined the edges of the skull wound. "With the amount of blood, I would say she was alive when this was done. There's gaping in the surrounding scalp tissue."

Walsh coughed. "God, it's one of the worst murders I've ever seen, and I cut my eyeteeth on the Gacy killings. Shootings, beatings, stabbings, I've been there to have a look at them all, but nothing could compare to this brutality."

I checked my watch: 2:33 A.M.

There was no sign of bruising, but on the top quadrant of her right breast, I found several small incisions. "Hey, Petey," I said to one of the detectives. "Got an extra glove with you?"

"Sure thing, Nicki." He dug in his coat pocket and launched a wad of latex at me. I swiped it out of the air and unraveled it, shoving the right one on. My fingers went to the corpse and I felt the design there: two adjacent circles, intersected at their converging point by a slash. Here, though, the flesh did not gape and there was only slight bleeding. It was a sure bet the cuts were made after death.

I fished through my purse, finding my scalpel case. Taking a blade from it, I moved to the point of lividity.

"Nicki," Walsh muffled. "I've got to check in with the watch commander. I'll be back in a few minutes."

I nodded absently as he escaped before I punctured the corpse. Pausing, I let the scents in the room hold my consideration. The supernatural energy of my undead disposition clicked on and spilled into my system like gall into an empty stomach.

All the standard crime scene observations are a form of guesswork, where I'm concerned. I gather useful clues from physical evidence, don't misunderstand, but after remarking on them, I have to rely on my own expertise to make, as Chief Anthony often says, "such astoundingly accurate time-of-death determinations."

The study of blood is my life, or my unlife, if you prefer. Contrary to all the legends and myths associated with hematomans, we're sensitive creatures, able to taste disease, chemical influences, and even mark blood type. We share a symbiosis with normal humans in that regard. I can tell the exact bouquet of the individual on whom I feed. In my own clan of bloodletters, I can usually figure out immediately who's been abusing himself by the flavor of the drink. Spectral array analysis can't be faster than me in determining what is in a person's bloodstream.

I smoothed back my long, straight hair with one hand as I made a small incision at the victim's ankle. A bubble of blood trickled out and I caught it on my forefinger.

Glancing around, I saw that no one paid me any attention, so I tasted it.

2

HER BLOOD HAD been cold and sour. Type O-positive. She had a cigarette shortly before her death. There was something else I sensed, too. Something strained through the platelets of this river, something unrecognizable.

I filled out the examiner's report and set the time of death for Thursday, November 12 at 4:00 P.M. Leaving for home, I stopped beneath the sidewalk awning at the apartment's entrance to watch the snow hit Pennsylvania Avenue in belching torrents. The glare from the orange ghetto lights outlined the mounds of homeless people clustering on steaming street gates. The wind surged down the avenue to hustle the cold along. Sand trucks thundered by, trying to erase the scudding snowdrifts.

I own a comfortable little brownstone in Southwest D.C., near L'Enfant Plaza. There I keep a home laboratory in the basement. Having a subterranean closet so close to the Potomac River is rare in Washington, and it took me years to find it. I like being near the water and it's a convenient solution to my daylight dilemma.

Considering it, there's another set of myths I'd like to explode about hematomans. We don't need to quarter in a casket and take on the small death until the moon rises. It's bullshit. We don't need to sleep at all, and we don't need to use the bathroom, either. Have you ever seriously wondered what a vampire does with the blood he consumes? I've got a whole library on the subject of undead nature, and not one of those volumes discuss how we eliminate drosses. Being undead is not a state of mind, you see. It's a physical way of existing, as carnal as any normal, mortal life is.

We do need a certain shield against the light, though, and in my basement I have this problem under control. There are simply no windows to expose me to the sun's energy. My whole house is protected with few portals and lots of dark curtains and blinds. As for illumination, well, technology has come through for most of us. Halogen lighting doesn't burn my eyes, despite its bright intensity. Since the bulbs became available, I've been able to enjoy more of the true color in my surroundings.

I stomped through the streets for over an hour until I finally reached home. Entering my walk-up, I kicked off the snow, feeling the wetness that had seeped into my tennis shoes. The foyer was lit by a hurricane lantern sitting on the claw-footed Victorian table. I adjusted the flame upward and removed my coat, throwing it over the peg on the hall tree.

"Ekua?" I called.

My friend appeared immediately at the head of the stairs. He smiled, his dark-toned, South African accent filling the space between us. "Art Anthony just called. He wants to know if you'll be available to attend him in the autopsy of Gitana O'Quinn. Shall I ring him back for you?"

I found Ekua in a Johannesburg dung heap in the late 1970s. He was a brazen black youth, wonderfully intelligent, and full of rebellious ideology. I felt sorry for his family, living as they were in the cardboard community right outside the glistening streets of the beautiful, white city.

When riots broke out and South Africa turned increasingly violent, I made the decision to deliver him into my undead world. I would have taken the whole bunch— mother, father, sisters, and brothers—had they not fled to parts unknown before I had the chance to work my magic. Ekua remained by my side, and for his loyalty, he escaped poverty to come with me as one of my clan members. Without him, I could not run the house.

Vampires collect into small family units led by a single strong individual who can protect the younger and weaker of our kind. Contrary to popular belief, not all hematomans are powerful and strong. The personality of the mortal life transfers to the immortal side, and if individuals are ineffectual as humans, they don't change much after death.

"I'll be in the living room," I said. "Please transfer the call in there."

He nodded. "There are some Italian ices in the bar refrigerator," he said. "I just made them a little while ago from the snow piling on the front stoop. Help yourself before Gale realizes they're there and eats them all."

"Don't worry about him. He's over at Alan's this month."

Ekua frowned. "Did you lose your bloodrights to him again?"

I hesitated, then after a few seconds, managed to throw up a small nod.

He grunted, turning away down the corridor. "You're going to have to stop this, Nicki," he said. I nodded again, and listened to his even footfalls above me.

I can't help the gambling. I know I should stop, or at least refrain from gambling away the services of my clan members to other vampire families, but tell me: Can an undead actually go to Gamblers Anonymous and be relieved of this compulsion? Immortal life suits me and that's a long time to try to be good.

I went to the fridge and opened it, taking out one of the covered plastic cups filled with frozen liquid. Ekua just loves Tupperware; he is forever experimenting with treats for me and packing them in the little holders. Flipping the lid, I immediately smelled the musk of his blood. The ice was deep red, almost indigo, whipped to the texture of custard. I licked a tongue across it and tasted fructose. My canines inched outward from my gums and the points of the teeth pricked my bottom lip. I grabbed a spoon from behind the mahogany counter and dove into the dessert.

The intercom buzzed just as I finished, and I picked up the telephone extension, sitting down heavily into my ratty, blue recliner. It was Chief Medical Examiner Arthur Anthony.

"Hey, Nicki, thanks for taking the look on this one for me," he said. "I finally managed to get as far as home. I had to leave the car by the side of the road, right in the middle of a snow emergency route. That'll be a bitchin' ticket when I get it."

"So, make it better. Talk to DMV. They'll fix it."

"Yeah, you're right." He paused, letting the silence emphasize his next question. "So, what'dya think?"

I started untying my shoes before answering. The cuffs of my jeans were soaked through and my socks were weighty with water. "Looks like we've got a surgically talented psychopath on our hands."

"That's the conclusion of the FBI, too. They ran a profile on him and he fits it pretty well."

"Those profiles are crap, sometimes. With enough stretching, you can make anyone slide into place."

"Yeah, well, it's the best news we have right now. The department can't pin a motive on this guy and that's the real titty-pincher." He went silent, then, "Sorry."

I laughed. "Don't be. Listen, Art, do you still have tissue and blood samples from the last two victims, or did your regular assistant get hold of them?"

"Now, Nicki, he's a good medical examiner."

"He's sloppy."

"He's also on the government rolls, so he's got to get the chance to work the case first."

"Are you tired of him, yet, then? Or do I walk? Makes no difference. I've got six months of work in the pocket already. New York City just hired me out in a professional fee bracket."

"You know I can't offer you that. Same rate as before, and you use your equipment."

I smiled to myself. "Since it's going to take my secretary a few days to receive the information and samples for the NYC investigation, I'll have a look into your problem. You know, if you're not careful, certain members of your team are going to get your ass tangled in the old hammock, A. A."

"Warning noted."

"Now, as to samples. What do you have?"

"I did a complete autopsy on each one of the victims. Straight-line computer analysis after that. I've got a walk-in icebox full of shit."

"Good. Are you doing the dissection on Gitana O'Quinn tomorrow?"

"Yeah. I'll give you the news when I have it. In the meantime, I'll set you up with the samples and you can do some magic for me."

3

Saturday, November 14

THE SAMPLES AND case reports arrived about 10:00 A.M. Diane, my clan's human confidante and class-A, number-one secretary, fetched them in from the delivery officer and brought them to me.

In this day and age, a vampire simply must have a daytime associate who can be trusted. The miracle of electronic technology serves us in vast ways, too, allowing it to seem as though we're active parts of the community at all hours, but to run a business like I do requires someone who can stand the heat of the sun.

"Gale called again," Diane said, handing me the folders and following me into the lab to store the samples in the fridge. "He's upset as hell, Nicki. He wants to come home."

"What did you tell him?"

"I told him you would call. I'm not getting into the middle of this fight."

My bloodrights to him wouldn't revert until the next full moon, and there was no way I was going to be able to convince Alan to give him up. "Fair enough. I'll talk to him later. Are you going to the store today?"

"Yes. What do you need?"

I sat down at the long table in the lab. My cat, Fuzzy Nuts, parked his butt next to the computer, clawed at the edge of the manila file folder, finally curling up to gather the exhaust warmth coming off the machine. I stroked his golden fur. "Get ol'liver lips, here, something good to eat, OK?"

Diane nodded, popping a jazz CD into the player before she left. I settled back, pausing a moment to listen to the strains of tenor sax fill the room before I opened the file.

The first of the Winter Man's victims had been a hooker named Maggie Kahn, aka, The Mage. Among the whores working the Fourteenth Street corridor, she was considered a lieutenant, a girl who had some amount of respect among her associates. From the interviews with colleagues, it became clear that Maggie was an expert with yuppie johns who were loose with their money and their sperm.

Maggie had been found in her own apartment, tied to the bed, and drilled through the skull. Music had been playing in the background when one of her associates discovered her. Champagne and caviar accompanied the carnage. A trephining saw, three scalpels, and a straight-edged razor were found. Each sported a scrimshaw handle decorated with a demon carving.

The Winter Man had sliced in at an approximate forty-five degree angle to core out a tunnel that ravaged her cerebrum, corpus callosum, and limbic system. According to the autopsy, the tiny, conical pineal gland buried deep in the tissue was not accounted for.

Why the pineal gland?

Blood analysis showed she had O-positive blood and confirmed that she had injected heroin several hours before death. Her phagocytic activity was abnormally high. Upon checking her spleen, the medical examiner found tumors and a darkening of the organ, suggesting the woman suffered from hemolytic disease. Her own scavenger cells, those that clean the blood of worn-out red cells, had lost their distinguishing power and were chewing up the normal ones. Had not the Winter Man gotten to her first, Maggie

Kahn would have been dead in a few months from a blood infection.

Moving down the page, I found the chemical breakdowns in order of importance. Her pH was off to the acidic side and cobalt counts for B^{12} verification were practically nil. It had been a while since she'd eaten meat. Her triglycerides were low, too. I scanned the page, pausing to study the differentials on her mineral and trace elements. The numbers were in a range consistent with the obvious spleen malfunction. She was on the low end of most concentrations: iron, zinc, and copper. She was on the high end of gold.

Gold. The word stopped me. Gold. Is that what I had tasted?

I flipped to the other file, the one on the man with grandkids. On the blood analysis, the tech had found gold in just about the same elevated concentrations.

I sat there wondering why the medical examiner hadn't noticed it. Both victims carried so much gold in their bodies that a jeweler could have made each a bracelet.

4

Sunday, November 15

CHIEF ANTHONY CALLED while I was watching the Redskins game. "I got your fax, and I have a suggestion for you. Change your transmittal cover sheet next time. 'What are your people doing besides playing with themselves?' pissed everyone off."

I laughed. "It's a legitimate question. How'd you miss the gold thing?"

"My assistant," he said.

"I told you that one day he was going to screw up big time."

"Yeah, yeah. Again and again." He cleared his throat. "I called to tell you I got Walsh on the phone right away after hearing from you. He'll meet you at six-thirty tonight."

"Good."

At that moment, the Redskins made a touchdown. Like most people in Washington, I had muted the television and turned on the radio to listen to the local announcers. I could hear the echo of Anthony's radio through the phone. We drew up into a short silence as we both paused to watch the instant replay. A moment of satisfaction fed my compulsive nature. I'd picked the Redskins by fourteen in the Medical Examiner's Office football pool.

"I took Dallas by ten," Art muttered. He continued a little louder. "Do you want to know the winning result of the autopsy on Gitana O'Quinn?"

"Let me guess. It was the same as the others. He dug in and sliced out her pineal gland."

"Ten points for the consultant. Now, tell me, my favorite blood technician, how that figures into his motives."

"I don't know, but I'll tell you one thing, Art. I analyzed tissue and bone marrow samples from each corpse and found that their internal organs and musculature were loaded with gold. The element is so heavy that it settled into the bodies before they could evacuate most of it from their systems. In the concentrations I found, these people had to be ingesting it for weeks before their deaths."

"So he stalked them."

"I'd say he knew each of them well."

"Slowly poisoning them. Another twist to the story."

"It blows the FBI profile all to hell, doesn't it?"

"Yeah. The Hooverheads just wanted to drop him into a slot and be done with it."

A fumble on the forty-two yard line broke our conversation once more.

"Ah, damn," Anthony whispered. "Dallas looks like shit this season." He sighed and continued. "The department thinks your theory about the scalpel marks being the Winter Man's signature is crap. That's too easy, you know."

"The picture he carved into the victim was some sort of symbol. I'm sure of it. I can't quite figure out where I've seen it before, but it's familiar."

Anthony snorted. "Nicki, my dear, you're trying to catch butterflies in the breeze."

5

BACK AT THE turn of the twentieth century, when I was just a kid, nice folks called a woman like Laura Roberts a strumpet. A walking disease, she could have been food for Jack the Ripper, bolstered as she was by frequent sips of Mad Dog and a convenient back alley wall. I liked her right off.

I stood with Lieutenant Walsh in the prostitute's filthy Sixth Street flat, listening to her whining rendition of how she'd found Gitana O'Quinn. Her bony hands shook and it drew my eye to her long, pink-sliced, resin-built nails. She wore several oversized rings, one a man's signet. The monogrammed side of the weighty trinket kept sliding toward the bottom of her hand. She fiddled with the band, her glance stuttering off to regard it.

I glanced around her apartment. There was a lumpy chair that was the same color as a rotting avocado. Bullets of dog poop plastered the linoleum floor and the kitchenette counter was a farm of plastic dishes supporting the dehydrating process of long-past meals.

Walsh seemed to ignore it all. He was in a nasty mood with a nasty cold, and his patience was souring. "Look, sister, we don't have all night, here. We need to get some specific questions answered or I'm going to run your ass downtown."

"I did that two days ago. I ain't got no more answers," Laura snapped.

I really don't like to use my supernatural powers during criminal investigations, but I could tell this girl was doing the shuffle. Walsh was starting to smart from his illness, and I wanted to get the hell out of there as soon as I could, so I angled slightly away from him and stepped toward Laura. She backed away, tensing at my approach. "Don't be afraid," I murmured. When she nodded, I turned on what I call my Dracula Stare.

The old movies have gotten this one right, about our ability to hypnotize with intensity. I avoid this talent for the most part, because I always feel like I've just transported into a Saturday fright matinee and the person I'm mesmerizing is Lou Costello. Somehow, I always expect Bud Abbot, the wolf-man, and Frankenstein's monster to come rolling into the scene.

I knew Walsh watched me. Without glancing at him, I also knew he was frowning, trying to figure out what I was up to.

Gently, I touched Laura on the arm and locked her with my strength. My nose picked up the scent of AIDS under her perfume. "Look at me," I commanded, in a low voice. "Look at me."

She did her best to disobey, but the vibrations I sent out creamed with my silent insistence until I overpowered her. She brought her head up to return my gaze with smeary, blue eyes. In that instant, I stole her will. Her mouth dropped open a little at the moment of impact; her fingers clenched in an effort to dispel me.

"Why were you visiting Gitana O'Quinn?"

Her answer came hauntingly slow. "We were friends. Just like I told the police, already."

"But she was an uptown girl and worked out of a nice apartment. You haul it down on Henley Park at street level. How did you come to know her?"

Laura's eyes cleared for a second as I lightened my hypnotizing hold. Her reply came faster and with more vitality. "I ain't always on the street, lady. My man, Jow Lord, he's an important guy. Sometimes he likes me to go with him to openings and stuff. He took me to the National Theater to see that Russian ballet dancer. You know— Barnikov."

"Baryshnikov," Walsh muttered.

"Is that when you met Gitana?" I asked.

"Yeah. She was nice. Always taking care of folks. She was supposed to take over The Mage's place on the street; it's what she said, anyway. But Jow thought better of it. That's how she got an apartment gig."

"The Mage, that's Maggie Kahn?"

Laura nodded.

"Did you know her, too?"

"Yeah, I did. She had a real gentle spirit, that one."

"Was Gitana seeing a doctor?" I asked.

She hesitated, and I renewed my Dracula Stare. She shook her head, blinking rapidly. "Yes."

"Do you know his name?"

"No."

"Think clearly, now. Did she ever mention his name to you?"

She bit her bottom lip. "I'm not sure," she whispered.

"Carefully. What was his name?"

"She talked about a Dr. Hanuman. But then, I don't know. He might have been one of her clients."

6

IT WAS 8:30 P.M. when I climbed off the Yellow Line at the
Gallery Place Metro station. I paused at the top of the
subway's escalator to stare at the burned-out buildings. I
needed a moment to regain my composure. Taking the
subterranean routes through the city always unsettles me. I
suppose it's the vampire thing, because I associate underground travel with life in coffins and tombs, but on rare
occasions it's just the easiest way to get to certain areas of
D.C.

I cut up H Street toward the Convention Center, strolling
slowly and doing some window shopping. Many people
don't realize that the nation's capital has its own Chinatown.
It's a tight, little section, unlike those of Philly or New York
City, but in these few streets, the tourist can find all the
normal clichés of such a neighborhood: golden dragon
restaurants, dry cleaning stores, the odors of kim chee and
ginger. There's even a friendship archway to mark the
boundary of this city-village.

Yet, to the observing eye, it's a blend of Civil War
buildings, martial arts dojos, and street signs lettered with
Oriental characters. I come often to buy silk and noodles
here. Diane loves my Canton pork surprise, and I love the
feel of my hand-stitched lounging robe.

The lights of the city were blooming: neon, halogen,
ghetto. Metro buses cranked by, splattering dirty slush onto
pedestrians. Street sellers were closing up shop, taking their
flimsy stalls of Redskin hats, belts, and souvenir tee shirts
with them for the night. Taxis gushed by, a snowplow dug

aimlessly at the ice congealing along the curb. It was a good night to go hunting.

When I need to make a kill for blood, I don't suffer any remorse. That emotion is a human conception, a way to gentle death in mortal eyes. I will admit, though, to one time feeling like a damned fool after inadvertently stalking and killing my favorite writer back in the 1940s.

I don't kill as often as some of my friends do. With the size of my clan, I don't need to hunt that much. We share our individual takes by adding to the communal blood pot. Still, a fresh infusion of fluid is always a nice change.

I chose a darker street, traveling in the shadows as best I could. The snow heaped on the sidewalks hindered my speed. Skidding along, I crossed ice patches and little white mountains. Once, I lingered beneath an awning to take deep draws of frigid air so that I might pick up a good scent. I wanted healthy prey tonight; no druggies, drunks, or diseases.

People don't think that the condition of the blood taken from a person affects a hematoman. It does. We're sensitive to drastic imbalances.

Attacking a person with disease presents a variety of complications for us. Suffice it to say, once you get an initial draw on the victim and taste the taint, it's up to the vampire to shuck off or continue. For myself, I never, never suck on a person who has high blood pressure, not because there is anything wrong with the blood itself, but because it's made way too rich by the intensity of the victim's metabolic heater. I get the hiccups from it, and beyond that, I get cranky as hell.

I passed an alley and stopped when I saw a young white kid pissing near a trash dumpster. He was maybe twenty years old, and primed for life. No drugs on this one; he looked too good for that. If anything, he was a dealer, and after taking him down I would find his goods, his gun, and his profits. The money I would pass on to the homeless. The gun and drugs would get flushed down some nearby sewer.

I hugged the darkness for a moment more, sending out a bounce of echolocation. He was ten point three meters on a west by northwest path from me. I hiked my purse strap firmly over my left shoulder and slowly stepped from the shadows.

He flinched when he noticed the movement, his hand reaching beneath his denim jacket, but when he saw that it was just a tiny, Chinese-looking woman, he relaxed. His stance went limp, and he slumped, hooking his thumb into a belt loop. It was this come-hither attitude, this vile, street representation of classic mating rites that made my fangs spout. The impudence in his manner stimulated my blood lust.

I paused a yard from him. "Are you holding, my man?" I asked.

"Depends," he husked. "What do you want?"

"I talked to some guy up the street who said to look for the skinny white hustler hiding behind Yong's Peking Palace. That would be you, I suppose."

"I ain't skinny; or are you just half-blind?"

"Well, you are white. What about the hustler part?"

"Don't know what you're saying, bitch."

I shrugged. "Hey, no problem. I didn't mean offense, buddy. You're the wrong guy. Sorry. Can you tell me where the right one is?"

He squinted at me and straightened his slump. "What do you want to buy?" he asked, lowering his voice.

"A lid of weed, if you got it."

"Shit, I got nothin' but chip on me. Ain't been no smoke in these parts for months. Can't make enough off of it anymore. Too hard to carry around. Sure you don't want the good stuff? Pure and wholesome. That's what I sell."

I pursed my lips like I was thinking hard about his offer. "A chip is about all I can afford, handsome."

He smiled. "Maybe we can take some of it off in trade. Before." He paused to give me his sexiest leer.

"Aren't you worried about AIDS?"

"Are you?"

I had to chuckle on that one, and not for the reason he thought. "No, I'm not. But no dally until I first get a glance at the rock."

He nodded and leaned close, fishing into his coat pocket. When he did, I grabbed him by the femoral artery in his neck, pinching hard. He snorted against the sudden pain, and I slammed a fist into his stomach. I'm small, but supernaturally powerful.

He sagged to his knees, and I felt him scrabble for the weapon I was sure sheltered in a shoulder holster. I kicked him in the groin, landing the toe of my tennis shoe right into his scrotum. He howled. I used the opportunity to pinch the other side of his neck and the pressure I exerted made the artery bulge. Ah, it was a beauty, indeed!

With no hesitation, I drove my fangs directly into this conduit, tasting in the first moments blood that was almost crystalline it was so clean. There was no aftertaste of a meat-eater, or one who indulged in cigarettes. There was only the subtle flavor of carbon dioxide in the stream. He'd recently chugged a soda pop of some sort.

Vampires are like mosquitos. Our bite injects a calming enzyme into the victim's body, along with an anticoagulant. These molecules we pass along attach to human chemical transmitters and it's only a matter of seconds before the prey becomes willing and compliant. My young stud-muffin was no exception. He was mine in a heartbeat.

I detached. "Follow me into the shadows," I whispered.

He moaned and crawled behind me to sit on a flattened cardboard box. I joined him, again pinching his jugular full and reinserting my canines.

Drinking blood is not such a big psychological deal for a vampire as storytellers and movie people would have you believe. You need it to survive, so you take feeders, but it doesn't inconvenience you around other humans. I don't lose control when I see or smell blood.

We do make sure that we're careful about killing. Most of us don't go on drinking rampages. We're selective. For myself, I wouldn't think of taking someone down who had a chance to make a difference in the world, but a dirt bag like the one I had here was a whole other matter. I think of it as cleaning up the shit on the streets.

For a good ten minutes, I gulped Mr. Sexy's life force. After a bit, the energy signature of the new blood lessened and I could relax as the flow slackened. It's during this phase of the kill when I experience the flush of my vampire powers, and communing with the soul of the victim sends me into a state of heightened meditation. My imagination gets a boost and my thoughts wander off. Sitting here with this youth, listening to his slowing breath, I started to think about the Winter Man.

The detectives had found many of the murder weapons at every crime scene: ivory-handled scalpels and trephining saws, each one delicately etched with the likeness of a mythological Hindu demon. Gorgeous and lethal, these tools were obviously handled with the precision that the instruments demanded. Each implement had been dipped in formaldehyde before surgery. Each had been wrapped in delicate, gauzy, parchment paper and tied up with a gold ribbon.

All these things they had discovered about the weapons,

save for the most important: who had used them. There were no prints and no molecular residue from rubber or leather gloves. There were skin flecks picked up by a view into the electron microscope, but all those did was announce that Gitana O'Quinn had been a busy whore. She wore the slough of black, white, and Hispanic johns.

I sucked hard on my young man's neck, and he groaned. His heart rate was down and his blood pressure had fallen on the lee side of seventy diastolic. Brushing a hand through his thick, black hair, I let my considerations float off again.

I imagined the Winter Man's fingers tracing the carved shank of his largest knife, following the raised pattern there. Slowly and lightly he caressed the design, discovering through touch alone the killing energy contained within the tools.

The blood coated my stomach and a flush came over me. I felt myself beginning to bloat from the liquid. My feeder abruptly stopped breathing.

I pushed him away, letting his body fall limply against the cardboard. The punctures I had made in his neck would disappear before he grew cold in death. Hematomans leave no fingerprints, much like the Winter Man, it seemed. Not even heat analysis can raise a smudge off a victim's body.

I took a wet wipe from my purse and cleaned myself up before I turned to pretty boy and searched his pockets, relieving him of his gun and his crack cocaine.

A stiff wind met me at the alley's entrance, but it did little to dispel the warmth I carried within me. I pushed against the gale and strolled up the avenue toward home and tried to remember where I had seen the design that had been carved into Gitana O'Quinn's breast.

7

Tuesday, November 17

THE POLICE FOUND Jow Lord's body in the underground parking garage of Techworld Plaza. The pimp had been shot through the head and his tongue cut out. From the crime scene report, he had lost his tongue before he had lost his life.

I received the gruesome notice along with Lieutenant Walsh as he joined me on a run over to see Edward Bunt's widow. Mr. Bunt was the man with the grandkids.

My associate pushed the patrol car through rush hour traffic, weaving along East Capitol Street toward Potomac Avenue.

"We checked the name Hanuman against AMA records and came up with zilch," he sniffled. "I think it's a dead end. He could be any kind of doctor, if the guy really exists. Laura Roberts is not what you call reliable."

"Have you checked the name out among Jow Lord's other girls?" I asked.

"We're working it, but I'll tell you, news travels fast in the District. We found the Vietnamese at four-ten A.M. By five-thirty, there wasn't one of his walkers left on the street. Someone signaled them and they charged for the four corners of this town. Now we've got to go round them up."

"He might have worked for Jow Lord."

"I think so, too, but right now we're in the minority on that opinion. The pimp kept books, I'm sure. If we find them, we'll see if he mentions him. Right now, the FBI is running up anyone with the first or last name of Hanuman." He sighed. "I'll be honest, I'm getting real tired of the Hooverheads stomping on my territory."

"Getting wrenched by the higher-ups, are you?"

"Yeah. I don't know how many senators and congressmen have called, worried as hell that they might be the Winter Man's next victim. Shows just how popular Jow Lord's ladies are with our elected officials."

"Did a run-through on Gitana O'Quinn's apartment turn up any pills?"

"All kinds. The lab is looking them over."

"If the gold was packed in a time-release vitamin, it would have dropped into the victim's system slowly and probably wouldn't have caused any noticeable effects until the level grew toxic."

"Those people must have gotten mighty sick before W. M. offed them."

"Yeah. A toxin like that would be like lead poisoning. It probably collected in the tight squeezes of their bodies. We have lots of nooks and crannies that can be silted up—joints and things."

He nodded and joined the cars crossing the Sousa Bridge into Anacostia. Once across the river, the whole flavor of the city changed. We entered one of the badlands of the District, a place where the houses were as chipped up as the streets. Glancing about, my eyes were assaulted with the sights: cracked neon signs of mom-and-pop liquor stores, rusted bars over broken windows, and cars that looked older than me. Young men and women clotted the sidewalks and the strong sound of rap added a counterpoint to the noises of loud mufflers and the chug of diesel buses.

I continued to stare out the window, noticing many of my own kind moving among the dense jungle of people. To see them, I thought of how I, too, enjoyed the raw sections of the world.

The earth has within it pulse points that a vampire can feel. The occultists of the twentieth century, those people who are into crystals and psychics and updated hippie beads, talk about how this vibration converges at certain places on the planet. They've got part of it right, but most of it wrong. These wrinkling flower children put their meditating hot spots in trendy, Club Med locations. The truth of it? Poverty brews the world's primal energy and it's in places like Southeast Washington where it can be claimed and directed.

Hematomans are masters at orchestrating this fire. The blood tastes far better when distilled over the flame of anger.

Walsh spoke, his graveled voice denting my reverie. "We better find the Winter Man soon," he said. "The weather report is calling for snow at the end of the week."

8

THE COMPOSITE WORKED up by the Medical Examiner's Office on the second victim read like the others. His name was Edward Bunt; he was black; an insulin diabetic; age fifty-eight when he had died. He worked on and off for Jow Lord, but his regular job was as a janitorial supervisor for the Smithsonian's night crew. Police had found his body in a flophouse near North Capitol Street, tied and murdered, with a hole punched through his head.

Edward Bunt's widow was named Marley Perkins Bunt. When Walsh and I arrived, she greeted us with a toothy smile and led us into her ramshackle home. Her walk was slowed by two wooden canes, and she sat heavily into a creaking recliner in a living room that was lit by the glow of a single lamp sporting a beaded shade.

Walsh and I took seats on a worn sofa with its arms covered in crocheted doilies. I smelled the lingering bouquet of cigar smoke and fried bacon.

Marley Perkins Bunt tucked at her short gray hair, sighing when she did, turning the weighty breath into a humming accompaniment to the radio playing in the kitchen. "Jesus counts on me," she sang in a low voice, before dropping out of harmony to stare straight at me.

"Eddie and I hadn't talked for years," she said. "We lived in the same house and all, but we never had so much as a civil word pass between us for as long as I can remember. Well, at least since our Freddie died, that is. He blamed me and I blamed him. It was his fault, you know. I'm a good, upstanding, church going woman and that's what I tried to teach my son. His father was a hell-raiser in his younger days, you see. Them stories he told of the streets and money and hustling and stuff got Freddie excited for the glamour life. Eddie said it was me who pushed him out the door with all my preaching. Don't matter, I suppose, because my boy got shot dead, anyway."

"We're sorry about your son, Mrs. Bunt," Walsh said. "I know the last few months have been difficult for you, but we must ask you some more questions. Another person has died in the same way that your late husband did."

"Lord, but I know. I read it in the *Post* on Sunday morning. You got to get this devil. He's Satan making a play for the innocents."

"Mrs. Bunt, I know the police detectives covered this ground before, but did you know a man named Jow Lord?"

"I never met that evil person, but I got to hear Eddie talk about him to Freddie a lot. My husband was driving his limousine, taking his whores and drug runners all through the city. That old man of mine thought that pimp was just like the savior himself. I told Eddie nothing but trouble would come from it, but he never listened. Thirty years of being married to him, and he never listened to a word I had to say. I thank the sweet Lord that my daughter saw the light and took to the church instead of the street, or I wouldn't have any children left at all."

I interrupted to ask a soft question. "Mrs. Bunt, did you ever meet a Dr. Hanuman?"

She shook her head. "No, but I got an earful about him right up front. He was some sort of miracle man, so Eddie said."

"Did he meet him through Jow Lord?" Walsh said.

"I suppose. I ain't sure."

"Was Dr. Hanuman treating your husband for a medical problem?"

"Oh, Lord, yes. I'd hear him and his no-account friends talking about how this man was going to make it so he wouldn't have to take his insulin ever again." She squinted at me. "He had sugar diabetes, you know."

"Yes, ma'am. Did Dr. Hanuman ever come here to see your husband?"

"No, indeed. Do doctors make house calls anymore?"

Walsh chuckled. "They haven't in a long time. We were just wondering if they were friendly enough to socialize with each other."

"Not that I know of. Eddie knew better than to bring his cronies into this house. These four walls are mine, given to me by my papa. It was a souring thing between us, you see." She shook her head. "Jow Lord had the gall to show up here one night, though, with a whole bunch of his whores. I called over to my brother, and he helped me toss them out of here. That was right after Eddie started driving for him. We started ignoring each other after that. About three months later, Freddie got cut down in a street shooting. I know he was delivering dope for him. I just know it, but Eddie denied it."

"Did Dr. Hanuman give your husband any medication?" I asked.

"Yes, indeed! Eddie would get on the phone with his loser friends and talk about the gold pills all the time."

I glanced at Walsh. His mouth dropped open by an inch and his next question came slowly. "Do you have some of these gold pills here?"

She frowned and pulled gently at one of her curls. "I believe I do," she answered.

9

WALSH LEFT ME off at my house on his way back to the station and a waiting lab technician. The front porch light was on. I thought it was for my return, but when I went inside, I saw why. Gale was there.

He sat in the living room drinking a glass of blood wine and talking to Ekua. His glance at me was filled with rage; I could see it clearly in those green eyes I had known for so many years.

I whipped a neutral tone into my voice. "Gale. What are you doing here?"

"I had to see you, since you won't return my phone calls."

"I've been busy working a case."

"Ah, yes, Ekua told me. The Winter Man. And knowing you as I do, you'll solve it where the frail humans cannot." He jittered a hand through his golden hair.

"Have you been mistreated by Alan? Is that why you've come home?"

Gale laughed darkly. "Alan. There's no telling where Alan is. I've been alone for a week, asked to serve as a house sitter. Again. He's afraid the street gangs are going to try and rob him while he and the regular members of his clan are off living it up in Rio. That's what his win over you bought him."

Ekua stood, pausing to rub his large hands together. "I'll be in the kitchen helping Diane," he said. "She's cooking and freezing food for our Thanksgiving donation to the homeless shelter."

I nodded as he padded by me. He paused to caress my

39

shoulder with a gentle squeeze from one of those incredible hands of his. "Work it out," he murmured at my ear. "Let's not lose Gale." Before I could answer, he disappeared from the room.

I sat down on the opposing sofa and tried to think what to do, but my brain short-circuited my efforts to come up with just the right words. Gale sipped his drink and when he tilted his head back, I saw the bulges beneath his upper lip. His fangs were out tonight.

"You've used me badly, Nicki," he said.

My heart puckered on me. I owed Gale a lot, and yes, my gambling problem had placed him in the position to repay my debts. We'd been together since the early 1920s, meeting soon after I had crossed over into vampirism. Gale was a being from another time, having gone undead after an encounter with a hematoman Parisian during a battle fought in the French and Indian War.

In those early years, I found that I was losing my mind and my discernment through unchecked blood lust. Being a vampire isn't as easy as most would think. You've got to learn respect, discipline, and caring for those victims you take, and for those humans you must deal with on a daily basis.

Gale's soul is that of an artist; he is an exceptional painter and sculptor, and through his gentle coercion, he showed me how to channel my frenzy, how to offer the daylight world some hope by establishing my own talents. He helped me to discover the wonder of my scientific, logical self.

"I never intended to hurt you," I whispered. "I love you more than all the others in my household. You know that."

He shook his head and blew a sigh through his nostrils. "The gambling. You have to do something about it. You can't keep losing your bloodrights to people like Alan."

"My problem is not that bad."

Gale slugged back the blood wine and slammed the glass onto the side table. "It is when it affects the members of your family." He rose from the chair and walked to the bar, smoothing his palm over the bare, dark wood. He turned back and spoke in a low voice. "I'm considering starting my own clan."

My chest tightened on my strictured heart when I heard those words, and panic trifled with my composure. I couldn't reply. My brain hammered out syllables for my tongue to take, but it was glued to the roof of my mouth.

My compassionate friend didn't have the stomach or the panache for the true vampire life and being a clan leader meant regular kills. Before we had hooked up, he lived in a garret, painting during the long nights and sending a manservant out during the day to collect animal blood from the corner butcher. I, on the other hand, had no problem attacking and drinking, and when he received a share of the blood I carried, the life force in him changed and his talents blossomed. He created masterpieces, then.

I rose and stepped to him, cupping my hands along his lovely, square jaw. How many, many times I opened a vein for him after I had killed, just to see his pale beauty flush up. "Please, my love, think about what you're doing. I need you; this clan needs you. Gale, you provide the balance for us. Without you, we do dangerous things."

"Exactly why it's time for me to exercise my powers over a clan of my own. There are vampires out there who would welcome my direction." He pulled from my small embrace. "I'm sorry, Nicki, but I can't live like this anymore."

10

GALE RETURNED TO Alan's house. He was true to his honor, that friend of mine. I'd lost his loyalty through my own stupidity, and someone had to show the vampire community that Clan Chim was worthy of its word. When Walsh called, I was feeling sorry for myself, sitting in the hot tub we have in the basement rec room, listening to Sting sing sad songs on the CD player and drinking bowls of pure blood pumped right out of Ekua. I kept dripping red tears over Gale, and it was starting to color the water.

Diane brought me the cellular phone, tenderly rubbing her hand across the top of my head as I took the instrument from her.

"Yes, Joe?" I said.

There was a moment of silence, then, "Sounds like you picked up my cold, Nicki. Sorry."

"Don't concern yourself. What can I do for you?"

"We got a report on Mrs. Bunt's gold pills. Pure aspirin in a time-release capsule."

Damn. "Could she have given us the wrong bottle?"

"I suppose, but I don't think so. The lab technician said they didn't look as though they were punched out of a mold. They were irregular sizes and contained various dosages. Analysis came back on containers found in Gitana O'Quinn's apartment, too. Same thing. There were no samples from Maggie Kahn's place."

"Then we're dealing with someone who has access to pharmaceutical supplies. He may have employed a different method to load up the first victim."

"Looks that way. I wish I could make sense of all this. I've seen ritual killings before, but this one is the winner in the esoteric category."

I didn't reply. The hot water calmed my thoughts as I absently listened to Walsh call down figures and blocks of information.

Gale had an esoteric streak in him. He often said it, but considering it right then in the midst of my guilt and pain, I couldn't put a finger on the particulars that defined the measure of such a personality. If the Winter Man had an appreciation for things esoteric, then was he on the same side of the stick as Gale or on the other end? Where my precious one sought mysteries of light and joy, the snow-storm killer obviously reveled in understanding and commanding black secrets.

"The gold is part of the ritual," I said, interrupting Walsh's monologue.

"What?"

"The motive, Joe."

"Nicki, what are you talking about?"

I sat forward in the tub, splashing water onto the phone. "We've been looking at this whole case from the perspective of a psychopath who has an undefined reason for killing; but when he murders, he follows a specific ritual. The motive has got to be tied to his sacrifices."

11

Wednesday, November 18

I SNUCK AWAY to the Wednesday night poker game after Ekua
and Diane had left to deliver the food to the homeless
shelter. Yolanda Raymond was hosting the party this time,
so I wasn't too worried about losing much. It was a cash
table. We play for bloodrights on the full moon, which only
comes once a month, except on those odd occasions when
there's a blue moon, and then the clan bets are set down
twice in four weeks.

Yolanda did it right with candlelight, new cards, and
shiny poker chips. Music pattered in the background and the
dog, a little, hairy brown fellow, came through to beg a taste
of our blood pudding hors d'oeuvres. I gave him a sample
from one of my squares and popped the rest into my mouth
as I glanced around to assess the mood of the players that
night.

Vampires are perfectly suited for the service industry.
Hell, most of my friends have practically kept D.C.'s
holistic movement alive. Since the late sixties when the
world opened up to new possibilities, it made perfect sense
to follow the lead of the fledgling New Age industry. Our
business is to meet humans, and for some, it's vital to meet
many, many humans. Take for instance, Yolanda. She
creamed into mainstream society by offering her talents as
a massage therapist.

Hematomans are unique creatures. We eliminate the blood we consume at different rates through the pores of our skin. Some folks, like Yolanda, metabolize at a furious speed and can't get enough energy simply by drinking blood from victims. Contrary to the fiction about us, you just can't go around killing people all the time to satisfy your needs, and animal blood, while a good substitute, usually has an old flavor and doesn't contain the same vibratory properties that we need to maintain undead health.

There are those who have other ways of taking a snack during the day. While Yolanda is giving her client a wonderful massage, she leeches blood from the tiny capillaries feeding their skin. She told me once that she can gather as much as a pint from a normal-sized woman and almost a quart from a large man. Her visitors go away feeling drained, yes, but she convinces them that it is relaxation and stress relief.

Glancing at my buddy, Duval, I smiled, thinking on how he worked the night shift at his own acupuncture clinic, and how the constant touching while inserting the needles gave him this extra blood jolt straight through the tips of his fingers.

"I'm in for twenty," Yolanda said, throwing her chips into the growing pile.

"I'll raise you five," Hardy answered.

"Going for ten more," Teresa chimed.

The bets continued the round until everyone faced off with a new pick from the dealer. Sizing up my opponents, I waited for the chatter to begin again.

"Nicki," Duval said, "how come you haven't come down to get your acupuncture treatment yet?"

"Was I supposed to do that?"

"What's the matter, you're brain rotting on you? Don't

you remember? You won a freebie from me five or six games ago."

"It slipped my mind. I've been busy."

"When I called you today, Ekua said you were working on the Winter Man case," Yolanda said.

"Yeah. The police are up against a deadline here. This guy kills with the snowfall and this season looks to be turning bad already."

"The acupuncture appointment, Nicki," Duval prodded. "I'd like to schedule it with you." He smiled, juggling his cards. "You should try this new procedure I've invented. I call it, The Snap Method. I dip the needles in a synthetic epinephrine mixture, punch them in, and then attach the stickers to a mild electrical current. The infusion of the chemicals combined with the pulse stimulation moves throughout the body to mimic the actions of the adrenal glands. You know, those little, pink things perched above your kidneys; those things that don't work anymore."

"Don't talk down to me, Du. I'm not stupid." The adrenals controlled metabolism and worked to pump adrenaline into a human's system when he required it.

"Oh, Nicki," Yolanda breathed, "you should try it. Epinephrine literally primes your heater and gives you a rush like you haven't had since you were mortal."

"Of course, when you finish, you'll be so pumped from the adrenaline, you'll need to drain down a victim, but I guarantee, you'll hold that blood charge longer."

Duval's eyes grew wide as he spoke about his new treatment. I couldn't help a chuckle. "Maybe it's what I need right now," I said.

"Good. Friday night all right with you?"

"Yeah. Call Diane and ask her to put it on the appointment calendar, or I'll forget, sure as hell." I threw in a card and turned to glance at Riley.

"So, tell me, Rog, how goes the dentistry business?"

"Got lots of folks needing root canals, lately."

I nodded, folding for the hand. If a vampire knew anything besides blood, it was teeth.

12

Thursday, November 19

WHEN I LEFT the poker game, the sidewalks were empty, and dawn already misted the dark clouds with a vibrant salmon hue, the new day's color smearing away the stars. My pockets were full, but my mood floated along at a lower level, somewhere between the tops of the melting snow piles and the stream of water spilling from them into the street gutter. I glanced down and saw cigarette butts, like miniature ships, each dashing toward some underground sea. Yes, that was right. At the moment, I was the captain of one of those ships destined to explore the sewer worlds if I didn't get a handle on my gambling.

Ekua, Diane, Michael, and Ilea, everyone but Gale, met me at the door, worry showing in the lines of their faces. Again, I had caused them concern by fording the currents of dawn to spend a minute mocking the sun. Satisfied that I wasn't crippled by the light, they moved off into the shadows of the house and I went down to the lab where I found my cat and yards of paper spilled from the fax machine. Fuzzy Nuts yowled at me while I picked off the message from Chief Anthony.

According to his transmittal, my theory that the killer's motive was intertwined with ritual had set well with the police department and the FBI. Apparently, they'd all had the idea at the same exact moment as I did. Art's cover sheet explained how suddenly, everyone was trying to make different connections in the case, and how the "Hoover-heads now engaged in butting their skulls against the concrete walls of that ugly, goddamned building they work out of."

I sat down at the table and pushed off a stack of library books Diane had gotten for me. Shuffling the papers, I followed his summary into the autopsy protocol on Jow Lord. Fuzzy Nuts decided it was the perfect opportunity to jump into my lap for a long overdue scratching.

The Vietnamese died of shock trauma after his tongue had been cut out. There were abrasions on his wrists and ankles, indicating that he had been tied prior to his demise. The wound to the head came after he'd leaked into death. His tissue and blood analyses showed no sign of recent alcohol consumption but did indicate an elevated level of tetrahydrocannabinol, the active ingredient in marijuana. He had just finished smoking a joint.

Stab wounds were placed about the body and his chest was lacerated. With the numbers coming up, it was easy to tell that the pimp had fought for his life. I wondered if, in this mixture of cuts and slashes, the Winter Man's design could be found. Making a note, I promised myself I would call for permission to look over the photos of the body.

The hematologist doing the workup had discovered no gold in the blood, but Art Anthony, who did the autopsy, found a gold bullet in Jow Lord's brain.

13

Friday, November 20

ONCE IN A while the weather over D.C. cooperates. It happens a lot in the winter. Cold fronts coming in from the west stall on the other side of the Blue Ridge Mountains and then the warm air from the south comes billowing up the coast to give us rain. Walsh's scheduled snowstorm never materialized.

I left about nine P.M. to go over to Duval's for my acupuncture appointment. He lives and works out of a ritzy place up near Embassy Row. As I entered his house, I passed his last client, who smiled absently and sighed as she left. When my friend greeted me, he had a blood flush on and was grinning wide enough for me to see his fangs. He hiked up the sleeves of his sweater before nodding a chin after his unsuspecting victim.

"She comes twice a week for treatments for nervous anxiety. I jab a needle in her parietal meridian point and she starts snoring on me. Well, I can't let an opportunity like that pass, now can I?"

I followed him into his treatment room. "Don't get any ideas on me, Du," I said. "I'm dry as a Thanksgiving turkey heading for leftovers."

He squinted at me. "You do look a trifle washed-out."

Since succumbing to the poker table on Wednesday night, my guilt and self-hatred had forced me into a blood fast. I kept thinking about Gale and the turbulence of these

51

considerations soldered into my growing preoccupation with the Winter Man.

"You'll need at least a quart of blood to help transmit the epinephrine," Duval said. "I have some red in the freezer. Human blood, too. Got it from a guy over at Sibley Hospital. Nice bouquet and everything. Let me go pop it into the microwave oven."

"That's fine, but nothing fancy. I'm booked with appointments this evening."

"Got a date or something?"

My mind's eye went immediately to Gale. "Yes. I have business to take care of."

"Well, then, undress and hop on the table while I get my needles and your drink ready."

I obeyed his orders and slid onto the paper liner covering the examining board. Sitting there, I glanced about his office, noticing the framed diplomas and degrees. These things were trappings for human consumption; things to make the victims feel like they were getting a square deal from Duval. He carried through the decorating theme to the bitter end, displaying a certain medical proficiency with a modern sterilizer kit and disposable needles.

He returned, bringing me a pitcher of blood and a tumbler. Handing me the drink, he paused to run his eyes over me. "My, my, Nicki, you have one lovely body, if I may say so."

I ignored his compliment to slug down the contents of the tumbler. Pouring a refill, I asked, "Have you tried this little adrenaline trick on humans?"

"No. I think it would do more harm than good. Maybe once or twice it would give them a hell of a buzz, but I wouldn't take it any farther than that. An overabundance of the hormone in the human system would probably fry a person from the inside out. Get enough adrenaline going through somebody, and you could give them a stroke or a heart attack." He turned toward his worktable to fiddle with his needles. "Of course, adrenaline is one of the things a vampire just can't hold on to for long, so I don't think there's a thing to worry about for us."

"Oh, I don't know. I might not be able to handle my heart pumping again."

He laughed, but did not turn from his preparations. Several minutes later he had the stickers out of their paper packets and was ready to insert them.

Duval doesn't joke when he says he invents treatments. The old boy plays with things, creating mechanical devices, like Edison conjured up his light bulb. In this case, he had devised a variation on an old theme. Using the delicate golden needles fashioned by the Chinese, he slides a cylinder around each one after passing the tip into the nerve point. The tubes are loaded with synthetic epinephrine, a hormone normally secreted by the adrenal glands in humans. Attaching a small electrode to this metal straw, he hits the juice, sending a tiny charge that transmits into the nerve as it washes the chemical down along the needle, until eventually it finds its way into the feeder capillaries of the skin and on into the bloodstream.

He had me lie on my back and he inserted a pin into my thoracic duct. This canal is located in the chest cavity where most of the lymphatic vessels meet, and in a regular, functioning mortal, it's where lymph and chyle are conveyed into the blood. In a hematoman, this duct is dry of the necessary plasma and white cells usually found there. It's empty, of course, until fluid, like Duval's synthetic epinephrine is dripped into it.

My friend had just finished placing needles into other nerve points along my arms and legs when the adrenaline rush hit me.

I could feel my body wheeze, constricting in the places he had pricked. A tingling spritzed through me, and my heart, which hasn't given a bump in over seventy-five years, burped to life. I counted the beats and then lost it as a ringing in my ears encroached upon my attention.

The blood I had taken increased its speed inside my veins, and even though I held so little liquid, the combination with the hormone gave me a full, reanimated sensation. I must have moaned, because Duval touched me gently on the shoulder.

"Relax, Nicki," he murmured. "Give it a few more minutes, and you'll start to feel practically human again."

14

Duval was right. After his treatment, I felt almost human again. It had been so long since I had experienced the driving force of a living body that I didn't know quite what to do. I knew that it was artifically induced, knew that within hours the timbre of this marvelous sensation would fade.

I practically jumped from the table in my hurry to take fresh blood to keep the feeling going inside of me. Duval laughed at me as I launched off in my childish greed, saying as I pushed into my clothes that he would schedule me for treatment the following week. Of course, he added, it would cost next time.

Hitting Massachusetts Avenue, I found two victims straightaway, but in my excitement I wasn't my usual, careful self when it came to selecting my feeder. I bowled over two innocents—no street thugs, these killings. No, I pounced on two young professionals dressed in pinstripes and gold cuff links. Once full? I ran right to Gale.

Alan lives in a luxurious house near Georgetown with a view of the Potomac River. It's a rambling place, considering the prices of property in the area, and it reminds me of something Frank Lloyd Wright might design. Whenever I visit, I always expect a little waterfall to be gushing from the kitchen wall.

Gale met me at the door, a frown on his handsome face. Immediately, I knew from his high color that he was flush with blood. He wore a black flannel shirt opened down past the third button and jeans so tight I saw the ripples of his muscles as he leaned against the doorjamb to consider me.

"Are you alone?" I asked in low voice.

"Yes. Is something wrong?"

I shook my head. "I just wanted to see you. To apologize again."

He stared at me silently for a moment before backing away to let me inside. Shutting the door, he pointed to the living room. I stepped into the vast space and glanced around.

Alan is a vampire of exceptional taste. He told me that before entering his undead life in Egypt in the 1880s, he was an up-and-coming archaeologist. Actually, he had called himself a grave robber, but in the years since his adventures in Africa and South America, he'd managed to get an honest degree in antiquities and now worked for the Smithsonian Institution as a consultant.

He stuffed his house with many of the treasures from his explorations. Statues and pottery, gold doubloons, and even a tomb shroud shared space with the worn volumes of first-edition books. He fancied himself a rock hound, too, and displayed fossils and geodes on shelves fitted with recessed lighting. I stepped over to the ceiling-to-floor unit and picked up a small stone. Sliced in half, the interior looked like a tiny apricot-colored cave of crystals.

Gale moved to stand behind me, and without turning around, I knew he'd folded his arms across his chest in an effort to keep me at some sort of psychological distance. I turned and saw that I was right.

"I miss you, Gale," I said.

His arms loosened at the elbows, but still he didn't drop his defensive stance.

"I don't want you to leave my clan. Please, please, reconsider. I won't place you in another situation like this again, I promise."

He shook his head. "You can't promise that. Your gambling has become an addiction that you're not going to do anything about anytime soon. If I don't suffer from the fallout, then it'll be Ekua, or Michael, or even Diane."

"Give me a chance."

Gale finally unbuckled his arms. He stepped to the fireplace to stoke the flames popping and crackling in the hearth. I moved along with him and took the opportunity to place my hands on his shoulders as he bent before the chore. My adrenaline charge was starting to falter, the weird beating of a long-dead heart beginning to slow.

Gale is like a ferocious white tiger, sometimes. He has a feline fluidity that has always thrilled me, and though I'm the acknowledged clan leader, he knows how to transform me for a short time into his slave. That's the power of his hematoman sexuality.

Primed with blood, our sensitivity explodes, and we become more than wraiths of the night. While our lovemaking can't be described in any human way, it's far more intense than any mortal communion could be. We join in an emotional bonding that releases our lethal energies and through touch, we share these vibrations.

Gale turned on me so quickly, I couldn't stop his tiger attack. He pulled me into an embrace, his lips meeting mine so hard I felt the rub of his fangs against my front teeth. I returned his kiss, but before I closed my eyes to let him sweep me away into vampire-inspired lust, my gaze fell upon the picture above the mantelpiece.

It was the Winter Man's scalpel symbol displayed in gold filigree: two adjacent circles intersected with a slash.

My heart suddenly stopped beating when I saw that. Everything I'd experienced during the adrenaline evening gushed away. For a moment, I felt confused. The jolt literally flat-lined me, and though the press of Gale's body kept me smarting, I lost contact with the very reason I'd come. The epinephrine I carried leaked off at a furious rate. I could feel my skin burn from it.

Adding weight to all this were my thoughts on the Winter Man. They made me stop chewing on Gale's bottom lip, and when I did, he pulled back, scowling.

"What's the matter?" he asked.

Shaking my head, I pulled from his embrace. Fierce though he might be when his ardor is up, Gale suffers a fragile ego that needs more petting and rubbing than my cat does. "I'm sorry, my love, it's not you," I said in a low voice. "The picture over the mantel caught my eye."

His scowl swelled as he turned to look at it. When he angled back to consider me, his eyes had gathered a wild glint. After years of living with him, I knew it to be the prelude to what he termed righteous anger. "So, it's a picture," he murmured. "An ugly one, at that."

I nodded, but still I stepped over to examine it. Tracing the edge of the brass frame with my thumb, I leaned forward on my tiptoes to stick my nose up close. In the lower left corner, just above the green matting was a date: 1934. I pried it from its mooring nail to check the back for a label telling me the title or the artist's name. The paper was fragile, water-blotched, and old. It was also blank.

"Nicki," Gale whined.

"Did you say Alan is in Rio?" I asked.

"Yes." A hard pause, then, "Didn't you come to see me?"

I was about to plunge into a list of detailed demands when, arriving at the brink of my outburst, his question stalled me. Sometimes I get caught up in my own business and drag my clan members along. Right then, I knew it was best to sever my interest in the picture, but I couldn't. The dregs of the adrenaline high still had hold of my tongue.

"Do you have a telephone number where he can be reached?" I asked.

He hesitated. His anger feinted with his curiosity, yet, in the end, his pride won out and he cursed me. Yanking the picture from my hold, he slammed it back over its peg before letting his hands slide down the wall to grasp the edge of the mantel. So full of blood was he, and gripping the wood so tightly, I saw the pores in his fingers blossom tiny, red drops. "Get out," he whispered.

15

Saturday, November 21

AFTER MY FIGHT with Gale, I came home and hid in the kitchen. I didn't want to go down to the lab with all the darkness and electronic vibrations of the place. I wanted to be around people, but the only one at the house was Diane. Ekua was spending the daylight hours with another hemato-man living in Alexandria, Virginia, and there was just no telling where the others of my clan were.

Diane puttered at the stove, cooking something that made my mouth water, it smelled so good. Popular belief has it that vampires only drink blood, that we don't eat solids of any kind. We do eat on rare occasions, so that's another myth I explode. The problem comes in our method of elimination. Food in our bodies will immediately begin to putrefy. Thankfully, the strength of our metabolic heaters is such that they don't allow gravity the time to take over and the matter to reach our intestines before we can rid ourselves of the waste. We don't get any energy from it—an undead doesn't need to extract minerals or vitamins—so we pass off all this excess through our pores. Unfortunately, the smell of rotting flesh goes along with it. We get a case of body odor to beat all hell.

I sipped at a mug of hot mulled blood, waiting for the phone to ring. At the moment, helpless to heal the breech between Gale and myself, my idea was to concentrate on my work by trying to track down Alan's whereabouts. Diane had been on the horn for me all morning, calling Yolanda, Duval, Rog, and anyone else she could think of who might know his number in Rio. She found out from Nancy that he had a huge house in the lakeside town of Alfenas, just west of the city, and before leaving, Alan had mentioned that he would use it as a starting point for some Amazonian adventure he planned to take.

Diane finally managed to get through. How she found the right number is beyond me. The Portuguese language confounded her attempts at communication, and I couldn't be of any help at all. I watched her there on the phone and had to laugh. She resorted to a pidgin, high school Spanish, using her hands for emphasis. Finally, as with any great admin assistant, she came through for me and placed the call, reaching Alan's companion, Maria. It was just before dawn, and Alan was out hunting, but Maria assured Diane that she would have him call as soon as he returned.

It was during this second, interminable wait that I noticed the stack of mail sitting on the far end of the table. I pulled it to me, absently flipping through it to keep my mind from replaying the battle I'd had with Gale. Mixed in among the advertisements, magazines, and gossip papers picked up by Diane during her grocery store run, were several bills. Electric, gas, and credit card duns awaited my attention, but when I came across my new issue of *Lottery Player Magazine,* I decided to check out the latest contests going on around the world.

Diane played at the stove while we waited for Alan's return call, putting one of her stewpots on to simmer. She sat down at the table, bringing along a box of sourdough pretzels and her current entertainment tabloid.

She loves to read those things and will often argue with us that the journalism in these rags is based on the truth. Now you tell me: The one she read at that moment sported a headline that read, "Vampire Baby Exhumed Alive from Coffin." The picture accompanying the article showed a creature with a bald head and what I assumed were bat ears; huge, bulging, round eyes; and a gaping mouth filled with rows of pointy teeth.

If I had a kid that looked like that I would purposely leave him out in the sun.

According to the mortal world, we don't exist, so being make-believe, we're the brunt of jokes and sick stories. In fact, hematomans are considered right up there with bug-eyed aliens. In the minds of sane, rational humans, we're considered fantasy and folklore. If they could only see what was right under their noses.

Diane knew I was watching her, but she ignored my critical look at the newspaper, crunching on her salty treats, using what I like to call her pretzel protocol: delicately biting the two nubs off the bottom before sucking on the rest of it.

The phone rang, making us both jump.

I picked it up and heard the crackling resonance of an international call. "Nicki Chim," I said, loudly.

There was a momentary drop in the static and then, "Hey, Nicki, baby, how's it going?"

Alan's flamboyant style irritated me immediately. "It ain't going good," I growled.

"And you called to Rio just to tell me? What happened, did Gale let the house get robbed?"

"No, I called about something else. I was visiting last night when I saw a certain picture above your mantel and I was wondering if you could tell me about it."

There was a bluster in the line noise. I heard, "What picture?"

"It looks like a piece of gold ribbon fashioned into two

circles and intersected by a straight piece. There's a date on it: 1934. Can you tell me what it is?"

"I might, if I knew what you were talking about," he answered. "I seem to remember not having anything hanging above the mantel. Hold on; let me ask Maria."

I glanced at Diane and though she kept her face toward the paper, she whispered, "Don't forget about Gale."

"Nicki? My home decorator, here, says she hung the picture before we left. Why is it so important, anyway?"

"It might help me with an investigation I've gotten myself involved in. What is the thing, Alan?"

"It's a little something I found when I was doing a tomb excavation near Trujillo, Peru. It's Moche."

"Moche? I don't know the term."

"Indians, love, Indians. Right up there with the Inca and Aztec dynasties. Not a lot is known about them because they didn't have writing, but despite that, they were marvels when it came to working with precious metals and stones. Beautiful, delicate stuff, Nicki. For hundreds of years the Peruvian peasants looted the burial spots, and during the 1920s, pieces began to turn up in private collections. That's what got me interested. I went down and did my thing, but sometimes I have rotten luck. Some bastard made me for a vampire while I was there. It was a dicey time for a while and I barely got out of Peru without a severe sunburn. That little piece of ribbon was all I could get out of the country. As it was, I had to do the Bela Lugosi trick and ride back in a coffin. Jesus, it gives me the shivers to think about it."

"Do you have any idea what it is?"

"I would say it was a hair ornament for the deceased. The Moche were crazy about earrings and necklaces and stuff."

"Do you think it carried any particular symbolism?"

"Sure, but without written records, no one knows what kind. If you're really interested, why don't you go over to the Smithsonian? I hear they've teamed with the National Geographic Society to do some work in Peru." Static choked the connection for a moment, then, "Ah, but Nicki?"

"Yes?"

"Don't show them the picture. I don't want to get hauled off to jail for harboring something that might be considered a national treasure, if you know what I mean."

"Don't worry. Talking to you helps a little. At least, I know where to go next."

"Well, if I can be of any more assistance . . ."

"Alan?"

"Yes?"

"You can."

"Tell me how, Nicki, my dear."

"I want Gale back. Now."

16

AT 8:05 P.M., I sat in the interrogation room observation gallery with Art Anthony at the main police precinct watching Walsh grill Jow Lord's successor. As soon as the word hit the street about the new pimp, Metro Police scraped him up for an interview.

He was a Korean-American from Brooklyn, a guy named, Han Lee. He sported a head full of spiky black hair and a round face ridged with cheekbones that were even higher than mine. He wore dark jeans and a navy blue pullover shirt that looked like it had been thrown into the wash with a pair of white socks. From where I sat, I could see tiny lint balls stuck to it. This guy didn't have any of the suavity you figure a pimp needs to attract the right girls and clientele. He was belligerent and nasty, and he reminded me of a few New York cabbies I've met in my time. Yet, for all his coarse bravado, there was one remarkable thing about him. He was a hematoman. I could tell right off.

It's rare that one of our kind will find himself in a lockup. We're usually too quick and agile to be caught by humans, but occasionally, we get sloppy. It can come from any number of things: stress, depression, night anxiety. Han Lee had purposely announced his ascension to the head of the wolf pack, which, for a vampire, was a pretty stupid thing to do. Any sensible person would know that after a murder, the golden boy would be the cops' first suspect. I wondered if a little New York fatalism hadn't overcome this particular undead and he wanted to be caught. Life, or in our cases, unlife, is what you make it. Some folks aren't very good at dealing with either.

People who have a choice about becoming a hematoman don't often think about the drawbacks to immortality. There are physical and mental things that follow a person on the crossover. Take tattoos, for instance. If you're a man, and the way you showed your virility was to have a huge American eagle tattooed on your chest, then when you step into forever, that blasted bird goes with you. A woman can have myriad problems, too. Consider cellulite. The puckety-pucketies don't go away because you start drinking blood. Or what if you have hair above your lip? Waxing it off every day can get mighty old after a while.

People also make the mistake of assuming that once they're undead, all the normal worries of day-to-day exist-ence will vanish, but the reality is different. The emotional baggage you hauled around in mortal life doesn't get lost like your suitcase at National Airport. In other words, your feelings don't go to Sheboygan without you. Since death is a philosophical abstract for most of us anyway, the prospect of moving through eternity with the fetters of guilt, shame, or self-loathing can truly be defined as hell.

Looking at Han Lee, I could see a being who had jumped on the plane lifting off for immortality with more than his share of carry-on luggage.

Walsh's cold was down in his chest and he hacked between questions. "Did you kill Jow Lord?" he husked.

"I want my lawyer," Han Lee answered.

"Gary Lambert? Is that his name?"

"Yeah."

"He was arrested a couple days ago for contempt of court. I think I could arrange for you to share a cell with him."

For the first time in the interview, the hematoman showed a spark of panic. He sat forward in the chair and yanked at the three sets of plastic bindings cuffing his wrists. I could hear one of them pop as his strength broke through.

"You should never leave a message on your lawyer's answering machine," Walsh said, grinning and tucking at the bill of his Washington Bullets cap. "You wasted a whole quarter. That's the taxpayer's money, you know."

"I don't say nothing without my lawyer."

"Cooperate a little and we might let you back out on the street before morning."

Han Lee squinted at Walsh. "Why?" he asked.

"Because our business isn't with you," he said. "We want to find the man who's been killing Jow Lord's people. Maybe find him before he gets to you next. Now, wouldn't you like that?"

Han Lee tossed him a lizard look and suddenly burst out laughing. His maniacal guffaws made him stretch his arms and he broke a second plastic cuff. Walsh shook his head, turning to the uniformed officer guarding the door.

"Get a couple more bands," he ordered. "This bastard's pulled another one apart."

He padded over to the one-way glass, smiling and shaking his head. Walsh was a handsome man with a hard physique. Sitting there concealed by the glazed window, I thought of how well he would fit into hematoman society and into my own clan. Perhaps I entertained the fantasy because of my current fight with Gale. Whatever it was, I kneaded the image in my mind for a few seconds before again concentrating on the interview.

The officer tied up Han Lee with three new straps, and Walsh continued the interview. He turned slowly, dragging out his words as he spun on his heel. "I could let you rot in one of our special cells for a few months," he said. "No windows, no bed, no visitors. Not even a bare bulb to keep you company. I understand it's like a tomb. How about that?"

The hematoman fidgeted in the chair, casting a glance around the room, finally letting his gaze linger on the casement windows set high in the wall. Pink sweat beaded on his forehead. He licked his thick lips and then ran his tongue along his canine teeth. He was probably wishing the old stories were true and he could turn into a vampire bat and fly through the window.

"I'm going to give you a single opportunity to be released," Walsh said.

"What is it, then?"

Walsh leaned close to the prisoner. "Do you know a Dr. Hanuman?"

Han Lee blinked at him, looking like a cobra ready to spit. "Yeah, I do."

Walsh straightened. "Who is he?"

"You guarantee I can get out of here before morning?"

"Make it a good answer and we'll see."

"He was some guy Jow met through one of his regular clients. A weird bastard, if you ask me. Came around in the evenings to talk shit with the boss while they drank Chinese herb medicine."

"Chinese herb medicine? Was Hanuman Oriental?"

"No. He's white."

"Was he a medical doctor?"

"How the hell would I know?"

Walsh sat down at the table. His words plopped out slowly again. "Was he a medical doctor?"

Han Lee hesitated before answering. "No. I don't think so. He was into herbs and holistic crap. One night he burned incense and said chants to drive off evil spirits that he swore were plaguing Jow and giving him a stomachache." He snorted. "Evil spirits. Jow Lord had an ulcer so big the Grand Canyon could have fit through it."

"Did his cure seem to work?"

"Jow thought so. He was sucking down the Chinese tea like there was no tomorrow. I figure there was something in the blend that was good for the pain, but my boss insisted it was Hanuman's balancing of his yin-yang energies."

"Did he treat Maggie Kahn and Edward Bunt?"

"Yeah, I think so."

"Gitana O'Quinn?"

"I guess." Lee squinted at Walsh. "How about letting me out of here now?"

Walsh grinned. "I will. Right after you help the police artist to do a composite drawing of Hanuman."

"When will that be?"

"About five-thirty A.M. Give it a couple of hours, and you'll be back on the street in time for breakfast."

The hematoman moaned, slumping in the chair.

Watching him, I wondered how the morning duty officer was going to explain Han Lee's mysterious death during his shift. Spontaneous combustion was my guess.

17

How DO YOU tell someone that their only witness is going to turn into a grease spot the moment the sun shines through the bars of the jail cell window? Since I couldn't think of any way to do it, I just let it go by leaving Anthony and Walsh outside Metro Headquarters to discuss the merits of the Rib Pit Carry-Out and Charlie Turner's North Carolina barbecue sauce. Walking up the street toward Chinatown, I tucked copies of the Jow Lord crime scene photos into my purse, along with a couple of the gold pills taken from Edward Bunt's medicine cabinet.

The temperature had risen sometime during the evening. Between the evaporating snow and the fog rolling in from the Potomac River, the city was swathed in so much mist it was easy to imagine that I was in London rather than Washington, D.C. The moon clung to the backside of dark, autumn clouds, and the glare from the street lights was gentled. It was perfect hunting weather, but unfortunately, I didn't feel like going to all the trouble of stalking a victim. I didn't feel like going home either, so I decided to visit my friend, Sam Short.

Sam is one of the few non-Asians operating a business in Chinatown. The reason he's tolerated by folks living and working on Eighth Street NW is because of the service he offers. His storefront is simply marked with a cracked, blue neon sign that announces it as a Café.

When Han Lee mentioned that the Winter Man pushed herbal remedies and holistic healing, I thought of my friend. Sam knows a lot about traditional Oriental medicine. He serves health foods, those dishes specifically prepared to meet the culinary prescriptions written for patients by Chinese healers practicing the ancient arts. Since the Asian mind-set deals with balancing the body's yin and yang, the positive and negative energies, some of these cures call for strange ingredients that don't necessarily meet the standards placed on restaurants by the Department of Health. So, for those seeking an old-fashioned treatment, Sam's is one of the places in D.C. where a person can buy stir-fried rhinoceros balls seasoned with fresh ginseng, ground deer antler, and packed in a Styrofoam container accompanied by duck sauce and disposable chopsticks.

Serving rats soaked in zebra milk offends American sensibilities. For years, the D.C. government has known about these back-room establishments, but in Chinatown, it's impossible to keep them from operating. Because of this illegality, Sam, like his counterparts in the business, is a man with two kitchens. One fronts the other, serving food for discriminating patrons who pig out on his dim sum and spare ribs soaked in rice vinegar, but off behind the ladies' room, there's a second restaurant. It's a carry-out in the truest sense of the word: a couple of woks and fresh ingredients brought in nightly and used up right down to the last hyena's toenail. Sam has to be able to pack up quickly when the health inspectors pound at the door. He needs easy knock-down and an inventory that can go out in a rucksack and some paper bags.

I could see the flickering sign still inviting customers into his establishment. Entering through a steamed-up glass door marked with Chinese characters, I paused to look around.

The main dining hall was a profusion of papier-mâché dragons and black lacquered lanterns. Red and gold washed the place, and elephant's ear plants accented several cracked, white formica tables. I counted ten people, each one the solitary master of his own little greasy booth. In the far corner, there was hooker and a cop ignoring their snug proximity by diving into bowls of soup and deep-fried wonton. A Hindu wearing a brown turban broke with his beliefs to eat a plate of pepper steak.

A waiter approached me and bowed slightly.

"I'd like to speak to Sam Short, please," I asked, trying out my Cantonese.

He nodded. "Who should I tell him calls?"

"My name is Nicki Chim. He knows me."

"A moment, please." The man bowed again and slid away.

Sam is the biggest black man I've ever met. When he comes into the room, he's all rolling bulk and blood-stained apron. He's usually sweating a waterfall from hours of standing over steaming pots, and on this visit, I wasn't the least bit disappointed. He appeared exactly as I expected. The waiter never returned.

"Hello, Nicki," Sam said, shaking my hand. "It's been a long time."

"How've you been?" I asked.

"Fine. Just got back from mainland China. I took Sarah to see her grandmother."

"Restaurant business must be good."

"Tourists. We had a lot in D.C. last summer and I managed to get a deal on advertising." He pointed to a table. "Have a seat. Did you want something to eat, or did you come just to talk?"

"You know soy sauce gives me indigestion."

"I told you I have a tea that will help."

I nodded. "Thanks, I remember. Tea, though is actually why I'm here." We slid into a lonely booth, curtained by one of the ugly, big-eared bushes standing sentinel in the dining room. "I'm working a case: the Winter Man. Have you been keeping up with it?"

"I've been reading about it in the *Post*. Pretty gruesome stuff."

"Yeah. Confusing investigation, too. There are a whole lot of weird clues that are stretching some brains over at Metro and at the FBI."

"The guy is crazy, right? Weird and crazy go together. Aren't the feds and the cops supposed to be experts on serial murderers like Jeffrey Dahmer?" He snorted. "He had a fridge full of body parts. Talk about your health foods."

"Well, I was hoping you could help me help them."

"Now, how can I possibly do that?"

"For being a round-eye, you have access to the most exotic foods and herbs available in the D.C. area. True?"

"That's right. You know that. I only use stuff that has been locally grown. It has to be that way. My customers want freshness for their money. As for my dried products, I buy the best. People can tell by the way the cure works when you've skimped on the ingredients."

"Do you ever sell herbals wholesale, say to local Chinese healers?"

"Once in a while."

"Do you know, offhand, if a white man calling himself Dr. Hanuman has bought any products from you recently?"

"The name's not familiar, but that doesn't mean anything. Sarah handles the legal side of this venture, if you know what I mean. She keeps the books. I know she's made some big orders out here lately, but I'm not sure who they went to. Sales go up whenever we come back from Asia."

"All right. What about Jow Lord? Do you know him? He's a Chinatown fixture, I understand."

Sam frowned. "That bastard. Doesn't everyone know him? Yeah, he's been in a bunch of times in the last couple of months. Always has his whores hanging on him. My regulars get all pissed off, but that guy is dangerous, so I can't just throw him out. I got kids to think about, you know?"

"Does he ever bring other guests besides his girls?"

"You mean like white men?"

"Yes."

"Just before we left for China, he did. A couple of pinstripe types—clients, I guess." He wiped sweat from his right eyebrow. "Then, there's the guy with the red gloves."

"Red gloves?"

"Yeah. They come in for lunch about once a week. This guy always wears red gloves. Sometimes they're leather, sometimes edged in lace like they did in Victorian times."

"Besides wearing red gloves, what did he look like? Can you remember?"

"Long, grayish blond hair, cut all shaggy like they did back in the seventies. Big guy. Can't seem to recall what he wore, though." He grinned, his mouth brightening with teeth. "I got the case of the ass when I saw Jow Lord come in with him last time, so Sarah made me go back into the kitchen. She's good at handling his type. He's a demanding SOB."

"Were they drinking herbal teas?"

"By the tubful. My wife kept coming in for refills. She said this fellow was pushing the ginseng into Jow."

"Is she here, now?"

"No, she's home with the little ones."

I sat back in the chair and, taking a pen from my purse, I jotted down Joe Walsh's telephone number. I slid it toward him. "Do me a favor, will you, Sam? Have Sarah go down to police headquarters and give a description of this man with the red gloves. It's important."

18

Sunday, November 22

WHEN A PERSON is converted from human to hematoman, he dies of shock, which is nothing more than a state where the body has an inadequate supply of blood to feed the vital organs. In clinical death, there's usually a lapse of time between when the heart stops and the brain flatlines. It's in these few moments when the transfiguration takes place. For those seeking immortality, this is where they'll find it and this is where they'll exist.

The brain so saved from death is changed somehow, providing us with heightened sensitivities such as acute taste, hearing, and smell. It also fosters extreme emotional states that can make great chapters for abnormal psychology textbooks.

It was 2:30 A.M., and I expected Gale to be home. When he wasn't, depression swamped me, and I knew all too well that if I didn't get a handle on it, the mood would gravitate into rage.

Alan had consented to release his bloodrights to Gale if I provided him with a round-the-clock guard to watch his precious house, so I called my friend Vance. The security business is another service industry that draws a lot of interest from hematomans. Vance has been in the sentry trade for a long time, using his clan members to fill the graveyard billets at museums and office buildings. He was more than happy to charge me an exorbitant fee to send someone over. I had done it immediately with no hesitation, demanding that for my payment, the guy arrive as soon as possible after sunset so that my lover could come home right away. It was foolish of me to think that Gale would hurry back.

Concentrating on the murder case was the only thing I could do to stall my growing annoyance with him. I retreated into my lab, leaving the door wide open, so I could hear the house settle in around me. Ekua serenaded us with old African flute lullabies and Diane was following the natural tick of her circadian clock, wide awake and singing the words to the songs in her usual off-key soprano. Michael and Ilea were home, too, confined to one of the bedrooms, probably licking each other's tonsils in some attempt at hot sex. Fuzzy Nuts plopped down the steps, greeting me with a yowl as he curled up by the computer.

I flipped on the halogens, flooding the basement with light. There was some comfort to be gleaned from the brightness, and I turned to get a plasma cocktail from the fridge. I could tell Diane had made up the drinks. She had decorated the glasses with celery swizzle sticks.

Taking a sip, I dug through my purse one-handed, pulling out the bottle of sample capsules taken from Mrs. Bunt. Cracking the container, a sweet almond odor flushed out so strong, it almost knocked me over.

Art Anthony's group had analyzed these pills, and their report stated that the contents was comprised mainly of acetylsalicylic acid, common, household aspirin.

I split one of the capsules open with a scalpel to have a look. Inside, I found a sticky, pulverized, pink substance. It had no special taste that I could detect, but the smell could have overwhelmed my senses to the point that the tip of my tongue had lost its usual acuity.

I sprinkled a little of the gooey powder onto a differential slide and ran it through the chemical analyzer. Several moments passed as the computer identified the compound's structure along with a graphic representation of the residue. The readings came up in a long chemical string that I didn't immediately recognize.

I tapped into the computer's database and demanded to know the name of the formula. The answer struck me as strange: salicin. I stared at the blocky letters on the monitor's screen, trying to recall what I knew about the compound, when Gale stepped into the lab and broke my concentration.

From the way his feet hit the stairs, I could tell he was in a sulking mood. The rifle through my brain's repository ended as I turned in my seat to look at him, trying to paste on a casual expression.

He carried Alan's mantel picture with him and set it near the computer. "I thought you could use this somehow," he said. "Alan won't be back for a couple of days. He'll never miss it."

Fuzzy Nuts came to his feet and did a feline stretch. Gale reached out to stroke him and his purr motor surged.

"I'm glad you're back," I murmured.

He shook his head and tucked a sideways glance at me. "What I said the other night about having my own clan hasn't changed, Nicki. I need to change the situations in my unlife, desperately, right now." He inserted a pause before finishing with the kicker. "I've scheduled interviews for prospective members beginning tomorrow morning."

19

MY HEMATOMAN ANGER was finally unleashed by Gale's words, but instead of venting my aggravation on him, I turned it on Art Anthony.

Forensic medicine has been in a deplorable state for many years. The problems are all budget-related. Murder investigations usually fall to the local authorities and in a lot of cases there simply isn't the funding to hire proper support. Most medical examiners are brought on as consultants to help with the overload. Washington, D.C. is no different. The city has pathologists who can do a serviceable autopsy, but they wouldn't know how to track the trajectory of a bullet if they got inside the body with it.

I've seen plenty of bungled investigations because the ME either didn't care or didn't know, and once the cutting is done and the protocol written up, it's rare that the determination of death will be changed.

I'm not saying I'm perfect. I've missed things on occasion; that's only human—or in my case, inhuman. My mistakes usually come from the fact that I've relied on the initial ME report rather than using my intuition to search further for the right answer. Once in a while you'll pull an investigation that's full of complex nuances, and every little thing has to be double-checked. Such things as erratic scalpel marks could be a sign of a disorganized lunatic, but it could also be the proof of a brilliant killer who's rolling with his genius. As for computers and twenty-first century technology, if you don't read the results, what you've got is pure, useless poop.

Art's sleepy voice responded to the fifth ring of the telephone. "Better be important," he muttered. "Who is this?"

"Your assistant is a dickhead," I said.

A moment's silence, then, "Oh, Nicki. Charming to the last. What the hell are you talking about now?"

"I'm talking about that stunner of an ME you've got working over there. You ought to fire his ass before it's too late."

Art sighed. "It's six o'clock in the morning. Can't this tirade wait until a later hour? Say, sometime after two cups of coffee and a chocolate croissant?"

"Did your boy even bother to open up these capsules taken from Edward Bunt's widow?"

"Sure. We had to do a breakdown on the compound."

"Then, how the hell did he get acetylsalicylic acid out of this shit? It's salicin. You know, the stuff they gave people two hundred years ago to help relieve pain."

"You're talking about willow bark?"

"Bravo, you're finally awake. Only my books on the subject describe the compound as being derived from the buds of the meadowsweet flower."

"OK, the meadowsweet flower. This is supposed to mean something to me?"

"For Christ's sake, Art, wake up and listen to me. Salicin was used as a powerful anti-inflammatory back in the last century. So think about it: the Winter Man was feeding these people gold. Like any foreign matter, the metal is an irritant to the system and it's going to settle in the body's joints and cavities. He's masking the buildup in their systems and at the same time, keeping their blood flowing easily through their arteries. Mrs. Bunt didn't mean they were gold pills; she meant they were pills for the gold treatments."

20

GALE WAS GOOD to his word and his clan member interviews began promptly at 10:00 A.M. All day, people tromped through the house to talk to him, and from what Diane said, they were hanging around outside, too. I expected a few hematomans to stop by, youngsters like Michael and Ilea, but what a surprise when all these folks dressed in leather, punked-out hair, and black lipstick showed up.

I can't understand why there are so many people who wish to be undead. Immortality is no different than mortality, in that you still have to pay the rent every month.

I retreated to the back porch just after dusk to enjoy the rise of the moon. The night noises offered me a private symphony and blended with the sound of a 747 taking off overhead. I had a wonderful, nocturnal concert going when Diane placed a hand on my shoulder. I started, betraying the fact that my preoccupation had dulled my senses. I never heard her open the back door.

"Are you all right?" she asked gently.

I shook my head. "No."

She sighed. "Didn't you once tell me that Gale has acted up like this before? He threatened to leave another time, didn't he? When was that? Back in the sixties?"

"Yes. He wasn't getting along with a new clan member we had. I finally had to make a choice between them. It was not a pretty scene."

"Well, what makes you think he's going to go through with it now? He could be bluffing. I've seen him do that."

"I don't know. He's different, somehow. More determined. He's not just blowing smoke. Maybe my gambling has finally driven him over the edge."

"Even if he does go, you can always put the clan back together," she said. "Ekua and I are staying. We won't leave."

I slipped an arm about her chunky waist, feeling comfort in the solidity of her form. "Where are Michael and Ilea this evening?"

She got a pained look on her face. "They're out looking for a new place to rent."

"Figures." I dropped my hold on her and entered the house, trying to think of something pleasant so as to not let my depression and anger overwhelm me.

Inside, the kitchen was warm. A pot of chili simmered on the stove, accenting the heat with a snappy smell. Blood loaf cooled on the counter nearby. Sometime during the day, Diane had bought deep blue orchids from a street vendor and decorated the table in Victorian charm. Balancing this homey effect was her usual setup: a box of sourdough pretzels, a cup of hazelnut coffee, and the latest soap opera review.

Diane is the Donna Reed of the hematoman set.

The thought made me gush. "Anytime you're ready to become one of us, I promise you, I'll make it a beautiful experience."

She tut-tutted me and said, "I told you before, the minute I can lose this weight, I'll cross over. Why would I want to spend eternity as a size eighteen?"

"You're not getting any younger."

"I'm also not getting any thinner."

I chuckled. "So tell me, once you do lose the weight and are ready to leap into eternity, what will be your last human request?"

She smiled. "What else? A plate of prime rib and french

fries." She pointed to the door. "Now, go, there's an interesting one in there waiting to talk to our blond-haired fool. He's not a vampire, either, but meeting him might help your mood."

Gale had placed a quick ad in *Night Argosy,* an underground newspaper run by humans who fancy themselves vampires. They're the people who have yet to step into the night, but who play out their warped fantasies by wearing leather capes, slave bracelets, starched hair, and safety pins pierced through their chins. I've met some who do it for kinky sex and a chance to suck on animal entrails. They say these games heighten their sensitivities, pushing them closer in their imitation to the real McCoy.

I went into the front parlor, expecting to see some of these cuties, but was met by only one man dressed conservatively in a midnight blue turtleneck sweater and stone-washed jeans. His back was to me as he caressed the lines of my Chinese Chippendale stand. When he heard me enter, he turned, and I saw that he had large hazel eyes, a sturdy jaw, and thin lips. He wore a dangling cross in his right ear.

Crosses—that's another untruth about the undead. It ranks right up there with garlic. In fact, I keep a crucifix collection displayed on the bureau in my bedroom. I've got some pretty old ones that are worth a dime or two. When I was caught up in the Bolshevik Revolution, I took the opportunity to test out my new hematoman abilities and, enjoying the irony of it, used my Dracula Stare to convince a frightened old aristocrat into selling his assortment of icons at a cheap price. We both needed to get out of Russia, and I could handle the extra baggage.

"Hello," I said, sitting down on the sofa. I casually adjusted my red silk robe to expose a little leg.

"Hi. Are you waiting for an interview?" he asked.

"Yes, in a manner of speaking. I've been trying to get into

see him all afternoon. What about you? Been waiting long?"

He nodded and sat down beside me. Diane had been right; he was human. His scent was Old Spice and fresh blood. Holding out a hand, he introduced himself. "My name is Justin Lang."

I shook his fingertips. "I'm Nicki Chim."

"Do you know Gale well, Nicki?"

"Yes. For many years. Do you know him?"

"No." He paused to release his squint as he appraised me. "What do you do for a living?"

For some reason, I couldn't resist making a flippant answer. "I'm a vampire. I bite people for a living. So does Gale."

He laughed. "You read that awful rag, then, and fancy yourself one of the supernatural wraiths?"

"You mean *Night Argosy*? No, I don't read it as a general rule, and I don't just fancy myself as an immortal. Isn't that why you're here—to answer Gale's ad for vampires interested in forming a clan?"

"No, though that sounds like a very nineties thing; counterculture stuff. It would get some interest, I suppose. You could get some amusing, creative individuals that way. And apparently that's what he wants. But vampires? His ad didn't say anything about that. What did you read, anyway?"

I shook my head and blew off his question with one of my own. "If you're not petitioning for membership in this newly forming clan, then why are you here, might I ask?"

"Business, primarily. I'm an antiques dealer and I have a showroom in Georgetown." He glanced toward the door as if expecting Gale to appear at any moment. "I just leased an adjoining storefront and have turned it into an art gallery. I'd like to put my first show together using his artwork." He moved his gaze back to me and paused to scrape a hand through his long, dark hair. "I found a page of the *Night Argosy* classified section stuffed in my mailbox this morning. His ad was circled in red pencil. I assumed it was a joke someone was trying to get over on me, but then I saw his name and knew who he was. What a talent, huh? Naturally, when I saw he was interviewing for associates, I called right away."

"I hadn't realized he was looking for partners."

He nodded and continued by leaning in to give me an appraising look. "So, if you're a vampire, like you say, why don't you show me your fangs?"

Impertinent SOB, wasn't he? I shook my head and countered his expression with one of my own. "Don't tempt me, friend. You may be in for a big surprise."

I rose as liquidly as possible and returned to the kitchen, my thoughts of Gale driving my steps hard down the hallway. Fuzzy Nuts was sitting on the table and Diane fed him a spoonful of canned salmon. They both watched silently as I moved to join them.

It was obvious now why Gale hadn't come home sooner when I released him from Alan. The time spent over at the Frank Lloyd Wright Memorial Rendition had given him a chance to plan his escape from me, and he was doing it in such a calculating way that I had almost missed it. He wasn't interested in enticing prospective clan members into joining a compassionate family unit; he was staffing a tiny empire of people to promote his work. He was as selfish as I, only in a different way. I, at least, admitted to playing the ponies and dragging loved ones into the problems this causes, but I hadn't figured Gale capable of a vindictiveness that was so glacial. It was almost as if he'd lost all his feelings for me.

21

WALSH CALLED AT 6:00 P.M. He invited me to meet him outside the Kennedy Center to share a cappuccino at the Espresso Cart, a vendor truck that you can regularly find parked by the building, summer and winter. The lady who owns the truck is a Washington institution, a person everyone knows by her face and her smile, though if you ask somebody what her real name is you'll get a blank stare. She calls herself Diva, as in the operatic kind. The story that goes along with this moniker is a tearjerker; on cold evenings it helps to push the coffee.

When I met Walsh at the corner of F Street and Virginia Avenue, a matinee performance had just dumped from the center and Diva's business was brisk. The line leading to the step van of java delights was a long one, so we hitched up in last place, using the minutes to talk.

I was in a stinky mood over the events of the day, and because of it, poor Walsh was in for a harassing. "Going to the Kennedy Center," I said. "I didn't figure you as a culture hound, Joe. Was it the ballet?"

He shook his head and threw me a snotty grin, already having picked up on my sneering attitude. "I like the ballet. Managed to get seats for the Moscow company performance last year." He paused to take a step closer to the coffeepot on wheels. "The President of the United States was there. He sat right beside me. Yeah, he did. We got to talking and he told me he didn't much care for Ruskie women. He said even their dancers have big asses."

I couldn't help a grin, and I couldn't think of an equally

witty reply. When I didn't answer, he went on to fill in the space between us. "I just met a lady who lives over in Hughes Mews. We took in an oldie at the American Film Institute. *Night of the Devils.* French. Nineteen seventy-two. I would have enjoyed it more if I'd been sitting at home watching it on cable."

"Hughes Mews. Classy section of town. I hope she paid."

He changed the subject. "The FBI finally coughed up the results of their rundown on the name Hanuman. They came up with four possibles, but two are a wash."

"Why?"

"One is a little old lady who lives over in Northeast. She worked as a secretary at the Department of State for about a hundred years."

"And the other?"

"Is a little old man who lives over in Southwest. He worked for forty-one years in the mail room of the Patent Office. Neither suspect can walk without the help of a cane and a live-in nurse."

"What about the two possibles who do look interesting?"

"There's a David Hanuman and a guy named Richard Hanuman," he answered. "David owns an import/export company. He has no priors, except for one, teeny altercation with a D.C. hooker a few years back. Assault."

"Ooh. That is interesting. What happened?"

"He was found guilty, forced to pay a fine, and do a hundred hours of community service. Do you know what he did for his restitution to society?"

"What?"

"He went to area schools, armed with condoms and a lecture on the proper ways to put on a rubber so you won't catch AIDS."

I laughed. "Did this guy invent his own gig or was it bestowed upon him by some smartass government official?"

"What do you think?"

We live in the political capital of the world. There was no question as to the answer. "So, who's the other suspect you have on tap?"

"Richard Hanuman. He used to work at the Smithsonian. The position title of his last assignment showed him to be a restorer. Six months ago, he left the job. The information ends at that point. In fact, the data we have on him is pretty damned sketchy. We don't even have a picture of him on file."

"No driver's license or anything?"

"Nothing. We do know, though, that he was adopted."

We finally reached Diva, who flashed us a charming smile, enhanced, I'm sure, by the number of joes going out of her cart.

"What do you want to drink, Nicki? It's my treat tonight."

"Thanks, but I can't handle caffeine too well. You go ahead, though. I'll be fine."

He gave Diva his order and in the span of some small talk about a new play coming to the center, he was served a hot cup of mocha royale. He blew at the froth, tentatively tasting the coffee, then, after a swallow, said, "I appreciate the lead on Sarah Short."

"You're welcome," I answered, and then in my most innocent voice, I asked, "Did it match up to the one Han Lee gave you?"

Walsh scowled, shaking his head. He started to walk up the street toward the Watergate Apartments. He tried to aim the conversation away by muttering, "I left my car along here somewhere."

I'm nothing if not persistent and when I'm being a crab, it's nice to share the feeling with someone I care about. "Didn't he give you a description?"

"No."

"Why not?"

"I'm not allowed to talk about it; not even to you."

"That bad, huh? What did you guys do? Beat him senseless? Or did you let him get away?"

"Nicki, just drop it, OK?"

"He could have sped up the process, and Metro dumped the opportunity?"

He sighed and nodded, but refused to openly counter my speculations.

I couldn't help smiling to myself. "All right, did you get a good picture from Sarah?"

"Yes. Mrs. Short was very helpful." He snorted. "She even brought Chinese carryout with her."

"Have you come across his mug shot in the database yet?"

"No, we're still running possible matches." He sipped his coffee, then held out a hand to help me over a mound of dirty snow. "I spent all goddamned day with my Hoover-head counterpart. What a little dink that guy is. He's straight out of Quantico. First assignment. You can tell how interested the FBI is in finding the Winter Man from the level of effort on their part. Mark my words, they're going to let Metro choke on it. When all our leads are exhausted, some office mole will surface to tell us who he is and where he can be found. My division will look like a bunch of idiots and Her Honor, the mayor, will not be a happy camper."

"So, what are you going to do next?"

"Have a talk with David Hanuman. I thought you might want to be in on this little talk."

"I would. Is he expecting us?"

"If he's psychic, he is."

"You're in a pissy mood tonight, aren't you, Joe?"

"It matches yours."

We both chuckled, but following the snicker, our conversation lulled into reflective silence.

A breeze kicked down the street, trundling by us. I looked up to see the orange gray color of the ghetto lights reflecting off a cast-iron sky. After a few minutes, we reached his car and climbed inside. He blasted the heat, shivering and cursing at the chill coming off the defroster.

"By the way," he said, through gritted teeth, "Art wanted you to know there's a job opening in his shop if you're interested. His assistant was dismissed early this morning." He put the car into gear and glanced at me. "The salicin catch was a good one. We're hunting down local herbal distributors and asking them for information on any sales of meadowsweet they might have made recently. Most of them tell us they don't handle the stuff."

"Meadowsweet is used in potpourri and floral arrangements. You see a lot of it in weddings."

"So check the florists, too, huh?"

"I would, if it were me."

"Do you know how long that could take?"

"Quite awhile, I would imagine."

He grunted. I could almost feel his growing inertia over the possibility. Walsh was tired and barely over his cold.

Putting the car in gear, we crossed over Memorial Bridge and took the George Washington Parkway, heading south to Alexandria, Virginia. Both Arlington and Alexandria are cities that shove D.C. up into the gut of Maryland. I do believe without the truss of suburbs, the District would slide off into the Chesapeake Bay.

Traffic in Old Town Alexandria was fierce for 7:30 at night. The Old Town section runs along Highway 1 and down to the Potomac River. It contains excerpts of Revolutionary War America, but each time I ride through the place, it seems that the original historic charm I remember so well is being slowly pasted into a modern motif. There are places like the Old Presbyterian Meeting House and Gadsby's Tavern sharing the same block with a Roy Rogers, which does business out of a storefront with a Georgian facade. Foreign cars park on cobblestone streets laid down by Hessian troops some two hundred years ago, and every block or two, there are signs indicating that the father of our country slept everywhere.

David Hanuman lived in a restored colonial home near the river. He answered the door wearing rubber gloves, holding a glass of champagne, and humming to the strains of Mozart playing in the background.

"Yes? May I help you?"

Walsh flashed his ID, introducing us. The fact that a cop and an ME were standing at his door didn't seem to dent his outward composure. He nodded and moved aside to let us in.

Entering, I was forced to shield my eyes from the bright, crystal light coming from a chandelier in the foyer. It took me a moment to adjust, and even at that, it was necessary for me to click on my echolocation system, so I didn't inadvertently run into things sitting in my path.

Since my radar was running, I used the opportunity to bounce a signal off Hanuman, too. I measured the man to be six feet four inches tall and weigh 250 pounds. The usual Washington cliché hit me hard and fast: He was so big, he could have been a linebacker for the Redskins.

"I'm trying to get one up on a dinner party tomorrow night," he said. "I hope you don't mind if we talk while I cook. I've got friends coming in from India. They're looking forward to a vegetable curry that I make."

Walsh mumbled a "No, sir" as we tagged along behind him. I tried to scrape up some impressions from the house, but the glare from the lights made me cast my glance down to the thick white carpet, instead. The kitchen, thankfully, was set on dim with Tiffany lamps and candles arranged along the counters and windowsill.

A gorgeous minx of a woman met us when we came into the room. It was obvious from her curves and her youth that she was in the relationship for more than love. My opinion was born out in an off-handed way as Hanuman introduced her as Ann Latrice, his new business partner. She smiled coyly at us while she stirred a wooden spoon in a steel pot, the scents of cumin and onion tickling my nose. "Can we offer you some champagne?" she asked politely.

We both declined, and Walsh went on to openly scan the room, his gaze finally settling on the table. A single red rose set in a small, fluted vase decorated it. He picked it up to glance at the bottom of the container. "Isn't that pretty," he said. Then, looking directly at Hanuman, he apologized, replacing the holder again. "Sorry, I'm irresistibly drawn to lovely things. Sometimes, I forget not to touch."

Hanuman smiled. "Quite all right, detective. I understand. It's the same with me."

"If you don't mind, we'd like to get right to the point of our visit, and unfortunately, I have to be blunt about the questions I'm asking."

"Yes," he answered. "What can I do for you?" He set his drink on the counter and moved to stand before the expensive-looking stove. By that time, I could again see well enough to notice that he punched a digital readout to set the burner on flame.

This place was elegant. When I'm presented with sur-roundings of wealth and affluence, I can't help but to think about my own home and how it's an amalgamation of junk: a few antiques, Gale's artwork, chairs that have been sat on through two World Wars, Korea, Vietnam, and Desert

Storm. The dishes are cracked and there's a litter box in the front bathroom. The towels don't match, and never will.

David Hanuman, in contrast, lived in dark wood and shades of beige natura.

"We need to ask you a few questions, if you don't mind," Walsh said.

Hanuman pulled the lid from a sauté pan. "Can you tell me what the investigation pertains to?"

Walsh massaged the brim of the fedora he wore and took a swallow that wobbled his Adam's apple. "It's a murder probe, sir."

Ann reacted with a surprised expression. "Surely, David's not a suspect?"

"We're not here to formally charge him. We have information that the murderer may have the last name of Hanuman. We're now conducting interviews in an attempt to narrow the list of possibles."

"Oh, I'm sorry I interrupted." She dunked her hands into a bowl of cooked rice and looked away from us.

"Who was killed?"

"I'm not at liberty to give out that information."

Hanuman picked up a boning knife. Now that my eyeballs were back on-line, I saw the reason for his rubber gloves—he was cutting up hot chilies. He used his hands deftly, though he had fingers the size of sausages. I watched as he sliced open a pepper and ran a thumb down the groove to push out the seeds. He moved back to a bowl where several others floated in water, snatched one out, and repeated the sequence, finally throwing the lot in the steaming pot.

"Tell me, Mr. Hanuman," I asked, "have you had training as a professional chef?"

He chuckled. "My lord, no. It's a hobby. Can't you tell by my size that I love to eat?"

Walsh spoke up. "We have information that you were a premed student for a while."

"Yes, but that didn't last. I hated the subject about as much as I hated the sight of blood."

"Why did you attempt to go for a medical degree, then?"

"I come from a family of doctors. My father was a psychiatrist, as was his father. My uncle was a surgeon and convinced my father that with my dexterity I ought to be a cutter. The first dissection I did on a human corpse left me in a—shall we say—frazzled state. I transferred my major to business the next day."

"When did you start Hanuman Imports?" Walsh asked.

"In 1975. Right after college graduation."

"What exactly do you import?"

"My goods come from Pakistan, China, and India. You know, hand-hammered woks, clothing, ceramics."

"How do you market it?"

"Regionally. Malls, specialty shops, anyplace that will buy in the metropolitan area."

"Do you sell to stores in Chinatown?"

"I have a few customers. Mostly the little junk shops that cater to the tourists."

"Have you ever had dealings with a man named Jow Lord?"

I thought his neck was going to crack, so atomically did he shake his head. I sensed a marginal rise in his blood pressure, but after a moment, his vital signs leveled out. "I've never heard of him."

"Weren't there charges placed against you for assault of a prostitute in Chinatown?"

His partner popped her head up from the bowl to glare at him. He ignored her. "It's a matter of public record."

"What exactly happened?"

"She tried to steal my wallet. I wasn't bargaining for her

services; she approached me on the street. I defended myself."

"The word has it you broke her jaw and fractured her skull."

"And for that, I paid with money and public service."

Walsh nodded. "I'm required to ask these questions, you understand. We're trying to establish a motive in the murder investigation."

"I can't imagine what you're looking for."

"We're not sure, ourselves." Walsh flipped open the little spiral notebook he keeps with him at all times. He licked the tip of a pencil he pulled from his pocket and scribbled a few words on the tiny page. "Let's go back to discussing your business," he said. "How do you market your goods?"

"Are you asking if I sell my wares door-to-door like a Fuller Brush man?"

"Yes."

"I don't leave my office. I hire people to pound the pavement."

Walsh juggled his pad to fish inside his coat pocket. He shook open the composite picture put together with Sarah Short's help, and leaned in between Hanuman and his babe. "Do you recognize this man? Is he in your employ?"

Hanuman studied the drawing. He grew a furrow on his forehead, and his pulse rate thumped up. When he answered, his voice cracked. "No, I don't have anybody who looks like that. Not with all that shaggy hair. My salesmen are clean-cut and conservative."

Ann angled in for a peek, bits of rice flying from her hands. "Ugly man. And such high cheekbones he has. He looks like he could be a killer."

I couldn't stop a small smile. I pack the Himalayas in my face and no one has ever said to me that I look like I could be a killer.

Everyone drew back at the same time.

"Why do you ask if he's one of my salesmen?" Hanuman said.

"Occasionally, people will use the names of an employer as an alias. We just want to be certain you don't know him."

"I can guarantee that." Then, looking right at me, he said, "Ms. Chim, would you be so kind as to fetch the bottle of thyme from that spice cupboard by the refrigerator? I have a few more chilies to cut up and my darling Ann is up to her elbows in risotto."

"Of course," I said, opening the pantry door. When I did, my eye fell upon the carved, ivory handled knife lying on the bottom shelf. If my heart could have thumped it would have done a drum roll. I picked it out and held it up for Walsh to see the Hindu demon dancing on it. "How lovely," I managed to say.

Hanuman nodded, his heart rate noticeably settling down. "Oh, yes, isn't it? I found it in India, years ago." He glanced at Walsh. "Before the ivory ban, of course."

I turned it over. It was exactly the same as the murder weapons found at the crime scenes. "It looks like it was fashioned for some ritual," I managed to say. "Is that what it's used for?"

"Have you been to India?" he countered.

"A long time ago. Why?"

"You're right. That knife is a ritual item. Very old, actually. Fashioned sometime just after the Moguls took over the continent. Several hundred were made, I understand, by Hindu peasants for rich families. They would use them during feast days or when heads of state came for royal visits. These implements moved down through the generations, but when the empire started to break up, they found their way back into the mainstream culture."

"What does the carving mean?" I asked. "Do you know?"

"It's a picture of Hanuman, the monkey chief. He's a character in Hindu literature. He can fly and has an extremely long tail. Lots of stories have been written about him. One tells of the time when the god Rama sent him to bring healing herbs from a mountain before the rising moon. Hanuman couldn't find the herbs right away, so he carried back the entire mountain to Rama. Digging it up took so long that he couldn't complete his job before the moon hit the sky, so he ate the moon. Then, after he got the herbs, he disgorged the moon and replaced the mountain."

"Lovely story," Walsh said with a frown. "Did you import many like it?"

Hanuman turned to stare directly into the pot. His voice was low. "It's the only one I have," he said.

22

AFTER OUR VISIT to David Hanuman, Walsh decided he needed me along on the second interview, so we drove over to Arlington, taking the road that loops up around the Pentagon and then deep into the middle of Arlington National Cemetery. Flanking the drive were rows of identical white tombstones fanning out toward the high-rises of Rosslyn, a minicity complex of office buildings, restaurants, and a Metrorail dump-off point. I looked in that direction because the twin towers of the USA Today buildings drew my eye. They glistened like huge grain silos, and in this night of hard, cold November light, they shared the landscape with the wandering ghosts of dead soldiers.

Walsh made a right turn and parked at the Prospect House, a swanky condominium that overlooks the Potomac River and the National Mall. The desk manager buzzed us into a lobby of cherry wood paneling and Oriental screens. I couldn't help stopping to have a look at cloisonné vase used to decorate a small table. It seemed that bits of Chinatown had made it uptown.

"We're here to see Mrs. Barbara Pollack," Walsh said to him. "Suite eight-forty, please."

"Is she expecting you?" he asked.

"Nope." Walsh flashed his ID, laying it open on the counter.

The man settled a look on me before nodding and dialing the house phone. In a minute more we had permission to pack into a small, cherry-lined elevator. We shared the space with a fashionable young woman and a gentlemen that looked a lot like Larry King.

Mrs. Barbara Pollack opened the door immediately in response to Walsh's knock. Thin and elegant, she wore a plain silk shift in a pale blue hue with small bone buttons. A chunky silver chain roped her long neck like a slender yoke for a horse, and she nervously patted this jewelry when she saw our IDs. I noticed she had a profusion of age spots on her hands. The long, red nails and cocktail rings did nothing to hide them.

Mrs. Pollack shut the door and led us up a short flight of steps into a living room with a dead-on view of the Lincoln Memorial, Washington Monument, and the Mall. I stopped to gaze out her two-story glass wall, marveling at the beauty of the nation's Capitol Building.

She invited us to sit on two white Italian leather sofas arranged about a large, glass-topped coffee table. "Is Harry all right?" she asked, in a breathy voice.

"Harry, ma'am?" Walsh said.

"My husband. He's away on a company trip. I thought when Carson called up from downstairs that it concerned him."

"No, ma'am. We're not here about your husband."

"What a relief. What is it that you want?"

"We're here to ask you a few questions about Richard Hanuman."

She frowned and her tongue came out to taste her red lipstick. "Richard Hanuman?"

"Yes, ma'am. You're the head of personnel for the Museum of Natural History at the Smithsonian. Is that correct?"

"Yes."

"Richard Hanuman was an employee, there. Is that correct?"

"Well, the name is familiar. I oversee several hundred employees and I'm not on a first-name basis with many of them."

"Please do what you can to remember, Mrs. Pollack. It's

important that we locate this individual. Would you mind if we establish some validating criteria here, first?"

She shrugged. Her expression deepened into concern.

"You're a general manager, grade fifteen civil servant for the Smithsonian Institution. You've been there since 1978."

"Yes. I didn't start handling the Natural History Museum until 1992, though. Before that, I did personnel work for the Air and Space Museum and the Museum of American History." Her hand stuttered about her silver collar.

"Richard Hanuman's civil service title listed him as a restorer. He was a grade twelve and had been with the Smithsonian since 1980. Shortly after you were made chief, Mr. Hanuman voluntarily quit. Is that correct?"

She nodded. "Yes, I believe so. I would have to check the records to be sure, though."

"Do you remember why he left?"

"I don't know," she answered. "I can't remember what reason he gave on his resignation papers."

"Could there be a professional reason for his departure that you're aware of—a new job, or perhaps some undesirable situation with a coworker?"

"I would assume he had a new job."

"Do you have his letter of resignation on file?"

"We require one upon departure."

"What exactly did Richard Hanuman do?"

"Do? I'd have to check to see what particular projects he worked on." She glanced at me but spoke to Walsh. "Those who serve in positions designated as restorers do just that. They work to recreate the pieces we use in exhibits. Sometimes they reconstruct articles that are in poor shape by matching fibers and paint. That type of thing. General restoration duties."

"Any idea what projects he might have worked on?"

"I'm not sure. We rotate these individuals every few

months. They could work on anything from a diorama of ancient Egyptians to cleaning up fossil bones. They go wherever we need their expertise, and their duties change with the mission. As I said, I just don't know the specifics on Mr. Hanuman, so I can't tell you much about him."

Walsh fished into his coat pocket and brought out a copy of the picture done by the police artist. "Do you recognize this man?"

She took the paper. The minute she laid eyes on it, I could feel a change in her body's vibrations. She shook on the inside, and after a few seconds managed a softly spoken no. Then, suddenly, she narrowed her look. "Why are you asking me, anyway? Why aren't you talking to Richard Hanuman, instead?"

"We can't locate him. The forwarding address taken from his last federal tax filing specified an apartment in Northwest Washington, but it was abandoned about eight months ago, according to the leasing company."

"What has this man done?"

"We want to talk to him concerning an ongoing investigation. We feel he may have some current information that might allow us to apprehend a murderer."

"A murderer?"

"Yes, ma'am. It's of a serial nature, so time is of the essence. Anything you may know about him could help us."

She rose, moving to stare out the glass wall. Walsh looked at me and stifled a sigh, before turning to address Mrs. Pollack's butt. "We would like to see your personnel records on Richard Hanuman."

She spun around to look at him. "Unless you have a warrant, I can't release the files. The Privacy Act forbids it."

23

Monday, November 23

THE LAST DREAM I ever had was a nightmare. In it, I was walking a train track, wearing, as I often did in those days, a long, black skirt and a red blouse with a Chinese collar. The train came along and blew its whistle to warn me of its approach, but for some reason I couldn't get off the rails. It was like the soles of my shoes had melted, gotten all gluey, and stuck me where I had stopped. The train smacked me head-on and rolled right over me. The very next evening I had the fateful run-in with my hematoman mentor.

It was late afternoon, and sitting in the living room staring at one of Diane's soap operas, I remembered my nocturnal fantasy with a rather warped sense of delight. Hematomans don't sleep, so we don't dream. My assistant had given up on the television and instead caught a catnap on the couch. I'll admit to feeling a tinge of jealousy for her ability to go into a fantasy land created wholly out of her subconscious mind. As for me? I was trapped with my constant, jackhammer thoughts.

Gale was going on with his interviews again. There were weirdos of every assortment waiting in the front parlor to see him: a biker mama with tattoos of snakes going down her arms, a couple of Vincent Price types, and a woman who looked like she would be at home living in a Gypsy wagon. This circus was starting to piss me off. So, to avoid another argument, I was just about to click off the TV and retreat into the darkness of my lab. The phone rang, though, before I could. Diane never even moved.

"Nicki Chim," I whispered into the receiver.

"It's Walsh," came the familiar, graveled voice. "I thought you might like to know that I just spoke to the owner of Wine and Roses," he said.

"What's that, Joe?"

"Wine and Roses is a little floral shop in Northwest, up near Dupont Circle. It's a specialty store with a unique concept. They cater fancy occasions: things like weddings, anniversaries, and birthdays. They provide flowers and, get this, champagne and caviar."

"Why the interest in this particular place?"

"Remember when we were visiting David Hanuman, and I picked up the bud vase?"

"Yes. So?"

"There was a label on the bottom of it with the name of the shop."

I smiled to myself. "Did you talk to them?"

"Yeah. With a little persuasion, I managed to coax the owner into giving up some information. Hanuman orders several arrangements per month from them. Only last week, he had several bouquets made up, two of which were composed mainly of meadowsweet, blooming sage, and baby's breath. He also ordered a case of Korbell champagne, smoked salmon, and beluga. He had these nice little gifts delivered to various people across the city." I heard him take a deep breath just before he shot me the clincher to his report. "I also have a list of names here that you might find interesting."

"He's not the same man Sarah Short identified for us."

"I know, but she could be mistaken. She may have heard Jow Lord mention the name Hanuman while talking to the guy whose composite we're flashing."

Diane snorted and turned over, her movement drawing my attention away for a second. "What about Richard Hanuman? Have you tracked him down?"

"Not yet. I'm working on it. I'll give you a call later if I come up with anything. The guy has literally gone underground. There's no trace of him."

We hung up. I continued to sit in my lumpy old chair, listening to Diane snore and the freaks talking among themselves in the next room. When evening finally arrived, I got the hell out of the house by going over to Duval's for an acupuncture treatment.

I rushed through town, taking the Metrorail all the way, and before I knew it, I was lying on the table in his consultation room. He burned candles instead of the fluorescent lights, and to further set my relaxed mood, he simmered a mixture of herbs in a beaker that sat atop a Bunsen burner designed to look like an Egyptian pyramid.

"So, the first time we did this treatment, the epinephrine really slammed you, huh?" he said.

"Yes. I was in such a rage, I could barely control myself."

"I see you're back, too."

"I want to see if I can slow the drain down. It only lasted a few hours last time."

Duval sucked at his lips before speaking. "All right. Maybe I can help with that. Fewer needles along the adrenal pathway might make the respondent nerves work a little harder to pick up the electric pulses."

"Do you ever feel like Dr. Frankenstein?" I asked.

"Great, isn't it? Bringing the undead to life." He leaned over me and squinted. "You know, I could shoot the epinephrine through the lymph nodes in your neck. Going in through the thoracic duct is a major jolt into the bloodstream. Tying up the strength and the speed of the adrenaline by making it work through the filtering network of your glands might slow the process in the system and evenly distribute it."

The moment I heard his words, I got a jolt without his assistance. I suddenly knew how the Winter Man got the gold into his victims' systems.

I sat up and pushed him back as I jumped to the floor. Naked and sizzling inside, I cast a circle looking for a telephone. Duval did nothing but watch me in amused silence. He didn't even offer to direct me to his desk where the thing sat. I had to clear a path through my jostling thoughts to eventually make my way to it.

Edward Bunt had been an insulin diabetic and it could have been possible that he was sharing his used needles with the Winter Man. The killer, in turn, would have had a ready source of hypodermics, and theoretically, he could have injected the gold into his victims through their lymph glands. The nodes cluster in different areas of the body and are connected by lympathic vessels, which feed the tissues and cleanse the bloodstream of carbon dioxide. Given in small doses, enough of the gold would still pass through the cleansing glands to slowly build up in the organs and muscles.

I dialed the Medical Examiner's Office and was patched through to Art Anthony.

"Do you have any meat left on Gitana O'Quinn?" I asked him.

"I've still got a good bit of her on ice. No one's claimed the body. Why?"

"Would you take a dermal scraping from her neck, underarms, and groin sections, especially in the general area of the lymph node sites?"

"Yeah, sure." Then, "I take it gold capsules are out now, huh? Hypodermics are in?"

"The Winter Man could have been bartering his so-called

treatments, making deals about the method of payment for his services. He could have been taking the things he needed for his killing ritual directly from his victims. Edward Bunt had a ready supply of insulin needles."

"All right, Nicki," Art said. "I'll get on it right away. I'll fax you the results."

I hung up and climbed back onto the table so Duval could pin me up and get my own treatment under way.

Duval punched my neck glands with the epinephrine and flipped me over to place the needles down the ridge of my spine. He was right; the adrenaline smack was gentled by its delivery through my neck. It was like ice water slowly trickling down my nerve endings to give me a cool, crisp sensation throughout my body. By the time I left Duval's little clinic, I practically quivered with lethality. I needed to drink, but I didn't have that same ballistic feeling as I'd had after the other appointment. More than craving blood, I had a desire to use some hematoman powers that I routinely ignore. It was time to go back and see Mrs. Pollack.

24

I HOPPED BACK on the Metrorail, and fifteen minutes later, I climbed across a windswept Wilson Boulevard to head toward Prospect House.

Though a hematoman can't turn into a bat or suddenly grow suction cups on his fingers for scaling sheer walls upside down, he can do other things attributed to vampires. These talents seem to lie within enhanced vibrational abilities. When a person enters unlife, the energy levels shift, as though existing in this state of clinical death gives the brain more freedom to access special resources since it doesn't have to worry about the bodily functions.

One of my best-developed skills is that of invisibility. I'm not really invisible, mind you. It's just that I can somehow cycle my personal frequency pattern so that folks don't actually notice I'm there. Accomplishing this feat is a little like a waking meditation. You have to concentrate on being invisible. It can get so intense that I sometimes lose track of what is happening around me and where I'm going. That's why it's so important to be focused. Invisibility doesn't keep you from running facefirst into closed doors.

Ekua can do this little trick as well as I. He attributes this undead dexterity to the fact that we're able to march into the middle of Einstein's Theory of Relativity—we bend light by jerking the gravitational fields surrounding each one of us. In other words, we curve the space-time continuum. Diane says Ekua has a scientific mind. Personally, I think she means that he has a science fiction mind.

Whatever the reason, invisibility works, once you figure

out how to do it. Like most hematomans, I tried for a good twenty years before I managed to accomplish this ability that most vampire mythologists consider as natural for us as sleeping in a coffin.

Arriving at the front entrance of Mrs. Pollack's apartment house, I turned on my juice as I buzzed the lobby manager. He hit the admit button to unlock the door and I walked inside. You can imagine the man's expression. To begin with, he looked like Harpo Marx, and when I came through, his hand sought one of his curly red locks. He scowled and then went wide-eyed. If he'd had a little horn to toot, I might have lost my concealment in laughter. As it was, I couldn't help a chuckle. He heard me and his hand stretched for the phone. As I moved passed him, I whispered, "The number you want is nine one one."

The thing about having all those little gravitons and electrons bouncing around is this: I can manipulate my size. A crack is all I need to slide through. It's sort of like being one of those alien jelly people you see nowadays in the movies and on television. Movement becomes fluid and a bit slimy feeling.

Good as that is, the invisible state can cause problems, too. My vision tends to get blurry and if I stay under wraps, I'm subject to experiencing waves of dizziness. That's why people associate vampires and shadows, you see. More often than not, we use the darkness to cloak our presence.

I went to Mrs. Pollack's apartment. The interview with her had bothered me, and like Laura Roberts, I figured she needed a little help in giving up the answers from her obviously selective memory. As a personnel supervisor, she would have had to remember more than she indicated during our talk.

She answered my knock after a bit, tentatively confirming the vacant view from her peephole by opening the door the width of the chain lock. It was all I needed to enter, so I grabbed up all my flinging atoms and squeezed through to slip into her living room.

When she turned around, I had already dumped my invisibility and stood right next to her in the tight space of the foyer. I clamped a hand over her mouth to stall the scream I saw coming, and immediately leveled her right out with my most fearsome Dracula Stare. After a moment, the mesmerization caught and I freed her.

"Are you alone?" I asked.

"Yes," she said.

"Where's your husband?"

"Out . . . of . . . town . . . still."

"You'll be alone this evening?"

"Yes."

"Good. You'll be glad to know that you and I will begin a new relationship tonight. Go into the living room and sit on the sofa."

She moved to do my bidding. Her body jerked under my influence and as bony as she was, she looked like one of those paper skeletons the kids hang from the front doors during Halloween. I followed and stood before her, continuing with my Dracula Stare to the point where I could feel her will begin to evaporate.

The movies and books are right on another thing about us: We do keep "blood feeders." These are folks who are initially hostile toward hematomans and only join our company through coercion, but after about three days of pulling a few pints from them, they can't resist us and we can then claim not only their volition, but their loyalty.

I've always found maintaining a feeder to be a sensual experience for both parties. I have several across the city who willingly allow me to take their blood. As I said, I'm strong supernaturally, and this benefit stretches to my ability to control several human servants at one time. When I need something done during the daylight hours and Diane is so busy she can't accommodate me, I go to one of my feeders. After giving them a moment of pleasure by clamping down on their carotid artery, they practically grovel at my feet to be allowed to do my bidding.

Most of my feeders are male, and none so refined or wealthy as Mrs. Pollack seemed to be. I could use this alliance to my advantage.

Sitting beside her, I didn't hesitate, but pinched up the vein in her neck and drove my fangs in hard, sucking down just enough to give her a warm, fuzzy feeling. Her breath rasped and she blinked against my biting hold, but in the end, she relaxed, giving off a little moan when she did.

I sucked off and ran a finger over my lips to catch any dribbles. "Mrs. Pollack," I said quietly, "I want you to tell me about Richard Hanuman."

"He used to work at the Smithsonian," she answered dreamily.

"What exactly did he do while he was there? Not his official title. I want to know what he did."

"He was an artist. He helped to create the exhibits on ancient cultures."

"Did he do things like paint the backdrops for the dioramas?"

She nodded. "Yes, and more. His specialty was paleon-tological reconstruction."

"What's that?"

"He would take skull bones brought in by the field scientists and make molds of them. Then he would build up the features of the individual by using clay. That way, we got a realistic presentation of what people looked like in the culture we were attempting to recreate."

"He would have to have knowledge of human anatomy to do that."

"Yes, he did. He was good. He had an appreciation for ancient people and the various world races."

"It sounds like he liked his job. Why did he quit?"

"He—he didn't quit. He was fired."

"The reason?"

"We had many different problems with him. His coworkers avoided him. He had harassment grievances filed against him. One woman in particular was out to get him."

"What was her name?"

"Catherine Forest."

"What else did he do to cause you to fire him?"

"He stole things."

"What things?"

Mrs. Pollack hesitated, and I had to lay on the Dracula Stare to force her to speak. "What things did he steal?"

"We had to cover it up," she said. "It wouldn't have looked good for us. Congress might have cut our appropriations during the next fiscal year. I had too many years in civil service to let anyone find out."

Once in a while, you come across something so sensitive to the person's survival that it's like pulling fangs to get an answer. "What did Richard Hanuman steal?" I demanded, in a harsh tone.

She wrung her knotty little hands together before answering. "We have several warehouses where we catalog and store the finds from archaeological digs: articles of clothing, pottery, jewelry. We usually make copies of these things for our displays. The valuable finds are always locked in vaults. Things started coming up missing." She halted in her dialogue again. I was just about to yank it out of her when the words started to flood forth.

"Richard Hanuman had access to the warehouses. His

supervisor, Melvin Kingsley, was diagnosed with lung cancer and about the time he started getting too sick to work, he made Richard a temporary unit leader. I don't know why he did, either. Melvin didn't like Richard, as far as I could tell."

"Why not?"

"He thought he was a troublemaker. Richard would submit papers he had written for inclusion in his personnel record. They were far from scholarly, if you understand me. Word got out, and it made Melvin look bad, as though it was his choice to keep this crank working in his division. There was nothing he could do legally to have him removed, so before he left, he tried talking to him, but he couldn't convince Hanuman to stop writing his reports."

"Then what happened?"

"Melvin went on terminal leave, and before he did, he appointed Richard to a supervisory slot. He told me that all the aggravation concerning this employee had hastened the advancement of his disease, and personnel was going to have to deal with the lunatic from then on. It was like he was getting the last laugh."

"But you didn't take steps to fire him or have him demoted?"

"Not right away. I thought maybe he would calm down and stop sending in his absurd reports, so I had him issued a clearance to enter the storage vaults, when necessary."

"Did he keep writing his papers?"

"He did, but less frequently. He faded somewhat into the background, until we were preparing for the yearly inspection by the Smithsonian auditing service. If it hadn't been for that, we wouldn't have discovered the ten vials missing."

"What was in the vials?"

"Gold dust."

I almost choked on my hold over her. Scraping together

my composure, I managed to reestablish our bond without losing control. "Did you question Hanuman about the missing articles?"

"Yes. He denied it, but by that time, I was sure it was he who was responsible for the theft. He looked like a thief to me. Always wearing gloves."

"Why?"

"I understand he was severely burned as a child, but still, it's what I thought."

"What did you do to have him released from his position?"

"I put the pressure on my own supervisor, but he was afraid to make an issue out of it. Funding. You have to be careful about the funding."

"What finally changed his mind?"

"Catherine Forest's complaint. We wanted to avoid an investigation. She threatened to go the *Post* if nothing was done. Last year alone, we had twenty-seven sexual harassment grievances."

"What happened about Catherine's complaint?"

"Nothing. It was shuffled. After a while, she agreed to drop the charges provided she received an in-grade salary increase. When we finally released Hanuman, I made her unit leader just to keep her quiet."

I reached into my purse, thinking I had the composite picture drawn by the police artist, but I had left the house without my copy. "Do you keep an employee roster here at home?"

"Yes."

"Good. Give me Catherine's address. I want to visit her."

Mrs. Pollack stood slowly, reminding me of a wooden toy hinged at the joints. She went to a mahogany secretary and opened a drawer, pulling out a thick sheaf of papers. With a jerky hand, she wrote down the address. I took it from her and doubling up my hematoman charm, gathered in more of her cooperation.

"Tell me, Barbara, how do you keep files on your employees? Paper copies or computer disk?"

"Both."

"What about Richard Hanuman? Do you still have something on him, or have you archived it?"

"I have records. At the office."

"I want a copy of everything you have. Get your coat. Let's go over to the museum and get it."

"Yes, yes, of course. Anything you want."

She disappeared into the bedroom and a moment later came out wearing a black wrap trimmed in mink. Standing before me, I got the impression she was waiting for inspection. The only thing she gained was my envy. I've always wanted a coat like that.

25

THE NIGHT WAS frigid. Temperatures were cold enough to freeze the balls on a caveman. The sidewalks and streets were fun, too, because a diaphanous cloak of ice covered the District. Few people were out on this night and those who were could be classified as either hematoman or homeless. Mrs. Pollack and I arrived downtown in the backseat of an old taxicab driven by a Nigerian who wanted to practice his English. After I got it through his head that we didn't want to take a tour of Northwest Washington, he gave up on trying to turn an extra buck and finally dropped us off at the corner of Fourteenth and Constitution Avenue. From there, we slipped and slid our way toward her museum office.

Even if you've never been to the nation's capital, you probably still know what the Mall looks like. I'm sure everybody has at one time or the other seen a picture of the place. It's one photo that has decorated calendar covers handed out by realtors and insurance agents for years, showing the straight-arrow lineup of the Lincoln Memorial, the Washington Monument, the reflecting pool, and the lovely manicured green leading straight down the pike to the U.S. Capitol Building. The buildings that flank this promenade belong to the Smithsonian Institution.

There's the famous Castle, the National Gallery of Art, the Air and Space Museum, and the Hirshhorn, just to name a few. There are even museums that have been built underground, because topside real estate is at such a premium. Among the most famous marble temples devoted to man and his achievements is the National Museum of Natural History.

Walking into the rotunda of this building, the visitor is immediately stopped in his tracks by a view of an eight-ton, thirteen-foot-high stuffed Angolan elephant. The eyelashes on this thing are incredible. They've got to be three inches long and curl so prettily you would think someone had used a crimper on them just that morning.

It's a big place in every respect, and the elephant is just for starters. One room offers a look at dinosaurs, and another holds a giant squid that beached on the shore of Plum Island, Massachusetts. There's also an 860-pound Bengal tiger, and a gift shop that will sell you the plush toy version of it. Separate halls will let you study Egyptian and Peruvian mummies, moon rocks, evolution, and the major cultures of the world, but I suppose as far as the kids are concerned, the biggest exhibit draw is the bug room. There, the visitor will find an assortment of live insects, everything from African horned beetles to honey bees and roaches. They feed the tarantula spiders weekdays at 10:30 A.M. and again at 11:30 and 1:30 P.M. I would really like to see that, but unfortunately, the bug feeders go home before the sun sets.

Mrs. Pollack and I paused at the bottom of the stone steps leading to the museum. It was important for me to reinforce my control over her, but I couldn't take any more blood. She was two pints low and looked like she could hardly afford that.

"Give me your hand," I ordered, and she did.

Pulling back her coat sleeve, I lifted her wrist to my mouth, pricking the tips of my fangs into the artery there. I didn't want to draw fluid, just inject more of my enzymes into her. The tiny points of contact would quickly scab over to close off the canals.

With a sigh, she was again totally mine.

"Let's go inside, Barbara. I want you to take me to where you keep the information."

She nodded and I went invisible, just to be on the safe side. I didn't want anyone asking her who I was, especially someone from the FBI side of the investigation. The Hooverheads didn't need to know that I was overstepping the bounds of my responsibility as far as the probe was concerned.

She buzzed the guard at the main entrance, who admitted us with a remote control device designed to open the massive doors. He nodded and pushed a clipboard in her direction, but beyond that, he hardly noticed her, consumed as he was by the conversation he was having on the phone. While she signed in, I moved back a ways to position myself in the eye of the surveillance camera.

I can't help myself. Every time I see one of those cameras, I have to screw with it and with the poor guy whose job it is to review the films. Duval's epinephrine package made me feel playful, so I switched myself on and off like a lighthouse beacon. One second I was there; one second I was gone.

I did a little jig as I played, waving, and finally bowing. Watching this videotape was going to give someone a hell of a headache. In the end, they would say it was a glitch in the electronics, but the fellow seeing all the tomfoolery will swear until he's dead that the Smithsonian has a ghost who wears jeans and athletic shoes.

After showing the guard her ID, Mrs. Pollack walked away from the desk with a purposeful step. I followed her as she clicked past the elephant and made a turn toward the east wing, whereupon I felt it was marginally safe to come back into full visibility. The lights were dimmed in this section, the surveillance units giving way, it seemed, to the occasional pass of a night guard. The really expensive stuff, like the Hope Diamond and the moon rocks brought back during one of the Apollo space missions, was housed on the second floor. That's where the high-tech security systems could be found.

Mrs. Pollack cut beneath a hundred-foot replica of a sperm whale suspended from the ceiling. I get the creeps walking under things that could fall on me. I'm not sure where this phobia comes from, but it's right up there with being buried alive, so while she showed her nonchalance, I took a wide berth and followed her by taking the route closest to the display of the giant squid. At least it was noodled around a stand that sat on the floor.

Just beyond the open jawbone of a great white shark was a nondescript steel door, simply marked with the word Associates. I thought it was a bathroom for a moment, but Mrs. Pollack stopped before it. Fumbling inside her purse, she brought out a magnetic card and slid it through the strip reader hanging from the wall near the knob. There was a buzz announcing access, and she pushed the door open.

We entered another shadowy corridor, this one plushly accommodated with good-grade brown carpeting. A few more steps and she stopped at a door to swipe her card through another magnetic reader. Without a word, we entered.

Inside, I could tell Mrs. Pollack lived her days here. The space looked like it belonged to her: a beige-on-beige hideaway. Light wood, pale fabrics, delicate lines. Manila folders fanned across the desk next to a neat stack of cream-colored paper. There were no whimsical coffee mugs, no cutsie pictures, nothing to tell an employee that this person could be approached for a raise by using a light touch and a sense of humor. The walls were adorned with copies of Chinese prints that were washed in harmony, solitude, and blandness. Her choice of furnishings gave a new meaning to the word conservative.

"Take your coat off and sit down before the computer," I ordered.

She did as I said, perching herself at the desk and turning on the IBM clone.

"I want all the information you have on Richard Hanuman and the projects he worked on."

"Yes, of course."

"Dump it to a blank disk when you find it."

Her skinny fingers played the keys for several minutes. Occasionally, she would grunt when some security flag slowed her progress. Stepping behind her, I watched as she wound through the network, retrieving data by slamming in her password and moving down electronic streets that would have made any good hacker drool with delight.

"Can you access all his employment records?"

"Yes. We keep historical data files of SF–one seventy-ones."

SF-171s are standard government resume forms for civil service workers. "I want everything you can capture on him."

She tapped away and soon had downloaded everything to three floppy disks. I had her make a set for Walsh, placed them in my purse, and turned to go, but Mrs. Pollack didn't move from her chair.

I could have let her stay there. She would have eventually snapped out of the trance and wondered how she managed to get to her office. A certain amount of confusion follows when the enzymes wear off. Depending on the strength of the human's personality, this disorientation can range from mild to extreme, and I'm not so cruel as to let a person suffer even in a small way, especially after she's helped me.

"Barbara, you'll remember nothing of this evening. Do you understand?"

"Yes."

"Tomorrow, or the next day, the Metro Police may contact you for additional information on Richard Hanuman. You'll be cooperative in every way, as though you've never been approached, aside from the single interview Lieutenant Walsh and I held with you a few days ago. Is that clear, Barbara?"

"I will do as you wish."

"Good. Now, go home and go to bed. If anyone asked where you were, tell them you took in a movie."

"Yes."

She rose and followed me out of the office, pulling the door closed to engage the security latch.

We strolled through the museum. I decided right then and there I would keep Mrs. Pollack as one of my feeders, if only to allow me to visit this place during my own hours. Before leaving, we took a turn through the *Halls of Native Peoples of the Americas* to have a look at some of the dioramas. They showed in wax and paint how the cultures of the New World lived before Columbus and his cronies stopped in for that fateful visit in 1492.

I turned invisible as we reached the guard post at the entrance. The security watch had changed since our arrival. This sentry seemed a lonely sort and wanted to talk, but Mrs. Pollack only grunted in reply. After two failed attempts to gather her into conversation, he gave up, allowing his attention to be corrupted by a sandwich and a diet soda sitting on the desk before him. Amid the noise of her snapping heels, I heard him pop the top on the drink can as we left the building.

When we cleared the huge marble portico of the museum, I felt the slashing cold of freezing rain hit my face.

26

I CALLED WALSH and told him I had just met with Barbara Pollack and to come pick me up at the Crystal City Metrorail station. When I stepped from the subway, he was waiting right out front, idling his car in the fire zone. A surge of heat hit me as I slipped into the passenger's seat, and I just couldn't resist laying a cold palm against his face.

He winced, casting a sideways glance at me. "Lady Ice. Out enjoying a stroll in the nice weather?"

I laughed. I was still riding high on adrenaline and blood. "This is actually warm for me, Joe. My furnace is really cranking, tonight."

"Yes, but cranking out what? Frost, maybe?"

I ignored his remark and dug into my purse. I found the disk copy made so willingly by Mrs. Pollack and slid it into the glove box of his car. "We should find out all kinds of interesting things about Richard Hanuman with this data. Barbara had records that go back to his employment entry date. Did you bring the composite with you?"

He patted his coat pocket. "Right here." He put the car into gear and turned onto Highway 1, heading south. "Now tell me, Nicki, how did you manage to get any information out of that snotty bitch? She was damned uncooperative the last time we talked."

"I bought her dinner," I lied. Then, to spin the tale more, I added, "I've spent most of the day wondering about what she said in the initial interview, so I decided to take her to Paul's Pig Palace for barbecue and some general conversation."

He chuckled. "I can't believe she went. Paul's? Those belly busters explode in your stomach. It's like eating nitro. Not to mention the grease. They have the deep fat fryer positioned just behind the cash register. When you pay, you get a ritual anointing in rancid mist."

"Sounds like you eat there a lot."

"Saturdays, only. It's a treat. Right after my bowling league knocks down a few pins at the Shoot-a-Rama, we retire to Paul's for some seasoned cholesterol."

"I didn't take you for a bowler, Joe."

He threw me another sideways look. "And you better not." He grinned, and tucked at the bill of his Redskins cap.

We were going to pay a visit to Mrs. Pollack's disgruntled, sexually harassed employee, Catherine Forest. She lived near the subway line in a house in the Aurora Hills section of Arlington, up by the Pentagon. It was an old craftsman cottage, complete with dormers and a screened front porch. Even in the darkness, it was easy to see the place was in bad need of a paint job, and the small yard strapped in by a rusty, brown fence could have used a mow and edge trim. We went through the squeaky gate and up to the door where Walsh tapped a staccato tune with his knuckles. After a few seconds, a small black kid, about eight years old, appeared.

"You're not the pizza man," he said.

Walsh hunkered down to his eye level. "Naw, we're the cops."

The child's expression went wide. "My mom ain't done nothin' wrong."

"We know. We just want to talk to her. Is she home?"

He turned away and screeched, "Mom! Some people are here to see you." Catherine Forest came around the corner and stepped out on the porch, wiping her hands on a green dishtowel as she did. She frowned as Walsh flashed his ID to introduce us, and then bobbed her head at the boy. "Luke, go up to your room. Mama's got business with these folks."

"But the pizza is coming."

"Do as I say," she snapped. "In this weather, it's going to take the delivery man a half an hour to come six blocks. I'll make sure you get your share when he brings it."

"Don't forget, OK?"

She smiled and pushed him behind her. "I won't forget. I got you pineapple on top of it."

"Yum!" he squealed, and with pounding footsteps, headed back into the house.

"Won't you two come in, please?" she asked, leading the way.

It was a comfortable house on the inside, filled with family photographs and furniture of pressed wood and laminate. I sat on a rocker-recliner that reminded me of the one I have in my own home—more springs than stuffing. Walsh sat down on the sofa, and Catherine took her place in a wing chair across from us. While my partner fiddled with his notebook and pen, I had the opportunity to study the woman.

It was easy to see why anyone would be attracted to her. She was tall and shapely with good skin and good manners. She wore her clothes like they were made of leather rather than denim, and poked up under her dreads were long, coiling earrings that looked like they were made of titanium.

"What's the problem, detective?" she asked.

"We'd like to ask you a few questions about a man named Richard Hanuman. We understand he was a former associate of yours."

Her blood pressure thumped up a notch and I could smell the blood as it flushed into the tiny capillaries feeding her skin. Walsh sensed her wariness, too, and hastened to alleviate her tension.

"I believe you know the head of personnel responsible for your division," he said, "a Mrs. Barbara Pollack. She suggested that we see you concerning this gentleman."

She swallowed. "Well, if Mrs. Pollack has already talked to you, I guess the secrets are out, then. What do you want to know?"

Walsh opened with a generic question. "Can you tell us what sort of person he was?"

"He was strange. He used to say I was the reincarnation of an African princess. Do you believe it? I figured it was a come-on at first, and a creative one at that, but after awhile, I couldn't shake him." She paused to draw a deep breath before taking off in earnest. "I remember the first time I met him. I had just been transferred to the Division of Ancient Cultures from the Arts and Industries Building. I had just finished my degree in art restoration, and even though I was going in as a staff secretary, it was a good chance to work my way into a new slot. The museum was adding several new dioramas to the *Halls of Native Peoples of the Americas*. I was excited at first, because this was a good chance to get into a professional series, so I started using Hanuman's interest in me to learn the office politics, you know? But it didn't work like I thought it would. He started to really annoy me."

"We understand that you filed a complaint against him for sexual harassment. Is that correct?"

"Yeah."

"Will you please tell us what form this harassment took?"

She rubbed the tip of her small chin. "The usual kind. Like I said, I worked as a unit secretary for a while and he would stop by my desk to talk. Before he would go back to his cubicle, he'd say things about how nice he thought I dressed and what a good figure I have."

"That seems harmless enough," I said.

"I didn't think much of it, either. I've had men hitting on me since I was fourteen years old, and most of the time I just blow them off and go on with what I'm doing." She paused and then said, "It was the flowers that finally made me start to worry."

"Flowers?" Walsh asked, scribbling furiously in his notebook.

"I don't know what kind they were, but they were sickly sweet to smell. I'd come to work on Monday morning, and there'd be two or three vases full of them. They were huge bouquets, kind of like what you see at a funeral home. With the way the things stank, everybody got the same idea about that. People started asking Richard if he worked part time over at DeMaines Mortuary. They kidded him about stealing flowers from graves, too."

"What did he say to them when they gave him a hard time?"

"Nothing. It's like the jabs didn't bother him. He'd smile really politely and go back to his cubicle or into the lab. He never raised his voice; not that I ever saw."

Walsh added another note in his pad. As she continued to speak, I saw his brow cave in to a frown and his knuckles whiten from his ever-tightening hold on the pen.

"He stopped after a while with the flowers. Maybe the office jokes were bothering him and he never let on. I told him how flattered I was and all, but that I just wasn't interested in him on a sexual basis. He wouldn't give it up. A couple of months went by, and then he started to try to impress me by sculpting clay fetishes and setting them all over my desk when I was off making copies or doing something for the unit supervisor."

"Fetishes? Would you please explain that term to us?"

"Sure. A fetish is an object that contains magical powers. It's a figurine of sorts."

"What form did these fetishes take? Were they sexual in nature?"

"No, they were mostly pretty ugly." She licked her lips before continuing. "Remember I said our unit was involved in setting up the exhibits in the *Halls of Native Peoples of the Americas*?"

"Yes."

"The Native peoples used these fetishes all the time. They believed that these objects helped them control the world. They served as a supernatural bridge linking the tribe to the dimensions of the gods."

"So, what kind of fetishes did Hanuman give you?"

She rose and walked over to a curio cabinet sitting in the corner. Once there, she selected a statuette, which she showed to us upon her return to the couch. "This is one of the objects he made for me. It's a protection fetish."

"May I see it?" Walsh asked.

Handing it to him, she continued, "It's the only one I ever really cared for. You're lucky it was in the cabinet, too. My son usually has it mixed in with his toy soldiers. It's the monster, you know."

Walsh grinned, fingering the piece before passing it to me. It was a strange thing: a feminine caricature with pointy breasts and a bottom half that looked like it belonged on a sheep or goat. No more than four inches tall, it showed the figure carrying a lidded basket on its back. This little container opened, and with a simple twist, I saw how the artist had used his thumb to make a small well on the inside. The object had such wonderful detail right down to the curling hair on the legs and the grimacing look of the face that Gale would have been jealous to see this kind of fanciful work.

"Is it possible that the police department may borrow this

object?" Walsh asked. "It'll be cataloged and returned to you when we complete our investigation."

She snorted. "Sure." Then, "Hanuman got himself into deep shit, didn't he?" When Walsh was noncommittal, she said, "I'm not surprised."

"What exactly does a protection fetish do?" he said, attempting to change the subject.

"Many times ancient people would cremate their dead and then would mix a person's ashes with a bit of wild grass, stuff some in the basket, and close it back up. It symbolically trapped a small part of the ancestor's soul. The person who owned the fetish was assured that the deceased could never leave the death plane to come back to haunt him, because he would need his whole soul intact to enter heaven again. Personally, I think it was mainly to keep vampires away."

Her words startled me so, I almost dropped the figurine, but I managed to recover my composure without too much notice from either of them.

"How did you finally resolve the problem you had with Hanuman's harassment?"

"I went to my supervisor first, but that was a waste of words. The old saying is true: Nobody knows nothing. It's especially true in the federal government. I was willing to let everything drop if the boss would at least get him off my back, but the bastard didn't do anything. I finally had enough of the both of them and went to EEO and filed a grievance. They buried the complaint, sitting on it for months. In the meantime, his attention got more obvious. He tried to kiss me a bunch of times right there in the office. Once he managed to fondle my breast as we passed in a tight squeeze among the work cubicles. During this whole time, I tried for a transfer. I was willing to take a demotion to get out of there; anything, to get away from this creep."

She injected a sigh into her voice. "The day we really had it out came after he followed me into the ladies' room and tried to put those nasty hands down my pants."

"Nasty hands? Is that a figure of speech or was there something wrong with him?"

"He was burned when he was a kid. I never found out what exactly happened, but his hands were all scarred up. He used to wear gloves because he was self-conscious about the way they looked."

Walsh glanced at me and retrieved the composite picture from his jacket pocket. He unwrapped it and showed it to Catherine Forest. "Is this Richard Hanuman?"

She nodded. "That's a pretty good likeness, I'd say."

27

WALSH DROVE ME home immediately after leaving Catherine Forest's house, the whole while munching from a bag of bridge mix stuffed into the ashtray of his car.

"Richard Hanuman sounds like a real pain in the ass for everybody concerned," he said around a bite of caramel.

I nodded. "He does seem interesting. Do you mind if I hang on to the fetish for a couple of days before you log it?" I asked.

He pulled it out of his jacket and gave it to me. "Be my guest. I'll put a flag on the computer in the property room and write up a description. Just don't lose it, please? I don't think I could ever replace that thing."

I smiled. "I won't. I'd like Gale to take a look at it and see what he thinks."

"Why?"

"Maybe this guy has sold some of these things. If he has, Gale might know who bought them or how to get hold of Hanuman. He does have a lot of contacts in the art world, and according to him, he moves in esoteric circles. Whatever that means."

"Good idea. See if he knows anything." He popped another piece of candy and turned down Water Street before speaking again. "You know, anyone who can carve like that could handle a scalpel just as easily."

"I thought of that, too, and if he spent his days reconstructing the facial features on skull molds taken from ancient people, then, he'd have to have a good command of anatomy. He'd have to know where the musculature goes, the thickness of the dermis, even down to the width of the nose according to the depth of the sinus passages."

Our conversation lapsed again until we pulled up in front of my house. "I'll give you a call if I turn up any more pieces of the puzzle," he said. Then, as I was getting out of the car, he added, "Oh, Nicki, I almost forgot. Again."

"What?"

He leaned across the seat to rifle through the glove box, finally coming up with an envelope. "You won last week's football pool over at Metro. I've been carrying the money around for two days. Sorry, I forgot to give it to you."

Great. Just when I needed to stop gambling, I started to win. I pasted on a smile. "Thanks. I hadn't even thought about it."

"How do you do it, anyway?" he asked, putting the car into drive, but pedaling the brake. "I've been playing the pool for three years and haven't scraped one in yet."

I leaned back over the passenger's seat. "The secret is play according to jersey color. The team wearing the darker uniforms are dominant. They'll usually win."

He snorted. "Seriously?"

"Sure."

"Good night, Nicki."

"Good night, Joe." I turned away and hurried up the front stoop, pausing by the trash can. My mind was on the lid, and my conviction was right up there, too. It was better to dump the money, just for peace of mind, but as I was ready to throw the envelope away, Diane opened the front door.

"Oh, it's you," she said. "I thought it was another one of Gale's interviewees." She squinted at the trash can cover I held.

"I—I thought I saw a rat," I said, replacing the lid and entering the house.

Diane shook her head, closing the door behind me. I

shoved the envelope at her. "Here, give this to the community center to help with the Thanksgiving dinner for the homeless."

"You won again, huh?"

I sighed and removed my coat. "I don't want to talk about it. Just do something with it, OK?"

She nodded, leading off toward the kitchen. I followed her down the hall, glancing into the parlor to see the latest freak show waiting to have their interviews. I counted two women and three men. The females smelled of blood and I could tell they were human right off. The men, though, were undead, suave and sophisticated. When I looked into the room, one of them sensed I was his kind of people, so he curled his lip to expose the tips of his fangs.

"You have a visitor, too," Diane said.

"Me? Who?"

"Justin Lang. I put him downstairs in the lab. I've got more flakes running around this place than I know what to do with. I didn't want him in the way. There's not much down there he can get in trouble over."

"Did you lock the fridge?"

"Yes. He won't be snooping much."

"Do you know what he wants?"

"Not really. I thought he was here to see Gale, at first. He called a couple of times today to talk to him, but his majesty put him off. He came over; I guess hoping to see him right away, but when he got here, there was a line to see his excellency." She slowed her step to throw a look over her shoulder at me. "Do you know what's going on?"

"Gale hasn't told me much. I suppose he figures it's none of my business, since he won't be part of the clan. And, I'm too stubborn to ask."

"I just don't think he'll leave."

"I hope you're right."

She sat down at the table and picked up a book. I noticed that her reading material had gone from *Beauty Digest* to a computer manual. She saw me looking at her and said, "I got you back on-line with the modem. You can send E-mail again."

"Thank you, my electronic guru."

"Don't gurus get their feet kissed once in a while?"

I grinned. "Aren't clan leaders supposed to get their butts kissed once in a while, too?"

She placed a hand against her heart and groaned, surrendering. "Go do your thing. It'll take me a few minutes to make up a snappy comeback."

"Is the moody artist with anyone right now? I need to see him before tackling Lang."

"Yeah. Why don't you go interrupt him?" Then, with a sheepish smile lighting her face, she said, "I'm sure he'd be willing to kiss your butt."

I held up my hands in forfeiture, too, relinquishing the game of verbal jabs to go upstairs. I knocked on the studio door. It was following a curse that an answer came.

"Who is it?" Gale roared.

"It's Nicki."

He yanked the door open to glare at me. "I'm busy right now."

I looked beyond him to see one of the black leatherettes posed nude in the center of the room. Her hair was a mass of rainbow-colored points; she had a large tattoo of a white tiger slinking down one shoulder; and her right cheek, which she faced toward me, was pierced with safety pins that were joined by little silver chains.

"I'm sorry. I just wanted to ask if when you had time you could have a look at something for me."

"No!" he stormed. "I don't have time for you now!"

He displayed such ferocity in his expression that he

immediately pissed me off. Anger banged through me and came out in my voice. "Why the hell are you so hostile toward me? You're home, aren't you?"

I saw canines before he spoke, but like a bulb going out, his face changed into a look of concern. "Please, Nicki," he said in raw whisper, "go away. I'll be down in a little while." With that, he shut the door.

More than being furious, I was stunned. I stood there for several seconds trying to get my brain to send my legs a message about walking. After a bit, I stumbled downstairs. In the kitchen, Diane glanced up from her book.

"That was quick," she said.

I shook my head. "If I didn't know better, I'd say Gale is going off the deep end."

"He's just having a tantrum."

It was a small straw, but I grabbed it anyway. "Maybe, you're right."

"Hunk, huh?" I opened the door to the lab and Fuzzy Nuts shot out. Glancing at Diane, I said, "Discerning cat. He doesn't like hunks."

She snorted and went back to reading about bits and bytes.

Justin Lang was sitting at my worktable, staring at the crime scene photos I had laid out there. He was dressed in jeans and a white shirt and in the light from the halogen lamp, his long, sienna-colored hair glistened.

"Do you find the pictures interesting, Mr. Lang?"

He started and looked toward me as I descended the stairs. "Hello." His eyes followed me as my feet hit the floor. "I hope you don't mind me looking at them. It's the Winter Man case, isn't it?"

"You read the newspapers, then."

"Well, yes, but I'll admit, the conversation I had with Gale was flavored with a few inquiries about you and your business. He told me you're a freelance consultant for the Medical Examiner's Office, and that you're called in on the unusual investigations. He also told me that he's in love with you, but the relationship is at an end. Is that true?"

I moved to the fax machine, suddenly feeling irritable. Art's report curled from the slot to drip on the floor. "Mr. Lang, what do you want?" I asked, as I ripped the paper off.

"A couple of things."

"Which are?"

"I'd like to get to know you. I found you instantly fascinating the other night. You have a way of drawing an unsuspecting person in with just a few words. The vampire thing really got me. I'm afraid I haven't stopped thinking about you."

My irritability turned up a notch. "Give me a break, Romeo; what's the real reason you're here?"

He sighed lightly and ran a hand through his dark mane. It was an orchestrated pause, intended to entice me, but with my corrupted mood, I didn't enjoy this human game. "That is the real reason," he said in a low voice. "The other is Gale."

"Right. You want me to convince him that you could make him rich and famous."

"I could make us both rich and famous."

"I don't know what you're worried about. He was the one who put the copy of *Night Argosy* into your mail slot. He wants you as much as you want him."

"Are you sure? I can't believe I'm the only one he's approached. I've known about him for a long time and assumed he already had an artist's agent. The guy has one of those off-the-wall creative visions, like Andy Warhol." He stopped, cutting in a frown. "No, not Warhol. He's like Picasso, you know? Most people see a bicycle: Picasso saw a bull. That's the way Gale is. I wish I could paint and sculpt like he does. I dabble, mostly." He halted again, and it felt like he was casting around for a bit of sympathy over his lack of talent, but then he started up and I saw where he was leading. "I suppose my special skills are on the promotion end of it all. Whatever, Gale needs the kind of exposure I can give him. It wouldn't be long before he becomes a success." He popped in another pause. "Still, I have some reservations."

"Like what?"

"He told me he only works at night and is unavailable for showings where he might be required to attend during the day. He keeps telling me he's a vampire, too. Is it a weird game you two play?"

"Let's just call it an alternative lifestyle and leave it at that, shall we?"

He didn't. "I've seen no evidence—no blood, no fangs."

I decided to ignore him, and set my purse down on the chair. When I did, I heard the clunk of the clay object Catherine had loaned us. Since Gale wasn't interested in helping me, I thought of Lang and his professed skill in finding quality art as well as artists. It was also a way to draw him off the subject of unlife so, unzipping my bag, I pulled it out to show to him.

"Let see how good you are, Mr. Lang," I said, handing him the object. "Do you know anyone around town who makes these little gems?"

He angled the neck of the lamp close to him to study it. I noticed he had clean, trimmed nails, but his hands showed a ridge of calluses—the kind you get when you work a lot with clay at a potter's wheel.

"Off the top of my head, I can't say I do, but whoever did this has exceptional talent for creating miniatures. The detail is extraordinary." He paused. Then, as though he'd forgotten I was there, he launched into an opinion. "It's old."

"I'm told it's a recent copy."

He shrugged. "Maybe it is, but I don't believe it. Just looking at it, I'd wager that it comes from Central or South America and was made about the time of the Mayans or a little earlier. If it's a copy, then the artist should be applauded."

"Why?"

"Because the person who carved this has gone to some trouble to make it appear as though it's an antique."

He hunkered down over the fetish, adjusting the halogen light. "Ceremonial objects were often painted with natural pigments and used for different rituals. Afterward, they were cleaned up and prepared for another use. It looks as though that's what the artist was trying to do with this figurine. I'd say that at one time it was covered with a thin wash of color. There's paint collected in the design detail. If it's new, this effect does create a nice illusion. Without specific tests, I can't pinpoint anything. I know what you said, yet it still might be an antique and worth more than your house." He didn't look up from the fetish, but paused in his narration to hold out his hand. "Do you have an X-acto knife?" he asked.

"Will a scalpel do?"

That got his attention. His face bobbed up, wearing a frown. "Yeah, that's fine." He dipped back down toward the object as I gave him the cutter. Opening the basket lid, he scraped the knife along the inside of the well formed there. "Just as I thought—this thing has been painted with pigment. Red ochre, I believe." Finally, he glanced at me with a grin. "You have scalpels; do you have specimen bags?"

I pulled one out of the table's drawer and held it open while he upended the figurine over it. A tiny bit of reddish residue spilled from the container.

"If it's a copy, I could sell this thing for an easy five hundred," he said. "There's big money in good forgeries."

Lang went on to talk about fakes and big business in the art world, but I didn't hear much more after that. I started thinking about Mrs. Pollack's assertions that Richard Hanuman had been slowly and systematically ripping off the Smithsonian of its treasures.

28

Tuesday, November 24

THERE IS A medical condition known as purpura. The outward symptoms of this malady are characterized by purplish discolorations that are visible through the skin. It's caused by bleeding or the inflammation of the blood vessels within the affected tissue. It can also be a sign that there's a lack of platelets, particles necessary to help the blood clot. Purpura can come from various drugs used to thin the blood, such as aspirin and salicin. It can also be a sign of septicemia, which is simple blood poisoning. The reason I didn't see the evidence of purpura on Gitana O'Quinn's body during my cursory exam at the time of death was because the discolorations were localized and hidden in a forest of thick, black hair under her arms.

It was 5:00 A.M. I sat alone in the lab, reading the fax that Art Anthony had sent me earlier in the evening. I would have gotten to it sooner had it not been so hard to get Lang back upstairs with Diane, where she plied him with hazelnut coffee and pretzels until Gale decided to be civil enough to come down from the studio to talk to him. Even at that, it was impossible to concentrate with the commotion of the interviews. The TV blared; there was giggling and laughing; doors slammed; people tromped with heavy feet across the wooden floor. Finally, I lost my patience and threw everybody out of the house, including Lang. Gale was not speaking to me; Diane was asleep; Ekua was off staying with friends; Michael and Ilea were among the undead and missing. My only companion left this night was Fuzzy Nuts, and he demanded that I stroke his fur while I read the ME report.

It hadn't taken Art long to discover the pinhead-sized bruises on the body, once he had centered his hunt on the corpse's lymphatic zones. He'd taken a tissue patch from the area and slipped it under an electron microscope. With the help of modern technology and a computer he lovingly refers to as Fred, he discovered a transdermal residue consisting of dirt, the chemical breakdown of roll-on deodorant, dried sweat, and gold. The Winter Man had been plugging her in the armpits, and each time he did, he irritated the area, causing the tiny feeder vessels located just beneath the skin to rupture.

I got up from the table and poured a glass of whole blood. Just as I did, the phone rang, the noise of which startled me so that I almost dropped the glass. It was Sarah Short.

"Hi, Miss Nicki," she said, in a light voice. "I'm sorry to call you so early in the morning. Sam told me you worked at night. I thought I'd take the chance that you might still be up."

I smiled to myself, imagining the tiny Chinese woman on the other end of the phone. "You didn't disturb me, Sarah. How are you?"

"Pretty good. I called you because Sam said you were interested in whether we had any big herbal tea orders lately."

"Yes, I am. Did you?"

"We have the usual buyers every month—you know, the traditional healers down here in Chinatown. I started thinking about your interest in the man who wears the red gloves and I looked back over our receipts to see what he's had when he's come into the restaurant. He always orders a tea called Fo-Ti-Tieng."

"Fo-Ti-Tieng? I never heard of it. What's it good for?"

"It's thought to promote longevity. There's a legend that goes along with it that says the tea was used by a Chinese named Li Ching Yun. He lived to be two hundred and fifty-five years old. So they say."

"What's this stuff got in it?"

"Mostly superstition and an herb called gotu kola."

"I never heard of that, either."

"Gotu kola is good for healing burns. It helps with the scarring. You can make a tincture or a cream of it and rub your skin with it."

"Is that all this man orders?" I asked.

"For himself. From what I've seen, if he comes in with someone else, he usually bullies them into drinking ginseng."

"Did he ever talk to you, Sarah?"

"Directly, you mean?"

"Yes. Did he ever say why he was drinking all this Fo-Ti-Tieng tea?"

She was silent for a moment. Then, "No, but I used to listen to his conversations with Jow Lord and one night I heard him say that he needed to live a long time. There was something he needed to see through to the end before he died. I don't know what he was he talking about. That's about all I can remember right now. If I think of anything else, I'll call you."

Sarah is a wonderful woman, but like Sam, she has a heart made for gossip. "That sounds fine," I said. "So, tell me. Did you have any big orders of herbal tea lately?"

"Well, we always have some. We're getting a reputation for the purity of our products, you know. I had my assistant help me go over the books for the last three months and I see we've been sending out an order for Fo-Ti-Tieng. And get this," she added in a conspiratorial tone. "We've been sending a kilo of tea a month."

"Where are you sending it?"

"To an address in Virginia—a post office box in some town called, Dumfries."

I tried not to slather my words with spit when I spoke. "What's the name on the order?"

"David Hanuman," she said.

29

It was 5:30 p.m. when Walsh called me. "I'm on my way back over to pick you up," he said. "I've invited us over to see a lady named, Dolores Raoul. She's a medical artist at the Smithsonian and went out a few times with Richard Hanuman. Be ready when I get there."

Ten minutes later, we pushed toward Arlington once more.

"Where did you get Mrs. Raoul's name?" I asked.

"Off the list given to me by the owner of the Wine and Roses Floral Shop," he said. "According to her records, Mrs. Raoul used to regularly receive flowers, champagne, and caviar." He went silent while he negotiated a turn onto Independence Avenue, and continued talking only after he pressed the gas pedal to run the straightaway. "The gifts were ordered using David Hanuman's account."

"Were there notes with the deliveries?"

"No. I thought we'd ask Dolores about that."

We clipped off the conversation after that, each lost in our own considerations. I'm sure Walsh's mind was on the case, because he wore an intense expression as he clawed into a new bag of bridge mix spilling from the car's ashtray. As for myself I thought only of Gale and how many years it had been since he'd bought me flowers.

Dolores Raoul lived in a quiet garden-style apartment just off Columbia Pike. She answered the door immediately, inviting us inside even before Walsh could show her his badge. Mrs. Raoul was Hispanic, small boned, but not a great beauty. Yet, from the way she bounced through her living room, I would say she had a terminal case of perkiness. The last part annoyed me just a little, especially since I was feeling pretty lousy, myself.

"Would you like some coffee?" she said.

We didn't get a chance to answer before she went on. "I just finished baking some Amish friendship bread. Can you smell it? Would you each like a piece? Ah, it's luscious."

I shook my head no and Walsh shook his yes. He glanced at me as we sat down on the couch. "I'm hungry," he whispered sheepishly.

Her apartment was arranged so she could work at the kitchen counter and still talk to her guests, which she did while she sliced into a brown loaf cooling there. Her expression drooped a bit and her words came out flat-sounding. "Forgive me. I haven't had much company the last year or so. My parents live in Mexico, and we're not rich enough to afford to visit all the time. And since my husband Egardo died last January, I've realized how many friends I don't have. They were all his." She came around the counter and placed a mug and a dish on the glass coffee table. "I hope you enjoy it, detective."

He said thank you, stalling the start of the interview to take a bite of the bread. This space gave me a chance to check out Mrs. Raoul's apartment.

Her tastes leaned toward a Southwestern motif, the kind of adobe pink look that has become so popular with people who long for the freedom and space of the desert, but who are stuck with urban blight and traffic jams. She obviously liked bric-a-brac and seemed to collect coyote figurines. These little things were all over the place, accenting rather strangely, a large, terra-cotta tiled wall mural of Monument Valley, in Utah.

Following his snack, Walsh took out his notebook and

pen and launched right into his usual monologue. I dragged back my attention to concentrate on the interview.

"Mrs. Raoul," he said, "as I explained on the phone, we're trying to get some information on Richard Hanuman. Time may be of the essence and anything you can tell us about him will help. To begin, do you know where he currently resides?"

"Not now. Before he left the Smithsonian, he rented an apartment just off of K Street, Northwest."

The information went into the notebook. "Will you tell us about your relationship to him? Did he ever invite you to his residence, say for dinner or drinks?"

"No, he never did. We were just friends. Richard helped me through the first few months after Egardo's death. I was pretty close to suicide, and he saved me by getting me into counseling and by just coming whenever I needed a shoulder to cry on. Then one day he said he had to leave his job at the Smithsonian, and that was it. This past July was the last time I saw him." She pointed her gaze straight at Walsh. "What's happened to him? You said you would explain when you got here."

"Yes ma'am, I did. I'll lay it out for you, if you think you can handle the worst."

She smiled sadly. "Of course I can. What I've been through this year is as bad as it gets."

"All right, then. Richard Hanuman is a suspect in a multiple murder case."

She blinked. "No. You mean, you think he's a serial killer?"

"That's right."

Her head shook just a bit as she placed her cup on the table. "I can't believe it."

"Why?"

"Richard was so gentle and kind. He made me feel special again."

"Did he ever send you flowers?" Walsh asked.

"Yes. All the time. Champagne and caviar, too."

"Excuse me for asking, but did he ever include a note with them?"

"No. He would always call a few minutes after they arrived."

Walsh scribbled away. Then he shifted his line of questioning. "Would you say he was a quiet, unassuming man?"

"He had a certain grace about him, I thought. He was an intellectual. The people at the office though, they thought he was weird, because he had such unique ideas." She hoisted her mug again to take a sip, her hand once more steady. "When you sit in a lab all day and plaster up skulls, you get a lot of time to think. The stuff he came up with would have made Socrates proud."

Walsh frowned and stopped writing. "Socrates?"

"Yes. Richard was a philosopher in his own right. He had strong opinions about how the past and present determine the future."

"Would you please explain that?"

"We all worked in the *Halls of Native Peoples of the Americas*, and whenever we would prepare a new diorama on one of these cultures, he would make a personal study of it. During the lunch hour the whole place empties out, but he and I would stay behind to talk, drink herbal tea, and eat salads that he brought from home. He often told me that no matter how insignificant the culture was, it still played an important part in promoting the events of the future. In his mind, everyone—dead and living—was interconnected through eternity." She paused to look off into the middle distance; then quietly she added: "I suppose he talked about those things to make me feel better about my husband. It helped me with my loneliness and my sorrow."

"How did discussing these different cultures help you with your grief?" Walsh asked. "I don't understand."

"His words made me realize that by keeping Egardo in my memory, he wasn't truly gone, and someday we would share another lifetime together."

Walsh frowned slightly and she hurried to explain. "Richard believed in reincarnation. He claimed to be psychic about people and who and what they were in past incarnations. When he wasn't working at the museum, he would give past life readings to folks interested in the metaphysical. He would get fifty dollars for a half-hour. He could look at you and tell you if you were once a Roman, or a Greek, or if you were one of the original people belonging to the lost tribes of Israel. He never charged me, though, and he tuned in a lot on my past life lineage."

"Past life lineage?"

She put on an exasperated face, but cleared the expression quickly. "The soul remains the same throughout eternity; it's only the body that changes. So, yes, it can be considered a lineage, because one life is connected to another in that the spiritual essence, the real person, never changes. That way a soul can work out its karma."

"Karma?" Walsh said, flipping the page in the notebook.

"The credits and debits accrued in each life. It's like the old 'eye for an eye' theory of the Bible. In reincarnation, a person gets to experience both sides of the situation, even if these situations are hundreds of years and hundreds of lifetimes apart."

"What did he say about you?"

"He said I was once a high priestess for the Moche People of Peru, and that I have always found myself in service to the world, trying to promote good over evil through knowledge."

Hearing her words, I suddenly remembered Alan's gold ribbon, and experienced a moment of the willies. "What did he say about himself?" I asked.

She glanced at me and then back to Walsh. "He's reincarnated several times in Peru and India. He said he has always been a warrior in each incarnation."

"He's an artist in this one," I said. "And he was born in the United States."

"When he talked about being a warrior, he meant metaphysically. He felt that his soul's mission was to reincarnate down through the ages to make sure that evil didn't get out of hand. It's a basic principle, you know. We're all stewards of the world. Richard's assessment of himself in that, was humble. As for being born in the U.S., his soul saw the opportunities it needed here. The spirit will go where there are good chances for it to work through its lessons and grow toward perfection. Once perfection is attained, the soul will return to God."

Joe scratched furiously in his pad, cocking a look at me, indicating for me to take the helm of the questioning for a while.

"Mrs. Raoul, what do you know about his relationship to Catherine Forest?"

"Quite a bit. Richard was genuinely crazy about her, but she couldn't stand him. He would bring her gifts—handcarved things he would do, flowers, miniature paintings. Beautiful presents. But she wouldn't even give him a toss. He thought it was because of his hands."

"His hands?"

"They were burned. Right down to the point where he didn't have any fingerprints left on them."

Walsh cleared his throat, slugged on his coffee, but didn't say anything.

"Do you know what happened to him?" I asked.

"He told me that when he was a kid, he lived with his grandmother in the Appalachian Mountains of Virginia. The old woman was into fundamentalism. She would take him to this little church where people would handle poisonous snakes and spiders. He told me he saw folks who would allow themselves to be bitten by cottonmouths or rattlers and then undergo a divine transformation as God came down and drew the venom right out of them.

"When he was about six years old, his granny took him to one of these come-to-Jesus meetings. The subject was the cleansing of the soul by spiritual fire. They had a visiting preacher that night who brought in a charcoal bucket loaded with hot coals. Well, the old woman must have gone a little nuts with all the chanting and praying. The minister invited someone to step forward to show they were endowed with the protection of the Holy Spirit by plunging his or her hands into this cooker. Richard remembered him saying a pious man would be blessed with no harm to him, but the fire would burn a sinner. Before he knew what was happening, his grandmother led him to the pot and plunged his little hands down into it."

"What happened then?"

"Someone called the sheriff and they came and got him. He said he was shipped to Louisville where he stayed in a hospital for months."

"Whatever became of his grandmother?"

"He didn't know. He never knew any of his relatives, I don't think. At least he never mentioned them. I'm not sure, but I believe he mentioned that he was adopted."

"Do you know a man named David Hanuman?" Walsh asked.

She thought a moment. "No, I'm afraid not."

"All right, Mrs. Raoul, what about friends?" Walsh asked. "Did he know a man named, Edward Bunt?"

"Slick Eddie? We all knew him. He'd come into the labs pushing a dust mop just about every evening. What he was really doing was hiding from his supervisor by coming into our section to talk to Richard."

"What would they talk about?"

"I don't know. I didn't like him, so when I'd see him coming, I'd go into one of the annexes to do my work."

"Did they ever socialize that you know of?"

"Yes. They'd go to Chinatown a lot. Richard used to tell me stories about prostitutes and pimps."

Walsh looked at me. "Nicki, do you have any questions?"

"Yes," I said. "Let me borrow your pad and pen, Joe." I drew the Winter Man's scalpel signature on a blank page and held it up for her to see. "Have you ever seen this symbol before, Mrs. Raoul?"

She lipped the edge of her coffee mug before answering. "Yes."

"Did Richard Hanuman ever use it, maybe to sign his artwork with?"

"Yes." She pointed past me. "Look in the lower right side of the mural—the last tile. Richard painted that for me and signed it, too. He used the symbol a lot."

Standing up, I moved close to inspect the symbol. It was small, unobtrusive, and painted into a border of Indian pictographs.

"Do you know what it means?" I asked.

She nodded. "It's an old Moche design. Their civilization flourished about 700 B.C. A lot has been done on them lately. You might have noticed the articles in the *National Geographic* magazine. The Society helped to uncover some tombs that hadn't been razed by grave robbers. One of them was of the High Priestess of the Sacrifice."

"I'm afraid I missed those issues," Joe said.

"Apparently, the Moche raised guinea pigs for food, but the rodents they kept were infested with fleas. From what the scientists can surmise, the people had an outbreak of bubonic plague. You know, the Black Death?" She drained her cup. "Can I get you some more coffee, detective?"

Walsh nodded and she disappeared into the kitchen.

It's rare you'll find a disease that not even a hematoman can contain, but the bubonic plague is one of them. Most people think the sickness disappeared after it wiped out three-quarters of Europe during the Middle Ages, but the truth is, it's still around, especially in Asiatic countries. I know, because back in the 1980s I sucked down on a diseased victim while visiting Hong Kong. It was the one time in my unlife I can truly say I was sick. Bubonic plague matures within the lymphatic system where the blood is processed and then sent through to the organs and tissues. The infection is so severe that it literally taints the person's entire system and will make a responsible hematoman go temporarily crazy with a fever that can't be broken unless fresh blood is taken on.

Mrs. Raoul returned, handed Walsh his coffee, and continued with her explanation. "When the Moche started dying out, their priests immediately thought that the people had somehow displeased their great fanged deity."

I went on alert. "Fanged deity?"

"Yes. It was represented as half-feline and half-reptile. I saw some artifacts that made it into the hands of the Los Angeles Museum of Art and they showed the fanged deity biting people. Anyway, one of the tombs they uncovered was pristine. This particular burial spot was good and dry, and the mummies inside had held up well over the centuries.

The scientists managed to get some physical samples from the bodies. Richard said he had heard that they discovered traces of the disease in the tissue samples. I don't know much more about that end of it. I was going through a rough period over Egardo and didn't listen very well."

"So, what does this have to do with the symbol?" Walsh asked.

"The Moche were incredible goldsmiths, and they made funerary jars that were just gorgeous. Buried in the tomb with these folks were several containers etched with this symbol and pictures of the fanged deity."

"I take it Richard had an explanation for it?" I said.

"Of course," she answered, narrowing her eyes at me. "He was considered eccentric by our colleagues, but he was brilliant, nonetheless. And what he said made sense." She sipped more coffee before continuing. "The scientists thought it was an abstract representation of a piece of knotted string. They assumed it meant that the persons in the tomb had become tied to the Moche god in the afterlife—like slaves, you might say.

"Richard saw it differently. To him, the circles represented the mathematical symbol for infinity, the slash, then, represented the severing of eternity. He believed the Moche regarded the people who had the bubonic plague as being corrupted and the fanged deity had come to punish them. Because of it, their bloodline had to be ritualistically cut to ensure that the disease didn't enter society again through the wickedness of future generations." The cup went to her mouth a final time, as she drained off the liquid. After she swallowed, she said, "It's too bad no one believed him but me."

30

Wednesday, November 25

WALSH SHOWED UP on my doorstep at one o'clock the next afternoon. Diane let him into the house and parked him in the kitchen with Ekua, Gale, and a cup of hazelnut coffee while she came down into the lab to fetch me.

A hematoman household must be careful. Our situation is similar to those people who do social drugs. They appear normal to the outside world and then go home and do cocaine and pot. They have to make sure that the joints and the bongs and the crack pipes are put away in case their unsuspecting friends come over for a visit. It's the same way with us. We have to make sure the blood is out of sight and the fangs are jacked back up into our gums. We can't let on to being different, and this thought worried me as I came up the steps. With the way Gale was acting, he might tilt the boat just out of sheer spite.

Walsh sat slumped over the table, nodding at something Ekua was saying when I entered the kitchen. He glanced at me, and I could see he was exhausted. His face was about as pale as Gale's is when he's gone for a few days without a blood fill-up.

"Joe, you look like hell," I greeted.

He smiled, slightly. "Remember last night when I said I was going home to get some sleep?"

"Yeah."

"Well, when I got there, I found that my dog had had an

159

intestinal episode. There was shit all over my apartment."
He sipped at his coffee. "So I cleaned up, washed him, took
him to the vet's, and then went down to Headquarters. Do
you want to know what I found out when I got there?"

I sat down at the table. "Sure."

"David Hanuman had been arrested at three o'clock this
morning, charged with assault on a hooker."

"Did you talk to him?"

He shook his head. "Unfortunately, no. Metro Police has
its problems, and one of them is communications. Hanuman
was picked up by blues out of the Sixth District. He was
barely processed before his business partner had him freed
on bail. Money talks, even in the sacred halls of justice. The
only reason I found out about the pickup was because the
Homicide Division has a good secretary who scans the
booking information. She saw his name come up this
morning in the database. I sent a couple of boys around to
his house, but he wasn't home. Alexandria Police are
helping us to keep tabs on his residence, but I don't know.
I think he's gone."

Diane interjected to do her housemother routine. "Joe,
you look hungry. Can I make you a sandwich?"

He dragged his eyes toward her. "Ah, that'd be great.
Thanks."

"Look," Gale said, "why don't you just crash here for the
afternoon and get some sleep? We've got a spare room.
Then, you and Nicki can get going again this evening and
you'll be fresh for the hunt."

Walsh shook his head. "I appreciate it, but I can't. I've got
a meeting this afternoon with the watch commander to
explain how the Winter Man investigation is coming. I
suppose I'll get my weekly butt-chewing about other cases
we haven't solved yet. Boy, don't want to miss that." He
drew a sigh and glanced at me. "I just came by to get the

fetish. I want to log it, so I don't look like I'm withholding evidence in the probe."

I rose to go fetch it from the lab and he called after me.

"Sorry, Nicki. I've got to catalog it. I can't afford to get the Mayor's Office down on the division for something like illegal procedure. It would mean my nuts, if I did."

"I understand," I said, patting him on the shoulder when I passed on my way to the basement. I returned a few seconds later, and Diane had already given him a sandwich to gnaw on. I placed the figurine in the center of the table. Seeing it, both Gale and Ekua lost the lock on their bottom lips.

Gale picked it up and fixed a squint onto it. "Was this the thing you wanted me to see the other night?"

"That was it, but since you were busy, Lang looked it over for me and gave his opinion."

Ekua interrupted, doing it, I knew, just to avoid an argument. "It looks African."

"It's supposedly modeled after Native American art," I answered. "It's a protection fetish. Probably made to keep vampires away."

Gale's hold bobbled when he heard the words, but with his usual dexterity, he saved the piece from dropping with a thunk to the table. "Did the Winter Man do this?"

"Perhaps. We're not certain."

Ekua plucked the fetish from Gale's fingers. "This looks a lot like a figurine my grandmother used to carry around with her."

"Traditional art shares many of the same technical concepts," Gale said, launching into one of his favorite discourses. "Before television connected most people around the world, you could still go to different countries and find examples of art that seemed to be interchangeable. There are some things that are just universal: methods of carving and clay work, painting, and weaving."

"I guess," Ekua answered. "Still, it reminds me of her."

"Why did she carry it?" Diane asked.

"It was her soul keeper."

"What's that?"

"Well, if I remember correctly, her father carved it for her before she was born. My people used to observe certain rites of passage: birth, adulthood, death, all the usual stuff that folks will do to make life bearable and to give it some meaning. My particular tribe still holds naming ceremonies. Well, they used to, before most everybody was wiped out by the government." He looked forlorn for a moment. I was sure he was thinking back to the past and the violent events that had changed his young life forever. Then, as though he shook off the memories, he continued. "A name is considered very important because it defines the person's destiny."

I couldn't help asking. "What does yours mean?"

Here, he grinned. "The truth? Ekua means 'man who walks in the moonlight.'"

I thought Gale was going to laugh out loud, but he stalled it by placing a hand over his mouth. Jumping in, I kept the explanation going so Walsh wouldn't realize how funny we all thought it was. "So, your grandmother got a fetish when she was named while still in the womb. Is that right?"

He nodded. "After she was born, she was taught that it was important for her to carry it with her for her whole life."

"What made it so special?" Walsh asked around a bite.

"It actually held her soul."

He stopped chewing. "Huh?"

"She believed that her spirit was locked up in this figurine, because the human body was considered an inappropriate vessel to house the soul, so they make these little holders. The tribal shaman purifies them and then when the name is spoken for the first time, it allows the soul to come down from the realm of the gods to inhabit the charm."

"Why do your people believe that the body's no good to house the soul?" Walsh asked.

"We do rotten things to ourselves, don't we?" Ekua said. He pointed the sandwich. "We eat things better left untouched. We smoke. We have sex more than we should. We run ourselves down into the ground and make ourselves sick. The soul is a magical part of us that has to be kept pristine. By bottling it in a figurine, we're then allowed to abuse ourselves without ever tarnishing our souls." He rubbed a thumb along the fetish's basket. "My grandmother always said that if the object ever broke, her soul would be released and she'd die."

"Did it ever break?" Walsh asked.

Ekua nodded and sad look drew down his handsome face. "Yes. It broke and she did die a few days later."

"So, maybe it's not been made to keep away vampires, but to keep the life force in," Gale said.

Walsh finished his sandwich, washing it down with a gulp of coffee. He kicked back from the table and stood up. "That was good. I feel better already." He glanced at Ekua and grinned. "So does my soul." He took the fetish from him and placed it in his jacket pocket, turned to go, but stopped. Glancing at me, he said, "I did find one piece of information about David Hanuman that you might think is interesting."

"What's that?"

"He was born in Kentucky. A little place near the Cumberland Gap called Pathfork."

"Dolores Raoul mentioned that Richard Hanuman went to a hospital in Kentucky as a child," I said.

He thumbed the bill of his cap and managed a thin smile. "I know."

31

___

IF I HAD a menstrual period, I'd swear that what bothered me was PMS. My disposition was starting to remind me of my mother's fiendish attachment to her hormones, except I didn't have any to blame my witchiness on. So, to save everyone in the house from having to make the moral choice of whether to put me out into the sunshine or not, I gave them all a break. I took myself over to Our Lady of Victory for Wednesday night bingo.

Sitting there daubing the numbers on my playing sheets with a dried-up Magic Marker gave me time to try to relax and think over my family problems. I didn't have to worry about how to hide my winnings this time, either. I never walk off with anything when I play bingo. Besides, if I did, Our Lady of Victory makes sure that I get a donation envelope along with the cash.

The smoke in the hall was thick and curled up around the five-foot-long crucifix plastered to the wall behind the game caller. My luck was running its usual cruise down another stream and boredom had flattened the initial gambling rush I'd had. I was missing a lot of numbers because I couldn't stop staring at that sculpture of Christ on the cross.

When a person becomes undead, it tends to dampen his spirituality. Most hematomans are atheists by circumstance. Not that Heaven or Hell don't exist, mind you. It's just that unless we spontaneously combust, our souls aren't likely to meet yours at either gate.

Languishing in this supreme cowardice is the knowledge that if God wanted vampires mucking up the afterlife, he wouldn't have given us unlife. Simple as that. Outcasts, yes, but we're saved from the worry about the great beyond. We're already there.

Trying to untangle myself from this particular thought pattern, I turned slightly to watch the old lady playing next to me. Her name was Mrs. Javinski, and according to proper bingo etiquette, she offered me small talk before the game began. Yet, once the caller was shouting numbers, this nice, blue-haired, Jewish woman from Northwest Washington joined her cohorts to become a demonic bingo player.

Most folks think this game is a tame, harmless version of gambling, but it's not. When everyone is concentrating on the jackpot, there's no talking, no socializing, no laughing. Cigarettes burn to the filters in nearby ashtrays, ignored until that last number comes up. No one moves from their seat, lest they disturb an entire hall. I've often imagined that if a killer came storming into Our Lady of Victory brandishing an automatic weapon and demanding everyone's winnings, some lady like Mrs. Javinski would reach out a single, taloned hand, grab him by the ear, throw him bodily into a chair, and tell him to shut up until the round was over.

Before I could collect myself to daub a number that came up on my card, someone shouted, "Bingo!" and put an end to 599 individual dreams of winning the night's big prize. The caller announced a fifteen-minute intermission after he checked the numbers. Chairs scuffled on the linoleum floor, and I could hear the creak of bones as most of the little old ladies sharing the place with me rose to check the absorbency of their incontinence diapers. They formed a line to the bathrooms that went right past the snack bar. Church volunteers took advantage of the queue to reload the deep fat fryers and put burgers on the grill.

I remained in my seat and watched the ebb and flow of this paisley print crowd. They were all human; I was the only immortal among them. They never suspected that I could be other than a young Chinese woman with nothing better to do with my evenings than to gamble.

I sighed and pumped at the straw in my water cup. I never drink the stuff straight because it dilutes a good blood flush, but when I'm at places like Our Lady of Victory, where the air has gone dense from burning menthol one hundreds all evening, I have to appear like a normal, thirsty human being. Truth is, this leaded oxygen doesn't give me a dry throat, but I have noticed it dries out my skin, and I need an extra portion of blood to return the moisture.

Bringing my stare back to the crucifix brought my thoughts back to wonder about the immortal soul and what had actually happened to mine when I had died. Dolores Raoul had said Richard Hanuman believed in reincarnation. He thought it likely that the soul would be reborn in a new body over and over, and he attached esoteric concepts to this cyclic possibility, too; stuff like karma and dharma and nirvana.

Yet, as far as I can tell, when the last drop of blood was drawn from me on that fateful night in 1917, I died, but my soul didn't evaporate through the crown of my head in search of an available human vessel to inhabit. I don't know if the soul is represented by the personality, but I think it is. If this assumption is true, then mine stayed with me. It was there after I reanimated. Had I not returned to some form of recognizable life, I believe my soul would have been trapped in the oblivion of final, black death. For me, it's safe to say, that there is no River Styx, no Hades, no Happy Hunting Grounds.

My beeper went off just before intermission was over. I glanced at the number and recognized it to be my own. My cellular was home on the lab table where I'd left it after talking to Art Anthony, so collecting my purse and dumping

my unused playing sheets onto Mrs. Javinski's chair, I slid
out of Our Lady of Victory's bingo hall to use the pay phone
by the back entrance. Of course, I didn't have a quarter
handy, either, and had to take time digging through my
wallet looking for my calling card. Finally, I got the home
phone to ring. After one sounding, Diane answered.

"What's up?" I asked.

She squeezed my name into a whisper. "Nicki, you've got
to come home. Now. We've got big trouble here."

"Trouble?"

"One of those *Night Argosy* freaks; a young woman.
Gale's killed her. In the house."

My stomach bottomed out on me. "What?"

"He sucked out all her blood!"

"I know how he does it, for Christ's sake!" I shook my
head, but it didn't help me to clear up my thoughts.
"Where's Ekua?"

"He's playing flute at some club in Alexandria. Please,
Nicki. I'm scared shitless here. Gale's in his studio, sitting
on the floor." She groaned. "He's holding her head in his
lap." Then, in a whisper, "Oh, my God. I can't believe this
is happening."

I couldn't either. It wasn't like I didn't have enough
problems. Now I had to get rid of a body, too.

"Don't go near him," I said. "I'll be home in a few
minutes."

I slammed the phone down and took off at a dead run out
of the church. Our Lady of Victory is on the other side of
town from my house, and I panicked for a couple of
moments until I managed to hail a taxi. Waving a ten-spot
under the driver's nose, I dickered with him on the cost to
run red lights. After we settled on twenty for each, he
knocked the meter off and turned that Plymouth into a

rocket. Sixty dollars poorer, I found myself trying to break to impulse power as I screamed though my front door.

The place was dark and quiet. This silence made me downshift in midstep and do what I could to bury my anxiety and switch on my extrasensory abilities.

The water tap in the front bathroom had long needed a new washer and the drain snaked out. I heard the regular plip-plop of drops falling into the scum pond formed in this sink. Beyond that, there was only the tick of the grandfather's clock coming from the kitchen.

"Diane?" I murmured.

She didn't answer immediately, but my radar picked her up in the shadows of the dining room. She had the cat in her arms.

"Diane, it's Nicki. You're safe, darling. I won't let anything happen to you."

"He's killed her," she said. "I saw it happen. I didn't mean to, but I did."

"Go downstairs into the lab, Diane, and wait for me to come get you. It'll be all right."

Without a word, she was gone.

I climbed the steps to the second floor. The door to the studio was ajar, and I peered through the crack. Gale sat just as Diane had said, cradling a naked woman in his lap. It was the same black leatherette who had modeled for him the night I threw everybody out of the house.

Pushing the door open, I had a better view of his killing ground. He had taken some chalk and painted a pentagram on the linoleum floor. Five stubby white candles were placed in the corners of this symbol, each washing up enough light to burnish the room in gold. Orchid petals were strewn across the design. The strong smell of sandalwood incense clipped at my nostrils.

I took a step into the room, but Gale didn't acknowledge

my presence and it suddenly pissed me off. He was like Mr.
Potato Head: He had eyes, ears, nose, lips, and starch for
brains.

Stopping just to the far side of the pentagram, I placed my
hands on my hips and said, "Think what you have done, you
idiot son of a bitch."

Slowly, he raised his head. "She was a witch, you know,"
he murmured. "She wanted to be a vampire, but witches are
evil, so I had to kill her. We can't have her kind living
among us."

I stared at him for a long minute and my pause allowed
time for a frightening realization to crawl inside me. When
I fully comprehended the situation, I couldn't keep a
shudder from overtaking me.

There come moments in unlife when moving through
eternity gets to be too much. The thought of shuttling down
forever tends to wipe some hematomans away while others
get stronger. If you crossed over weak and neurotic,
counting the passing ages can turn you into a slug.

Few humans realize that disease is eternity's traveling
companion. As long as the universe remains stable and
doesn't collapse in on itself, we'll tread time, and disease
will be right there to accompany us. Nothing escapes it. If
you live, or rather, unlive, you still must have certain
physiological and mental processes functioning, and like the
engine of a beat-up, old Cadillac, some of your parts are
bound to get rusty.

Since the essence of a hematoman has to do with our
brain waves, we usually get hit with afflictions that include
derangement, multiple personalities, and good, old, every-
day schizophrenia. Think of the crazed blood lust shown in
movies about vampires. It's this same kind of monstrous
desire that can hit us during an eternity crisis, but, unlike the

cinema, needing the blood is secondary to needing a release from the stress.

Our brains, then, become sanctuaries for snapping demons. In ancient times, we called it the rise of the beast, but in the twentieth century, we just call it a nervous breakdown.

The disease occurs for the first time along about three hundred years of unlife, and as I stood over Gale, I had to admit that his behavior matched his age.

I reached out and smacked him hard in the face. The force dislodged him from his hematoman coma.

"What did you do that for?" he asked, blinking at me.

"Goddamn you, Gale!"

He looked confused, but after a second, he grinned. "I broke the house rules, didn't I?"

"Your behavior has put us all in danger."

He glanced back down at the corpse and caressed the jumble of safety pins piercing her cheek. "Isn't she beautiful? She wanted to be my model." He slowly raised his head to look at me again. "She wanted me to sculpt her, but I didn't do it in clay. I did it in my head."

32

THE SUM OF my problem was this: Death stinks. Add excessive heat, and death stinks harder and spreads farther, faster. Before killing the girl, Gale had turned the furnace up to eighty-five degrees. Why he did that, I'll never figure out.

I clicked down the thermostat and checked the kitchen cork board for a message on Ekua's whereabouts. He was playing at the 701 Club, so I punched in the number, asked to speak to him, and then waited. And waited. Finally, he came on the phone.

"I was right in the middle of a set, Nicki," he said. "This better be good."

"Gale's been an ass tonight. I need you home right now. Please."

"Can't it wait? I've got another ten songs to do, or I don't get paid."

"Ekua. Please. I have a real problem, here."

He grumbled, and then a little louder: "OK. I'll be home as soon as I can."

I hung up and leaned on the wall phone for a few moments, trying to calm myself, but I was unable to reach relaxation and serenity. I couldn't stop thinking about Gale.

It had taken me an hour to get the pig back in the poke. He kept trying to talk to me about his artistic vision, about how he was destined to search for and define the true nature of death. All the while, the girl rotted.

When his blood flush lessened, he finally snapped out of his hematoman stupor and asked me what we should do with the body. For an awful half-second, there, I wished he were the one who was decomposing from the heat.

Hanging up the phone with Ekua, I imagined it again. We were just lucky he went bonkers after all his interviewees had left the house.

I tried to turn from the feeling by going to the fridge and busying myself with particulars of a quick plan on how to keep the leatherette fresh for a little while longer. It was a simple concept: dump the body into the bathtub and pack it with bags of frozen blood.

I heard a thump as Gale cleaned up. After a few minutes, he came down smelling of her ripeness and looking sheepish. I stepped back from the chore of unpacking the freezer compartment to let him silently assume the job, and then I went downstairs to talk to Diane.

She cowered in the corner of the lab, still holding fast to the cat, crying and trying hard not to be hysterical. I drew a chair up to her and gently released the cat. He darted away to the safety of the utility room and his litter box. Diane was the first to speak, but her words bubbled with tears and she had to stop for a moment to let go of a sob.

"I didn't realize what it was like, Nicki," she whispered. "The actual killing. I watched Gale do it and he knew I was, and still, he kept going until . . . she died." She massaged both hands across her cheeks. "His eyes. They were so strange."

"Maybe it was good that you saw it," I answered.

"How could that be?"

"You've lived with us for close to ten years now, and you've been insulated from the reality of our existence that whole time. You're considering becoming one of us—well, unlife is not the romance and freedom most humans think it is. There's nothing romantic about death."

She scowled, shaking her head, and I knew if I didn't get in there with some more words, she'd explode.

"You have to remember, Diane, Gale's not human. His reactions are those of a passionate, hematoman male, and he's going through a tough time right now. It could happen to anyone."

"Happen to anyone? He killed a young woman in this house!"

"Is that what bothers you—that he did it here? Or that he did it at all?"

She shook her head, but didn't answer. I rose and fetched the box of tissues from the lab table, handing off a wad to her. She blew her nose with a little honking sound.

"Gale loves you," I said. "Just like I do, and Ekua, too. He would never do anything to harm you, even during crazed moments like you just witnessed."

She rubbed a hand through her hair and came out with a frustrated response. "Don't you understand? He took time to plan that whole absurd sacrifice. I saw the girl here before. She came the other night for one of his so-called interviews. The bastard is warped, I tell you. He's a cold-blooded murderer."

"So am I."

When I said it, she stopped raging and stared at me. I decided at that point to put the polish on my sentence. "You didn't think he was so awful this morning. You've been forced to see the truth about us, so you tell us: Is it impossible, then, to love a killer?"

33

Besides Diane, Ekua was the only one in the clan who knew how to drive. He didn't have a D.C. license, but he did know how to steer and work the brake. So, just before he got home, I came up with an idea of how to dispose of the junior miss currently stiffening in my bathtub. I would call Archie Mellons, who ran the night shift over at the District crematorium. Archie was a hematoman and a hell of a nice guy, with ethics you only get having come straight from Nosferatu country in old Romania. I would have Ekua drive the leatherette over to him. I was sure he'd take the flesh off my hands.

In the past, I had enough wits about me to pilfer a couple of body bags from the Medical Examiner's Office. It was into one of these black plastic designs that I helped Gale stuff the corpse. Ekua joined us in the upstairs john just as my plan was starting to fall into place. I was glad to see him at first, but all that changed when I noticed the expression on his face. I knew from the way he held his jaw, he wasn't too pleased by what he saw.

"What happened?" he demanded in a low growl.

An easy death and a grand funeral; that's the only true birthright a man can claim, but for most people, it's the only thing they're usually cheated out of. "Gale had an episode," I said.

Ekua glared at him. In the fluorescent light, I could see him spit as he spoke. Tiny globules of blood peppered his white shirt, but he didn't even notice, so furious was he with Gale. "An episode? An episode is when the cat poops on the

177

floor. This is lunacy. Can't you control yourself, anymore?" he bellowed. "What the hell is wrong with you?"

Gale snarled. It was then that I knew his sanity had completely returned once more. "Shut up, you bloody, black irritation!"

With that insult, Ekua was on top of him. They fell onto the body and under the impact, air jettisoned from the corpse. The squealing sound stopped Ekua from choking Gale long enough for me to knock my way between them.

My luck: To be stuffed into a five foot by six foot potty with two raging hematomans and the farting corpse of Miss Underground America.

"Cut out the bullshit!" I barked, for what good it did. They unsheathed their fangs and flared their nostrils, each trying to get to the other through me. I thought for sure they were going to drill for gold in my neck just to get me out of the way.

Belligerence was the only thing to save me. "If you two don't stop this crap, you're going to have the neighbors calling the cops on us." I yanked Ekua roughly off Gale.

They lay where they fell and the staring contest was on. I kept up my talking, praying that their hematoman anger would drain away. "We've got to solve this problem before we can sit down and logically discuss this."

"Discuss it?" Ekua rumbled. "I spent my youth running away from lions and white South Africans." His face slid into a squint. "When I joined the undead, I vowed I wouldn't run away from humans again. Now, because of your goddamned, moody artist, here, I might have to face that again, and I don't like it."

"Who gives two rats' asses about what you like?" Gale growled.

Ekua lurched toward him, but I halted his advance by grabbing his shirt collar.

"He's sick!" I said.

That stopped him. "What the hell are you talking about? We don't get sick. Nicki, you defend him too much. He's got to be responsible for his actions."

Gale's anger abruptly fizzed out and he looked at me with such an expression of pain that I thought I was going to get weepy over it. I started to turn away. It was a calculated action to better counter the swell of sympathy. I felt for him, but Ekua's deep voice swerved me back just as I got to the halfway point.

"Nicki?" he said. The fury was lost on him, too.

I sighed, sat down between them, and stalled before asking the unavoidable questions. "Gale, do you remember anything that happened with this young woman?"

"No," he murmured.

"What? How can that be?" Ekua asked.

Gale snorted. "How can anything be? It just is."

"What are we talking about here?" he said.

"We're talking about the rise of the beast," I answered.

"Are you sure?"

"I think so." Looking at Gale, I awaited confirmation and it came with a single sharp nod.

Ekua sat forward and stared at the both of us. "I thought it was a myth when you told me about it before I crossed over."

"We weren't kidding. We just didn't think it was going to ever happen."

Gale suddenly had a laughing fit. He leaned against the corpse, barely able to speak through this hysteria. For a minute, he tried, and then just as abruptly stopped with the guffaws to draw up a sad smile. He must have decided whatever was so funny was worth keeping a secret.

"You're serious," Ekua said, and there was fear in his eyes.

Gale's smile left as quickly as it had come. "I can't remember the act of killing the woman. I came to afterward. It was like I was flying on autopilot." He sat up and halfheartedly stuffed the corpse's hand back in the bag. "I kept seeing all these images in my head and it felt like I was fused to them. I couldn't separate myself from the visions."

"You scared Diane witless," I said, climbing to a stand.

"Did I? I never intended that."

"Let's talk more about this later." I glanced at Ekua. "I need your help tonight. Please, do as I ask. It's necessary."

After a second's consideration, he rose to silently help Gale carry the body down to the garage.

"Take her out through the utility room," I ordered. "Diane is in the lab and I don't want her scared any more than she already is."

Following them down the steps, I stopped at the phone in the kitchen. "Get the engine warmed up while I make a call."

I punched up the crematorium and found to my relief that Archie was on duty this night. I told him the situation and he laughed, the bastard. He did take the corpse, though, in exchange for an unspecified favor at a later date.

I checked on Diane before joining the men and found her hiding in her first-floor bedroom. I was a bit worried that she would become a leaper—one of those human assistants that can't take the strain and who leaps from hematoman society back into the mainstream, mortal world. I didn't want to aggravate the situation, so I didn't bother her beyond calling a gentle assurance that I would be here when she came out, and then hurried off to the garage.

In the early eighties, I had decided that I wanted to learn to drive, so thinking my skills would improve if I had a full-sized car in which I felt safe, I bought a 1978 Pontiac Bonneville with a trunk big enough to park a Mazda inside.

It was a sea-green beauty at one time, complete with power steering, electric windows, and a tape deck. Unfortunately, I could never see over the hood. On those occasions when Ekua would give me a lesson, I would spend the hour slapping up against other cars. I smashed the right front fender so badly that I had to replace it, and after that, I just lost interest. It wasn't until Diane came to live with us that the Bonneville got regular use.

I stepped up to my cohorts in crime. Gale sat on the lid of the trunk absently picking at a rust spot blossoming above the tail light.

"Archie Mellons is waiting for you over at the D.C. crematorium. He said to bring the body down to the west docking entrance."

"What if we get stopped on the way there?" Ekua asked.

"Drive carefully and you won't be. If a cop pulls you over, give him the Dracula Stare."

There was another protest forming on his lips, but I pushed him toward the car and spoke first. "Get going. When you guys get back, you can help me scrub down the house to get the stink out of here."

34

AFTER THE GUYS left the crematorium, I stuffed a Valium down Diane's throat and sent her to bed. For myself, I took a few minutes to chill down my veins once more by pouring a clotted-blood shake from a recent brew I found in the lab refrigerator. Turning toward the fax machine, I saw that Walsh had sent me information on Richard Hanuman while I had been out playing bingo. I decided it would help me relax from the events of the evening so, ripping the paper off the machine, I sat at the lab table, sipped my drink, and read his findings and considerations. My thoughts bounced around like they had kangaroo legs, though. It took a few minutes to gather the amount of concentration I needed to read.

My personal situations always seem to mimic some segment of the current investigation I'm working on. The more intensively I'm involved in a case, the more I notice the similarities between the parallel currents of life and unlife. Take, for instance, Gale. Here I was trying to find a fringe lunatic when I had my very own at home.

He had seen a new dimension in the way he killed, and it had changed his whole concept toward murder. Rather than hunting a victim for food, he hunted to increase the pleasure of his fantasy. Gale had mentioned that while he was out of his mind, he had created a piece of art, but the masterpiece could only be privately viewed, because it was locked away inside his head.

For the Winter Man, it would have to be the same thing. I let my eyes go back into focus, chugged my drink, and settled in, determined to plow this acreage of small print sent to me by my partner. He'd put together quite a profile.

Richard Hanuman was born in the town of Pathfork, near the Cumberland Gap in eastern Kentucky. His name was originally Richard Swinton, and he was the only son of Molly and Maurice Swinton.

A search of death certificates led to the state of Illinois where Molly and Maurice were killed by a drunken driver just outside of Chicago. Richard was then two years old. Going back through the records, Walsh had discovered that his maternal grandmother, a one Lucy Barbour, gained custody.

Lucy Barbour raised him in Virginia until he was age six, when the authorities removed him from her care. At the time, she was also charged with the malicious wounding of her grandson.

The next place Richard showed up was in his medical records. Following the tragedy in the hallelujah tent, he was shipped to a state-funded hospital in Kentucky where he was used as a research subject for new techniques in plastic surgery and split-thickness skin grafts to treat areas damaged by burns. When he was nine, he was released from the hospital into an orphanage.

At the age of eleven, he was removed from the orphanage and adopted by Dr. and Mrs. Carl Hanuman of Richmond, Virginia. Dr. Hanuman was a plastic surgeon and an consulting physician during Richard's stay at the state clinic.

Walsh had checked out Carl Hanuman, too, systematically picking through the computer database, stopping now and then to scribble a line in his handy notebook, and then continuing on to create a profile of the man.

Carl had gone from plastic surgery to opening and operating the Water's Edge Abortion Clinic at 102 King

Street, in Alexandria, Virginia. According to available information, he died almost a year before, a victim of a drive-by shooting. Through some bureaucratic goof-up, his physician's drug license hadn't been snatched off the system.

Walsh had talked with the administrator of the private clinic, asking her to explain the center's method of ordering pharmaceutical supplies. The woman explained that they dealt with a company called Intensa-Care, a local manufacturer in Rockville, Maryland. To verify it, she let him take a quick look at their financial receipts and showed off their ID and tax numbers. She denied that anyone from the group had used Carl's number to make an order recently.

Leaving Water's Edge, he visited Intensa-Care and with a little bullying managed to do a records check. He gave the database operator Carl's ID. When she fed it into the computer, the number came up as having been used as recently as October. Hypodermic needles, formaldehyde, and cotton swabs had been ordered and sent to a post office box in Dumfries, Virginia, a town thirty minutes south of D.C. It was the same one where Sarah Short had mailed her herbal teas.

I skimmed the rest of the page until I found information on his adoptive mother. She was living in a nursing home in a place called, Lakeridge, Virginia, where she was being treated for Alzheimer's disease. Staff reports showed that she had been incoherent for nearly a year.

Losing both parents to disease and murder in a short time span. That could undo the strongest person.

35

Thursday, November 26
Thanksgiving Day

At 8:00 A.M. I was still cloistered in the lab. I didn't feel like talking to Gale or Ekua, and Diane was lingering in her bedroom. I did want some companionship in an odd sort of way, so I called Walsh at Metro Headquarters. He spoke his name on the exhale of a deep breath and the sound rattled across the telephone. I could hear the weariness in that blow.

"I found your fax very interesting," I said. "Good job putting it together."

"Thanks. Did you have something for me, Nicki?"

"I just wanted to discuss some things about Richard Hanuman." I paused, waiting for him to answer. When he didn't, I said, "Is something wrong?"

"Nothing that a month in Fiji wouldn't cure." He hesitated, then after a moment, continued. "We had a staff meeting this morning. The mayor is pulling the plug on the Homicide Division. Budget cuts. We're going to lose at least half our unit so that they can keep the blues on streets."

"Are you one who'll get the ax?"

"I don't know. Won't know for a couple of weeks." He cleared his throat. "Never mind about it. You said you wanted to talk about the case."

As far as I'm concerned, there's no delicate way to discuss someone's potential financial disaster, and doing the "poor baby" routine is a waste of time. We all have to plot our own course, as harsh as that may sound, so I plunged into the business at hand.

"I opened the employment files we got from Barbara Pollack. Hanuman filed a claim with Blue Cross/Blue Shield for expenses incurred by seeing a psychologist. According to the description, he was undergoing grief counseling resulting from the death of his father. His supervisor recommended that he go."

"I missed that one," Walsh answered. "Do you have a name on this therapist?"

"Yes. Dr. Hari Balin."

"Sounds foreign."

"I agree. I may be out in the ball field's hot dog stand on this one, Joe, but I think he chose this therapist for just that reason."

"How do you figure?"

"Dolores Raoul said Richard had a lot of interest in exotic cultures and he believed in reincarnation. He's obviously eccentric, so why wouldn't he choose an analyst with a name that incites his interest in Hinduism?"

"That makes sense. I'll see if I can't convince this particular psychologist to make a house call down here at Metro. I'll try to schedule the visit around six o'clock tomorrow night. I'm not going to get hold of anybody today. Even this joint is like a ghost town, Nicki, because of the holiday. Homicide is functioning with a skeleton crew. There are just enough detectives on duty to respond to the gang murders that will happen this evening."

"No turkey dinner for you, then, huh?"

"Not unless I go down to the automat and get a sandwich. Is Friday evening good for you?"

"See you then." I couldn't think of any more to talk about, so I hung up. For the hundredth time I considered going upstairs to speak with Gale, but after a moment decided against it again.

I'm not a caregiver; I know this. Whining really gets on my nerves and I just knew I would lose my patience with him. It was better to concentrate on the case and stay out of the way today. So, instead of chancing a new battle, I opened the data file given up by Mrs. Pollack and continued to do my own reading on Richard Hanuman.

His last supervisor had really had it in for him. Hanuman considered himself to be a fine, literate writer, as well as an artist. He also fancied himself as having some qualifications to discuss archaeological and anthropological findings made by the Smithsonian. He penned some of the wackiest discourses I have ever read: long on verbiage and short on science. Apparently, he made a prolific nuisance of himself. At the beginning of the end, his boss had seen a way to rid the museum of this man. He collected all of Richard's reports and included them in his personnel file, sending along with them his recommendations for an employee dismissal.

Richard tended to blend societies and their traits and traditions. His particular favorites were the Peruvian Moche, the various Hindu cultures of India, and the ancient Egyptians. It was as if by mixing the contributions these cultures gave the world in the arts and sciences, he proved the interrelationship of bloodlines across the planet. He said these three distinct groups invented many of the same tools, held the same basic religious concepts, organized their governments similarly, and were all connected through time on a reincarnation level. It was the migratory world theory turned strangely in upon itself.

He envisioned a prehistory based on this global village, but instead of discussing Stone Age people meeting the Iron Age folks, he spiced his musings with reflections on the lost continent of Atlantis, the truth about Sinbad the Sailor, and the fact that the East African Dogon tribe came to earth via a UFO from a star system in the Sirius constellation.

To square his ideas and to lend them a certain amount of scientific credence, he wrote again and again about the immortal soul. He surmised, with a liberal use of ten-cent words, how humans were sparks of the Divine Creator. In the scheme of things, they were the alpha and the omega, each endowed with a soul that held providence over the world, but at some time in man's long history, the mission had become blurred and the balance between good and evil was now in jeopardy.

For ten years, Richard had layered wax and clay over plaster of Paris skulls. He mentioned this fact several times, as though it lent more weight to his flaky dissertations. Besides that, this statement eventually led to a discussion on trepanation, the art of cutting holes in the head.

This is what he said concerning the subject: "During ancient times, at least two and a half percent of the entire Peruvian population permitted healers to perform trephining operations on them. They used obsidian knives to bore the hole through the skull, occasionally switching to quartz, flint, or bronze, depending upon the status of the patron undergoing the surgery. Paleontologists surmise that the reason for trephining a patient was to release evil spirits, which the Indians believed were causing illness, such as insanity, epilepsy, and even the flu." On this last part, Hanuman added his own interpretation.

He felt that the reason scientists found so many trephined skulls was not due to belief in demons, but due, instead, to bubonic plague. Although there was no evidence of a full-scale outbreak like that which had occurred in Europe, he maintained that it did occur to the civilizations in Peru. A greater part of the population had forsaken the fanged deity, just as Moses' people had abandoned the one true God of the Hebrews. To him, these gods were the same, each using an alias belonging to the Divine Creator.

The people had flirted with evil and worshipped graven images, and because of this the deity struck them down with the Black Death. According to the edicts of their cosmology, the Peruvians decided that it was necessary to relieve the world of this horrible influence by drilling holes into the heads of those afflicted. They performed trepanation just prior to death when no hope existed for the patient, because the demons associated with the plague would create havoc in the soul and make it go violently crazy. This essence could transmigrate, meaning that it was capable of leaping from one body to the next. Too weak to fight off the disease, it was imperative to release the person's spirit before he died. Hanuman said that they believed it could shoot straight out through the crown of the head to invade another innocent body, but expelling it prior to the crossover would allow the soul to simply evaporate in the air. With the strength of the evil that had brought on the plague, it was hard to tell what terror might be unleashed had this not been done.

It didn't matter to him that the ages of the skulls had been cataloged by the Smithsonian to range from the dawn of man until the late eighteenth century, suggesting that not all two and half percent of the population had their heads hollowed between 700 A.D. and 900 A.D. It also didn't matter that many of these specimens showed signs of healing through identification of new bone growth at the incision points.

In a decade, not one supervisor thought to question this man's eccentricities; if they had, there was no record of it on the floppy. There were several letters of recommendation and a special service award for exemplary performance in his position. He was promoted five times, starting as a GS-7. Just before he was shoved into the unemployment line, he had worked his way up to a GS-14. When he had moved to the GS-12 position, he crossed occupational lines and served as a mission head on several dioramas for the museum. This job gave him an opportunity to select items for his presentations from the various Smithsonian warehouses.

It was about this time that his written ranting increased in volume. He was submitting them like they were weekly activity reports and toward the end of his tenure he used them as such, turning his ideas from fantasy into a know-it-all snottiness aimed at getting his way in the presentation of the dioramas.

He questioned the selection committee's decisions. In one particular dialogue, he was especially firm about why the concept of an exhibit on the ancient Moche of Peru should show the duties of a high priestess as she conveyed a golden goblet of blood to a waiting lord. Many of the trephined skulls held in the museum's warehouse should surround her. The whole exhibit should be devoted to showing this particular phase of Indian philosophy.

Archaeologists had uncovered an intact burial tomb they thought belonged to this priestess, confirming that she was, indeed, a living being who was represented on much of the pottery found at the various sites. Her importance in daily life among the Moche, and the fact that one of her burial attendants had a head that had several holes bored through it, confirmed his theories on their religious practices. Following that opinion, he went right back to the stuff about divine sparks and universal creation.

Further on in the data I found a reference indicating how unpleasant his supervisor had been to him regarding the matter of the priestess and the air-conditioned skulls. He had gone over his boss's head to submit the report directly to members of the decisions committee. Apparently, some bureaucratic asshole up the line took Hanuman seriously and provided funding and extra manpower to complete the project as outlined.

36

Friday, November 27

IT WAS LATE the next morning when I knocked on the door to Gale's studio. A moment passed before the lock was thrown and he let me inside. There was no greeting from him, no pause to let his eye range over me, no baring of fangs to let me know he might be sexually aroused at the sight of me in the see-through robe I wore. His nonchalance pricked my ego, but instead of deflating my confidence, as I'm sure he intended, it only let steam build up inside of me.

Hematomans don't get physically tired, but we do get mentally weary, and I was to this point. Dealing with Miss Underground America, Ekua's anger, and Diane's fear had exploded my patience to the max. Gale's pouting mood only served to enrich my annoyance with him, so I took a turn around the room to calm myself before I spoke.

The studio is wedged in the attic. There aren't any windows, so there are no worries about sunshine coming through a crack in the blinds. The space, though not huge, has a high ceiling, which allows him to create large sculptures and big paintings. It always smells of wet clay and acrylic, and I'll admit, I've grown used to this over the years. The linoleum floor is dusted with what Gales calls his whittles—tiny wood chips that fly from his carvings.

For my whole life and unlife, I have longed to be able to draw and paint, but I don't have any talent for the pencil or the brush. I make it possible for Gale to take advantage of his skills by supplying protection and a suitable environment. I do this willingly, not just because I'm the clan leader and it's my job, but because I take comfort in Gale's work, as though I had something to do with each piece he creates.

There's a free-standing, full-length mirror in the studio and I stopped before it. Mirrors—that's another myth in the world's vampire lore. It's said that we cast no reflection in shiny objects, but I think the story got started around the fact that a demon isn't supposed to be able to face its true nature. Thousands of years before we became fashionable, vampires were considered nothing more than interdimensional gutter slime, and so, of course, if the wraith chanced to look upon its own image, it would be destroyed by its own horror. Gale uses the mirror to see different angles when he's painting from a model.

He flicked on his potter's wheel and boarded the seat like it was a horse. The machine hummed, drawing my attention for a moment. I watched in silence as the glob of clay he plopped onto the pan began to take shape within his hands. It was an effort for me to not lapse into my usual trance. Rather than waiting expectantly to see what he formed, I turned to study the table running along the far wall. It was covered with several objects awaiting a final baking in his small kiln. There were bowls, vases, figurines, even an oversized chess board complete with the players. I stepped over to study it and found that the pieces were intricately sculpted and partially painted; the king was cut in the likeness of a mythological vampire. With the gold-edged cape and tiny fangs, it looked just like Bela Lugosi. Picking up the queen, I realized it was Elsa Lanchester from the *Bride of Frankenstein* and the knights flanking this royal duo were Lon Chaney werewolves, each one carved to show them in the midst of transformation.

"Did you and Lang come to a permanent arrangement?"

"Yes. He's working round the clock to set up for my show. He has some buyers who are going to be in town next week. They've displayed interest in my work."

"Next week? How can he get the exhibit done that quickly?"

"He's got a large staff of gallery designers who work with him."

"Did you tell him that you're undead?"

"Yes. He didn't believe me. It doesn't matter."

"Are you planning to woo him across the Devil's Bridge?"

"Eventually, I think. Right now, he'll afford me the opportunity to take care of myself without your help."

"Then what?"

"I'll get my clan together."

I retreated into silence again, caught for the second time staring at the way he moved his hands. He formed the double necks of a Native American marriage jug. After a couple of minutes, I finally managed to come out with what was on my mind. "What happened the other night, Gale?"

He glanced at me and stopped the wheel, taking a stretch of wire to slice off the pot. "I don't know. It was like I wasn't myself while I was killing the girl. I was a different person and I imagined that I was caught in a different set of circumstances." He took out a wedge of flat wood and began to chip a pattern into the lips of the jug's spouts. "I couldn't snap out of the fantasy. I tried. You're the one who finally delivered me back into reality."

"Is it the rise of the beast?"

"Yes. You were right from the start."

"Have you seen Nelson about it?" I asked. Nelson knew more about hematoman maladies than anyone in D.C.

Gale nodded. "It's what he determined."

"How long have you been suffering with these black-outs?"

"A couple of months; but before, I could always control the rage. The other night proves I'm past that point."

"How long does Nelson think this breakdown is going to take to work through?"

He snorted. "How can temporary insanity be worked through? One day it will just stop happening, and I'll be all right again. I just have to deal with the problems it presents."

"You've got that wrong. The clan has to deal with the problems it presents."

"Yes," he said.

"Nelson must have had some idea how long this discomfort would continue."

"He said for my age, I could probably plan for a year's worth of fun. Now do you see why I want to get away? I can't burden our family with this shit. I'm more unreliable than usual. It's not right for me to suck the unlife out of you all."

"Michael and Ilea are willing to follow you. That says something for what this clan will do for each other."

"Michael and Ilea are using me as an excuse to leave you, Nicki. The minute I'm established someplace else, they'll be gone doing their own thing."

My anger dissipated into a pout of my own. "Am I so awful to live with?"

"Sometimes," he answered.

It's true, those old Romanian sayings about vampires: Nosferatu, the undead, live in torment. Can you imagine facing eternity knowing that you've lost your best friend?

37

DESPITE PERIODS OF freezing rain, Justin Lang showed up around two in the afternoon. Diane answered the door, torn from her lifeless grazing of a pretzel box. She called for Gale, and then, no other sound from her.

I had returned to the lab again, but rather than the nice quiet I longed for, I was forced to listen to the muffled words between Gale and Lang as they sat at the kitchen table talking about art deals and antiques. Justin wanted Gale to sign an agent's contract allowing him exclusive rights to sell his work. Gale was hedging, and after a bit I heard chairs slide back across the floor. A moment later, there was a knock at the lab door. Lang begged an entrance.

"Negotiations at a halt?" I asked, as he kicked off the bottom step into the basement.

He hooked his thumbs in the belt loops of his jeans and took a walk around the room. "We're taking a short break, then it's back to our corners to continue this sparring match," he answered. "How are you this afternoon?"

"I'm fine. And I'm working."

He ignored my hint and ambled over to the lab table. Pausing to glance over the crime scene photos spread about, he winced when he got to one showing the hole in a victim's head. He passed it quickly and moved on to the picture of a trephining saw. He picked it up. "That's interesting. Ivory?"

"Yes."

"I love scrimshaw. Myself, I dabble in the medium, but this is extraordinary work."

That got my attention. Sometimes thoughts hit me like atoms hit Einstein and I immediately tread off down pathways I haven't before considered. "You carve scrimshaw like this?" I asked. "Where do you get the ivory?"

He turned his face away a bit, and gently tugged at his earring. "From elephants, of course."

"Do you sell much of your work?"

He smiled slightly. The expression drew my gaze to his caramel-colored eyes, and yes, right there, I decided he was as pretty as Gale. We stared at each other for a moment before he answered. "Not as much as I would like."

"Do you think anyone would be interested in buying something like that?"

"With or without the saw?"

"Without. Replace it with any kind of knife you want."

"Antique?"

"Who knows? That's your arena, isn't it?"

His smile broadened. "The design looks as though it's Hindu-influenced."

"That's what I understand."

"I don't know much about Hindu art; antique or otherwise, but I'd say if you want to get information on this object and candidates for buyers, go over the Internet."

He replaced the photo on the table. "I guess I better get back to the debate."

I'm not one to waste a good suggestion. By the time he reached the stairs, I was already initializing my modem to dial into the computer network. Halting, though, he turned back. "I usually get a consultation fee for what I just did, but I'll settle for a date." With that, he bumped up the steps, shutting the door lightly behind him.

My modem made the appropriate squeaks and pings, going through the dial-in tones like the siren on a volunteer fire station. After a moment, it connected to my local area network and then with a few curses and misdirection, I finally found my way on to the information superhighway.

There are months where I drop a bundle of money on computer communications. Not only do I join forums geared to my particular interests, access databases, and get a good recipe or two, I'm also linked up to folks who are primarily hematoman. It occurred during a computer session several months before, quite by accident. I had plugged into a bulletin board with a message concerning something I'd heard about a fantasy convention being held in San Francisco—a convention inviting those interested in private discussions about the lifestyles of modern-day vampires. I expected to hear from all the wanna-bes and kooks out there, and I did, but interspersed through the garbage were notes sent to my private computer address, complete with such handles as Fangface, Dark Darling, and Blood Knight. Following their nicknames was always the digits: six, six, six.

I know it's corny, using the biblical sign of the Devil, but after asking some of my more computer-literate hematoman friends, I found out it flagged honest-to-goodness undead participating on the net. Logging back on to have a conversation with a guy named, Thor, from Minneapolis, I realized how technology had actually pushed back the night for my kind. We've never had such freedom with our unlives.

I absently listened to Lang's voice drift down to me as I tapped a message to the art forum. When the communication was finished, I scanned the picture of the trephining saw, turning it into a digitized image, and sent both on their way down the electronic road to see how many hitchhikers they would pick up. In my message, I had said telephone inquiries would be accepted, but since I didn't want to be overly bothered by them, I gave the number to Lang Gallery instead of mine.

38

DIANE IS AMAZING. Sometimes I think she's made of rubber by the way she bounces back. When she starts up at the stove, I know she's again among the unliving. Lang was still visiting Gale and I was down in the lab when I heard her throw them both out of the kitchen. It was just about tea time.

I came up from my cave and sat down at the table, not wanting to begin the conversation, but impatient at waiting for her to do it. She spent five minutes nicking a lighter against the oven's pilot light valve before the broiler flamed on. As if I wasn't there, she carefully opened a package of chicken breasts, peeled away the skin from two, cut off all the fat, and washed them down. It was then she went to the icebox and poured me a glass of iced blood.

She joined me at the table with her coffee.

"I talked to Gale," she said. "He told me about this rise of the beast thing, and about how he went crazy. Ekua said you were the first to mention it, but he's not so sure that's what's wrong with him. He thought the whole thing was a myth until all the crap happened this week. Is it true, or did you make it up?" She leaned in and squinted directly into my eyes. "Don't pull any vampire shit on me, Nicki; no Dracula Stares."

My stomach sank, not from the fact that Gale had told her about the illness, but from the fact that she was worried I would lie to her.

I'll admit, I have on occasion, told some fibs. All junkies, those who gamble, drink, or do drugs will lie to protect their vices, but I wouldn't invent a story about something so serious as a nervous breakdown.

Diane sat back in the chair. "Well? Are you covering for Gale, as usual?"

I shook my head. "No. It's the real thing. When I found him, he'd already blown his gyro system. He had no idea where he was, or who I was."

"Well, to be honest, I have noticed him acting weird, lately."

"We've all been experiencing that."

"I don't mean his outbursts and moods."

"What do you mean, then?"

"Haven't you seen some of the painting he's been doing? I thought he was going into a new artistic phase, but I guess not, now that I know what's wrong with him."

"How has his stuff been different?"

"He's painting daytime landscapes, and he can't get the colors right. One day, he was so frustrated that he went into a rage and ripped a canvas to shreds." She took a sip of coffee. "I suppose he's been living in the night for so long, he can't remember what the day looks like anymore."

What she said suddenly slammed me right between the eyes. The best I could do was offer a blink in response. When I didn't speak, she frowned, but didn't add more. Instead, she slid back the chair and went to her chicken to lay it out on the broiler pan.

Mythologists often talk about the curse of the undead. Until the moment before, I had always thought the curse was linked to the fact that we had to drink blood from the living so we could survive, but what Diane said made more sense. How frightening it must be to have lived in the night for so long that the memory of the day fades and you can't recall the way the sunshine plays off an object, or the way the warmth feels when it hits your face. You transform into a totally different entity, a true creature of the darkness. The memories of being human become just that: memories.

Considering it, I got my first chill in years.

39

W H E N I A R R I V E D that evening at Metro Headquarters at
Walsh's invitation, I found out that he had arrested Hari
Balin, Ph.D., for operating a practice without the proper city
licenses. His green card turned out to be so old that it had
gone white from age, and Dr. Balin had never gone to
immigration to renew it. He claimed to be from Kampur, a
city in northern India, where he had been a traditional healer
for twenty years before coming to the United States. When
I met him in the interrogation room, he was wearing a red
turban and dirty-toothed grimace. He had a snot-colored
beard and among his many accomplishments, he could read
and he could write and had a university degree—at least,
according to his sidekick and interpreter, a bald dwarf who
stank like hashish and goat cheese slurry.

Against the grime and gray marble of the interrogation
room, this freak show performed their act flawlessly. I sat
next to Walsh and couldn't help a smile at seeing his
frustration. He kept plucking at the bill of what looked to be
a brand-new Redskins cap. His fingers would massage it for
about thirty seconds before he would pull it from his head
and run his hand through his sandy-colored hair.

The two detainees filled an important niche in black
market America, that of defrauding health insurance com-
panies by using just enough front paper to provide alternative medicine. It's an old and time-honored scam, and legal,
too, as long as you don't dispense medicine in any form,
only advice.

Walsh's introduction was clipped. "This is Dr. Hari Balin

and his associate, Azi Talli." Then, staring at the dwarf, he said, abruptly, "Do you know a man named Richard Hanuman?"

Azi Talli nodded, and cracked his mouth open to reveal a charred landscape where his teeth should have been. Seeing the state of his dentura, I was surprised when he answered in a refined British accent. "He's one of Dr. Balin's patients. A very sick man, suffering terribly from demons of grief. The good doctor prescribed meditation, prayer, and herbal teas in great quantities, so as to flush the demons from his body. He also prescribed natural tinctures, blessed with white light, of course. His aura needed strengthening. Dr. Balin sensed a failing in the energy field in the area of his third eye."

"Jesus," Walsh muttered, yanking at his cap, and putting on a threatening look. The hat came down, his expression grew dangerous, and his words came slowly. "Let me tell you something. I'm tired and my patience has long been used up. I've been working around the clock trying to find a serial killer. So, if you don't the cut the bullshit, I'm going to call our wonderful precinct cafeteria and have them bring you up a nice dinner of raw hamburger. Then, I'm going to sit back and watch your enlightened Hindu selves eat a cow. Understand?"

Azi Talli blinked and laid on a disapproving frown. "It's true then, this police brutality. I have read about it."

"It can be."

He sighed and held out his hands in surrender. "What exactly would you like to know?"

"Now, that's what I like to hear." Walsh pulled on a lizard smile and then continued. "Explain the term 'demons of grief,' please."

The dwarf hesitated, clicking his tongue against the roof of his mouth.

"Don't stop now," Walsh said. "Steak tartar is only a phone call away."

"One moment, if you please." He turned and spit off some unfamiliar phonics to the turbaned one. The man gibbered a reply. "I beg your pardon," he continued. "Richard Hanuman came regularly for treatments, but stopped about six months ago. His father had died, you see, and that was what plagued him so."

"Is that what he specifically came to discuss with you?"

"Yes. He was very close to his father and had many unresolved feelings at the time of his death."

"How did his father die?"

Azi Talli shook his head. "Tragically. A victim of random violence. He was shot by a zealot who protested his right to operate an abortion clinic."

"Was he?" Walsh said, innocently. "Just how did Richard feel about that?"

"Enraged, of course. Bloodshed only invites more bloodshed. He blamed it on those people who are ruled by evil and dark excesses. He referred to the differences between them and us."

"Them and us?" I said. "Does that mean those who believe in abortion and those who don't?"

"No, no. He was talking about the larger perspective of good and evil, I think."

"Do you remember how he phrased it?"

Azi Talli sighed again, looking rather weary, as though he was trying to communicate with a six-year-old. "He spoke of the eternal soul, and how from the beginning of creation each man chose the side with which he would associate." Staring at me, he added, "Women, too." Then, as if this simple explanation were not enough, he went farther. "There are those people who propagate wisdom, freedom, and light. Yet, this good is balanced by the bad. So, on the opposite side of this concept, there are those who would bring down darkness, fear, and violent death."

This last part sounded like some hematomans I have known. "You're saying, then, that we're all either inherently evil or inherently good?"

"Precisely."

Balin suddenly exploded into a phlegm-filled cough. His turban jiggled with his convulsion. After a few spits into a crusty handkerchief and a shudder from Walsh, we resumed the interrogation. "Let's take this a step farther. From what we know of Richard Hanuman, he believes in reincarnation. How does that philosophy fit with this good and evil thing?"

The dwarf shrugged. "Reincarnation stresses the attainment of the soul's perfection from the experiences associated with a series of physical lives." He stopped, clearing his own throat.

I glanced at Walsh. He had his chin jacked up and his hat pulled low over his eyes. With slow, deliberate actions, he swung his feet onto the gunmetal table, which supported our elbows. Rocking the chair into a bipedal state, he said, "Let me get this straight, then. Hanuman divided up everyone in the world as either good or evil. If we're all trying for perfection, then the good get better and the bad get worse. Is that right?"

"It was his concept of universal balance, yes."

I chimed in. "We understand that he had some unique thoughts on Armageddon. Did he explain his views on that?"

"From what we could tell, Mr. Hanuman was a literate man who spent his days reflecting on the mysteries of the universe. He told us, according to the studies he had made, that the fight at the end of the world would see each reincarnational line vying for ultimate control of the earth."

"How exactly would they do this?" Walsh demanded.

"A single, perfected soul would be born to the most powerful line. If it is the son of evil, then the world is doomed. If it is the son of good, then we're all saved."

Walsh pushed a hard breath through his nostrils. Standing, he wrestled his notebook from the front pocket of his tight jeans. He took a moment to flip through it before sitting down again. "Did he ever explain his thoughts on how an individual might work to prevent evil from winning the world?"

"I don't believe so."

"Did he ever share with you his ideas on how to corrupt the reincarnational line of evil so that the bad son wouldn't be born?"

"No, he did not."

"What's your personal opinion of Richard Hanuman?"

"From what we know of him, he was a gentle man of high intelligence. He was very unhappy about his father's death and felt that somehow he must continue the work that his elder had started."

"The work that his elder had started?" Walsh leaned close to the rot-mouthed old man and said, "Did Hanuman feel that with every abortion performed at the clinic, a soul who sided with evil was defeated from reincarnating?"

The answer came quickly. "Yes."

40

Right after he concluded the interview with Balin and Talli, Walsh had to go into a squad meeting with his watch commander to give him a rundown on the events of the investigation. This particular officer loved to hear himself talk, so it was a good bet Walsh would be detained for a while. I thought about going home to see if everything was all right there, and if Diane wanted to talk some more, but just as I hit the street I got a call on my cellular from Justin Lang.

"What are you doing?" he asked.

"Standing here on the street. What do you want?"

"What are you wearing?"

"Justin, I really don't feel like all this right now."

"What are you wearing?"

"Jeans, a sweater, and tennis shoes. Are you happy?"

My electronics picked up the sound of his chuckle. "This ought to be interesting," he murmured. Then, louder, "Meet me out in front of the Hirshhorn Museum on the Mall side, and please come as soon as you can. I have something you'll find interesting."

"It better be more than the moonrise, Justin."

"It is. Guaranteed."

"All right. I'll be there as soon as I can." I hung up and headed down the street.

Washington in the winter: there's nothing like it. The city was originally built over a swamp and though the bog was filled in, nothing could ever be done about the humidity. The place still mugs up, even in the cold months. When the weather comes in fierce from the south, you can literally walk through an urban bayou of brown slush and thick fog.

Temperatures hovered on the frigid side, and turning down Seventh Street, I found that there were no vacancies at the steam-grate motels, where renting accommodations required payment up front: a communal slug of Thunderbird and your own grocery cart and cardboard box. A few more blocks and I neared Constitution Avenue, where I passed the parked van belonging to the Hypothermia Hotline. Several volunteers from this organization sported brightly lettered jackets and concern for a man sitting on the sidewalk. They tried to make him take a cup of steaming coffee, a blanket, and advice about going to a shelter for the night, but he refused their help.

A little farther on, I passed a hematoman couple who were out hunting. To an untrained eye, they looked like lovers, but they weren't. It was a practice session of sorts. The female was teaching the male how to stalk prey. When I passed them, I could tell that he had just died, because the energy signature of this ultimate event still lingered on him. He stank with it: violence, fear, loathing.

Most humans believe that when a person becomes undead he knows immediately how to hunt. All the books and movies lend credence to this fallacy, too. Actually, the first time the fangs come out is a traumatic experience and that goes for every one of us.

I reached the National Mall and crossed the promenade toward Independence Avenue, slowing a bit as I walked beneath the skeletal canopy of oak trees, made remarkable by the draping fabric of ice. Letting my eye fall from the branches, I cut diagonally down the green toward Eighth and Independence, SW, where Lang was supposed to be waiting outside the Hirshhorn Museum, the Smithsonian's gallery of modern art.

The Hirshhorn Museum houses the complete six thousand–
piece private collection of American financier Joseph Hirshhorn. On his death, he gave the country this marvelous gift,
and here you can find works of Rodin, Gaugin, Salvador Dali,
and Jackson Pollack, but ask a Washingtonian if he's ever been
inside the museum, and he will probably say no. You see, the
gallery next store is the National Air and Space Museum.
Looking at Apollo space capsules and the Spirit of St. Louis is
a lot more engaging for the kids than splotches of paint on a
board.

Justin Lang was on the steps when I arrived. He wore a
black overcoat, but when I got up close to him, I realized he
wore a tuxedo beneath.

"God, it's miserable out and you're dressed for the ball,"
I said, in an effort to make a light-hearted greeting.

"I've always loved challenges," he answered, taking my
hand. Then, looking at me with a quick squint, he said,
"You're cold. Is it natural, or are you freezing your butt off,
like I am?"

"Natural," I said, adding another flirty smile. "Now, what
is it that you think I'll find so interesting?"

"Inside," he answered. He led me up the granite stairs and
into the museum, explaining as he went. "I'm here for a
fund-raiser to benefit one of the new homeless shelters in
the city. I didn't even get near the door tonight before I was
accosted by a gentleman who had read your computer forum
message regarding the scrimshaw." He glanced sideways at
me. "Why did you give out my gallery number on your
E-mail message? My secretary was going nuts with the
phone this afternoon."

"You said you wanted to get to know me. It's the kind of
person I am. I couldn't resist."

"How did you know I wouldn't cut you off and not give
you the information that came in?"

"You wouldn't withhold information concerning a murder investigation?"

"If what you did really impacted my business, I would."

"Well, consider it a test, then."

"What kind of test?"

"The kind that tells me what sort of guy you are and whether Gale could trust you to have his best interests at heart. If money is all you care about, I wouldn't hesitate to sway him away from you. I believe business associates should have more in common."

He halted in mid step to stare at me. "You do run that house, don't you? Gale said everyone living there was more family then roommates, and that you're the boss."

I smiled. "I make the mortgage payment." I started walking again, using it as a transition point to change the subject. "What about the guy who talked to you concerning the scrimshaw?"

"He's an expert. Jade and ivory."

Lang opened a door for me and we stopped just inside the room. Despite the weather, there was a large crowd, intermingling with Henry Moore sculptures and the abstract expressions of de Kooning. Silk and sequins, it was a vibrant, colorful, fancy party, and here I stood, wearing tight jeans and tennis shoes made with heels that lit neon every time I took a step.

Lang immediately introduced me to an old man named Hiam Yusuf. From the looks of him, I'd say he once enjoyed the pleasures of living under the Shah of Iran. He bowed and took my hand to his lips.

"Dr. Yusuf works for the Smithsonian. He's a professor of Indian history and a cataloger for the Institution's general collection of Indo-Islamic art. Last year, he catalogued several scrimshaw ivories like the one you blasted over the computer network."

Yusuf bowed slightly before asking me, "Do you have these pieces in your possession, Ms. Chim?"

"The Metro Police do. They're listed as evidence. What do you know about these ivories?"

"From the description, I'd say the police hold several rare objects that have been lost to the light of day for more than three hundred years. They show the carving of the monkey god, Hanuman, yes? And are used as handles for cutting implements?"

I nodded. "As far as we know."

"What you may have is the serving utensils taken from the house of Akbar."

"All right, I'll bite. Who's Akbar?"

"He was the greatest Mogul the continent of India has ever known. His reign was from 1556 to 1605. Those ivories have an estimated worth of five hundred thousand dollars."

My jaw dropped open. "You're kidding?"

He shook his head. "When Akbar died, his son Jahangir succeeded him. Jahangir drank heavily and lived luxuriously, but unlike his father, he did not show tolerance toward the Hindu population. It's been speculated that he sold off much of the Indian art his family held, using the funds to finance his debauched lifestyle. Some of the artwork was from the Gupta period, which if you know your history, is considered India's classic period."

I didn't, but nodded anyway. "What happened to the pieces after that?"

"They moved about the world in the possession of private collectors. The last suspected owner of these utensils was Ian Hunt."

"Who's he?"

"An industrialist of this century. He lived in Hong Kong and died there in 1989. It was said he sold the serving ware just before he died, but the buyer has remained anonymous."

"How did he get hold of the set?"

"That's a mystery that went to the grave with him."

"Well, then, how did the Institution get hold of them?"

"A private donation." Yusuf clasped his hands for a gentle emphasis. "We were thrilled. They were stored in a vault at one of the warehouses to be cleaned and then readied for display. I remember them well. It isn't often that you get to see such beauty and intricacy first hand, you know. I cataloged seventeen of an estimated total of twenty-five flat pieces. Each one was carved with the same Hindu demon and was fitted with either a gold-hammered knife or spoon. They were magnificent."

"What happened to them?"

"One day they all came up missing."

41

THERE IS A legend, which I think is Romanian and was carried across Europe in the back of a Gypsy wagon. It talks about the village of Closso, and the vampire infestation that had turned it into a war zone. People were popping off right and left: the chief, the healer, the blacksmith, and even the baker, so they called out for a warrior to come fight the vampires for them. A guy named Onan showed up in response to the ad.

Onan decided that he could stop these night wraiths by catering to their fixation of objects, and he demonstrated it by placing stuff like wheat chaff and rotted bean pods on the front stoop of every house. The vampires stopped at the front doors, unable to go on because they were so fascinated by this garbage. This simple defense held off the undead for a little while, but then the people got lax about trashing their front stoops each night, so the invaders returned.

Onan was called again, and he came up with a brilliant idea. He ordered the people to steal the left sock of every person lying in the grave who was suspected of being undead. When they returned with the lot, he put the socks in a bag and tied it to a rock in the creek. Then he sat back to wait for the vampires to come fetch their clothes.

The story goes, he destroyed the whole clan, because the legends tell that a vampire can't cross running water. He'll drown, even if it's a half-inch deep.

I think of Onan's tale each time I buy a lottery ticket and it makes me feel better about my gambling compulsion. I know it's an excuse, but you've got to agree: I'm not so bad compared to a fellow who stole the socks off of corpses to satisfy an obvious foot fetish.

I stood at the counter in Bay Shing's Chinatown Noodle Shop and rubbed off a twenty dollar roll of Pick Three numbers. I had the cellular up to my ear, calling Walsh, so no one could say I wasn't working. He growled an answer after the first ring.

"Has David Hanuman made it back home, yet?" I asked.

"No. We don't know where the hell he went and I still don't have enough manpower to devote to finding him." In a lower voice, he added, "The idiot watch commander underscheduled. Stupid SOB." Then, louder, again: "Why?"

"I just had an old Arab tell me that those ivory handles we're so familiar with are as rare as angel spit." He didn't answer right away and I didn't push him, because my attention was drawn off by a winning combination that came up on one of the tickets. I only had eighteen dollars left to go before I broke even. Finally, he said something.

"Is this old Arab a reliable source?"

"You bet. He'll testify, if we need him."

"Good. Are you on your way back to Headquarters to sit in on the interrogation?"

"I'll be there in about twenty minutes."

I closed down the connection and proceeded to find myself twelve dollars in the hole. After I collected the few bucks owed to me, I hurried off to Metro to discover Walsh leaning on the lee side of his desk talking in low tones on the telephone. He smiled slightly at what was being said. Nodding a final time, he hung up and laid that smile on me.

"You look like you just planned a hot date," I said.

"Better," he answered. Before explaining, he stepped around his desk and leaned down a bit to peer beneath it. "Come out of there, you," he said, in a low voice.

A skittering sound followed and then I heard clicking on

the linoleum. From this little office cave emerged a Scottish terrier. The dog paused to regard me with such a look of appraisal that I felt compelled to squat beside him. He did a few perfunctory sniffs and with the most regal highland tilt, he presented his head for petting.

Walsh sat down and crossed his ankles to take a long, slow stretch against the curve of the chair. Sighing, he said, "Meet my main partner, Nicki. This is Chester." At hearing his name, the dog marched over to check on the smell of his master's butt. He reached down to knuckle him gently along the back of the neck.

"Glad to meet you, Chester." I dropped my purse on the floor and took a seat in the leftover chair by his desk. "Tell me, Joe, what's your homeboy doing here?"

He crinkled on a sheepish look. "I haven't been home for any length of time in the last three weeks. Poor mutt was starving for affection."

I smiled. "Which poor mutt are we talking about? You or him?"

"Not funny, Nicki." He slipped our eye contact before he added, "It's why he pooped all over my apartment. I'm pretty sure." He paused to rub at the dark stubble cropping up on his chin before continuing. "I just heard from the owner of Wine and Roses. When I talked to her last week, I convinced her to call me when someone used the account David Hanuman keeps there. Well, someone did. They ordered a bouquet of meadowsweet and baby's breath."

"Where was it delivered?"

"It wasn't. A guy came to pick it up around noon. She said the shop was busy filling holiday orders, and it didn't occur to her until she was going over the books at the end of the day. The only thing she remembers about him was that he was wearing red gloves."

42

Saturday, November 28

I LEFT METRO Police Headquarters about 3:00 A.M. and went home. Diane was locked behind her bedroom door, Ekua was doing scales in his music room, Michael and Ilea were pretty much gone for good with all their stuff moved out, and Gale was in his studio suffering through his creative frustrations.

He responded to my knock, wielding a fan-shaped brush that dripped red acrylic. He returned to his canvas without a word of greeting. I followed him inside, a trifle fearful that the conversation I was about to hold with him would again breach the small connection we had made since the night of his killing madness.

"What are you painting?" I asked.

"A scene from memory. Old Montreal."

That got my attention. "From the window of the garret we used to share?"

He nodded.

For a moment, I worried he was experimenting with daytime colors, and if what Diane said was right, he might bend around the corner again over his inability to express himself. "May I see?"

"Of course."

He stepped back as I rounded the easel. I was pleasantly surprised to see a rendition featuring the full moon casting its gentle light through the french doors belonging to the apartment. Standing there, I was transported back to those early years. He had remembered the room in every detail.

"It's one of the pieces I'll be displaying in my exhibit at Lang's gallery," he said. "Do you like it?"

"Very much. Someone's sure to buy it right away." I turned to look at him, and he surprised me with a kiss to my lips.

"I love you, Nicki."

"And I, you." I moved off a little, just so his mouth wouldn't confound the purpose for which I'd come. "Are you still going to leave?"

He dabbed some paint to the picture before answering. "I'm not sure. I probably should. Ekua and you were right the other night: My behavior is endangering the clan." He snorted. "Diane stays about five feet from me at all times, now; and I can't say when one of those seizures might hit me again. Maybe it's better that I go. Start fresh."

"Is that the only reason? Or are you afraid I'll bet my bloodrights in the next poker game and send you off to house-sit for Alan?"

"That, too," he answered, tossing me a candid look as he did. "I'm really tired of it. I never know what to expect from you anymore. With Justin Lang, I've got a chance to make a little money and a name for myself. I'm the one who suffers when you gamble me off, not you. If it happens again, I could lose an awful lot as far as my freedom goes. You know it." He was silent for a moment. Then, "I think it might push me over the edge."

I couldn't deny what he said. Every nerve ending still active in my body tingled with pain at hearing his words. "You blame me for your predicament?"

"No, not entirely. It's been brewing for a long time, but the situation over the last few months has made me open my eyes to the truth of living with an obsessive gambler. Now, with the rise of the beast, I can't keep going along as if nothing is wrong. As bad as it is in my head right now, I have, at least, changed in that respect."

He sounded like he was turning into a Lon Chaney werewolf. Dropping his brush on his palette, he wiped his hands on a rag before continuing quietly, "When you're old enough, it'll happen to you, Nicki. Mark my words."

"I don't doubt it."

"You expect it, but you don't know what to expect of it. When it hits, you get an uninvited behavior modification."

"I know these desires must be strong, but can't you control the actions stemming from them?"

"Any more than you can stop playing a game of cards when you're winning?"

He had me there. I had no defense against the truth, so I turned and skimmed around the room, noticing how full it was with sculptures and paintings that had never sold. "It looks like you cleaned out the storage room," I said.

"Lang wants to see it all so he can decide what to display."

I took the tour slowly while trying to be nonchalant with my next question. "So, what is it like when the beast rises?"

He sighed. "Your whole being rebels. My personality, the thing that makes me recognizable as Gale, is subverted, and I'm totally submissive to whims I can't begin to explain. It's like I'm turned into a fire-breathing dragon." He picked up his brush again and jabbed at the canvas. "Each time it happens, it gets harder to recover my usual state of mind."

"Why?"

"Because it feels wonderful."

That surprised me. "Are you gaining new vampire powers?"

"Not unless open belligerence qualifies."

I didn't respond, because my eye had stalled on a

painting. It showed a naked woman lounging on the beach of a quiet South Pacific lagoon. Beside her was a tumbler of ice tea, partially buried in the sand. He had painted the sun as though it was setting over swaying palms and mountains. Gulls lazed on the air, and bending close, I marveled at his skill with perspective. Just down the beach, a machine gun bunker protected the shore, its presence camouflaged with vines of tropical flowers. All of this was laid on the canvas with short, even strokes that gave the image a surreal feel to it. I was reminded of looking at an old photograph that had faded into tones of sepia and beige.

I suddenly found myself wondering if he had intended for it to be that way.

43

Sunday, November 29

THE NEXT DAY was our annual holiday season get-together, and vampire killing or no vampire killing, Diane was determined to throw her version of a Norman Rockwell dinner.

Instead of turkey or ham, the traditional fare of our feast is rare filet mignon. She justifies this extravagance by telling me how much cheaper the meat is when she buys a whole tenderloin and then has the butcher slice it up. The guests, hematomans and their human counterparts, are supposed to bring a casserole or blood dish to add to this potluck feast. Still, it costs me a bundle by the time I add the bread, cheese, wine, and tankards of blood broth. My irritation over the expense is usually softened by the joviality of close friends, but this particular party was entirely too much of a pain in the ass to be any fun.

Alan was just in from South America and showed up to crash the party. He brought along a clutch of clotted blood and three of his people, one of whom was the editor of *Night Argosy*. The bastard was all over Gale, wanting to write an article for his vampire rag that featured his exhibit at Justin Lang's gallery. Gale became so puffed up over the thought that he began to display his excitement and feelings of power by being openly suggestive to me in front of everyone. Each time he could, he unsheathed his fangs to nip at my neck.

As if that weren't enough to piss me off from the start, Yolanda brought her damned dog along to pee on my carpet and scare the cat. Duval was there, too, filled to the gills with epinephrine and blood, cruising about six inches off the ground, and backing up Gale's advances with some of his own.

So, with all this, I was glad when Sam Short called to ask me to stop by. I promised I would, but waited until nine o'clock when the whole group gathered in the front parlor to listen to Ekua play. When they became enthralled, I snuck out the back and headed toward Chinatown.

Sam said a guy would be waiting at the entrance to take me back to the prescription kitchen. The fellow was indeed there, and he guided me without much ado through a quiet restaurant where only a few people dined, but once through the double sets of swinging doors, the action picked up immediately. Stepping inside, I paused to have a look around.

I hadn't been in an Oriental kitchen in a long time. The very air fizzed with the scents of garlic and ginger and red pepper. Taking a deep breath, I luxuriated a moment, remembering a visit Gale and I made to South China in the 1930s. We were routed out, along with some unfortunate humans, by the Communists. Gale never did like Asia after that.

Sam motioned me to join him at a restaurant-sized, cast-iron stove. He sweated over three woks, ladling water and wine into the stir-fries of what looked like chicken feet and calve's brains. He had four cooks on and they crowded into the small space with him, one of the guys handling a cleaver like he was making a Ginsu commercial. A noodle maker stood before his own board, and caught my attention when I saw him pour a few ounces of fresh, red blood into his pasta dough.

"What's he putting into the flour?" I asked Sam, pointing toward the man.

He followed the aim of my finger, even as he measured a palm of spice into the pot. "Yak blood. It strengthens the action of the lower bowel."

"The stuff makes you poop?"

"That's right." He snapped an order to one of his waiters in Cantonese. Turning to me, he switched to English. "Your man, the guy with the red gloves? He was in here tonight eating dinner."

"When?"

"About six o'clock."

"Did you call the cops?"

He shook his head.

"Why not?"

"I've got to think about my business, Nicki. If it weren't for this kitchen, we'd be hard-pressed, right now, to show a decent profit. Since they put in that new eatery over by the Convention Center, the main restaurant just isn't pulling its own. I can't afford to have a load of cops in here." Before going on, he dished up a portion of food from the wok, letting it splat into a paper carton sitting on the serving ledge. "You've got to understand. I help when I can."

I understood it better than he realized. "What can you tell me, then?"

"He ordered fried rice with bean curd and drank two carafes of Fo-Ti-Tieng."

"Did he come in with anyone?"

"No, but he did pick up someone while he was here. A hooker. She was eating at a nearby table. My waiter told me that they acted like old friends when they noticed each other."

"Did they leave together?"

"Yeah."

"Can you give an ID on the woman?"

He shook his head. "No. I wasn't paying much attention. I didn't even know she was eating in the restaurant. I have a new man on out there and he felt sorry for her, so he let her take the carryout into the dining room. You know my rules about that. Second kitchen stuff goes out the door. Period. I don't want a nosy health inspector seeing someone eating rat livers. Anyway, I came out to check the register and noticed your guy, but by that time they were heading for the door."

"What about the waiter? Can he give a description of the woman?"

"He could, but he won't. He's an IA from Vietnam."

IA—illegal alien. Chinatown would sink through the sidewalks were it not for this particular layer of humanity.

"Can you tell me anything at all about the hooker?" I asked. "Try to remember, Sam. She could be the Winter Man's next victim."

He didn't answer right away. Instead, he freshened up the wok with a couple of handfuls of butterfly wings, and then added some dandelion greens and soy sauce. He wiped his hands on his apron before he reached into his shirt pocket and pulled out a slip of paper smudged with grease and streaked with Chinese characters. "She came in with this. It's a prescription for revitalizing the chi energy. You might be able to look up the healer and see if he knows her name."

44

WHEN I GOT home, everyone was gone except for the *Night Argosy* turd who slobbered over Gale. The place smelled to high hell, and I was immediately put on the defensive. I walked into the front parlor and found Diane passed out on the couch from much too much champagne. She snored a feminine little rattle, and pulling a frayed, green coverlet over her, I stopped to wipe away a bit of dribble running from the corner of her mouth. Ekua was pacing the room. His anger surfaced as he explained about the awful odor.

"Gale and that guy have been in the kitchen for three hours," he said. "I walked in there, thinking to get a glass of blood. I understand they know each other from the times Gale has stayed over Alan's house, but I've never seen him act so weird. You should be proud of me, Nicki. I kept my calm and decided it was better to wait for you before I went in there and beat some sense into him."

"Good," I answered. "I don't want a repeat of the other night. What were they doing?"

He sat down heavily in a chair before replying. "They're sitting at the table. This guy is interviewing him—tape recorder's going and so is a whole lot of ego massage. While Gale's answering his questions, he's using one of your scalpels to whittle little pieces of raw steak into fancy designs, and then he's feeding them to that creep." He paused to squint at me. "Gale's really lost his mind. All the way. I thought maybe you should handle this. My temper would just make matters worse."

I went into the kitchen, and the stench immediately hit

me, but like I said before, being that I've smelled like that on occasion, the odor doesn't bother me. I was worried about the neighbors getting a whiff, though, and then, there was poor Diane to consider.

They had lighted candles and placed them all over the counters and on top of the microwave. Gale was, indeed, fashioning chunks of New York strip steaks into different shapes. The stinker sat so close to him at the table that their thighs were touching.

They both looked up when I entered, and they both smiled. Gale silently held out his palm for me to see a sliver of meat carved into the shape of a key. He angled the pitch of his hand and his buddy peeled it away to dip it in a goblet of blood. With a satisfied slurp, he downed his prize.

I stepped up to the table, and hearing the whirr of the tape recorder, I punched the pause button so I wouldn't be picked up in the interview.

"I can't remember your name," I said to him.

"Bryan. I'm one of Alan's consorts."

Despite the fact that he smelled like a garbage dump, he had a dark, Mediterranean beauty about him, complete with olive skin and a nose that was only slightly hooked at the bridge.

Gale busied himself whittling another protein design. "Bryan's doing an article on my upcoming show at Lang's gallery," he said. "He said a good third of the next *Night Argosy* issue will be devoted to it. That's great news, huh?"

"Wonderful," I muttered. Then, because I didn't want to piss off Gale too badly, I spoke with as much gentle force as I could. "Can you two take the interview outside?"

"Why?" Gale asked. There was such a look of perplexity on his face that I thought for a moment that he was serious.

My diplomacy evaporated. "What is it with you?" I asked. "Do you have some strange vampire sinus infection or something? This place reeks." I turned a glare on him. "Again."

He blinked at me, but didn't answer, so I went on. "The neighbors are going to smell it soon and call the cops on us. That's just what I need. Then, there's Diane. The minute she wakes up and gets a whiff of this stench, she's going to throw up right where she sits."

Gale suddenly exploded. "Stop ordering me around, Nicki! I'll sit here if I want."

His outburst ignited my own anger. I leaned on the table swiped the dish and the steak onto the floor. "Get out!" I yelled. "Come back when you can act sensibly again." I then turned a glare onto Bryan. "You, sir, have displayed disgusting behavior this evening, as well, with your indulgence in raw meat. I will be discussing this matter with your clan leader."

Gale was about to react again, but Bryan placed a restraining hand on his shoulder. "She's right," he said in a low voice. "We didn't consider the human female or the neighbors." He rose, picking up his tape recorder. "Come on, Gale. I've got some friends over in Southeast who want to meet you. The stink won't bother them."

He ducked out the back way, but Gale lingered to offer one parting volley. "You're trying to destroy my success before I even get started."

"No," I answered. "If anything, your actions these last few weeks will serve to destroy your success. I'm not going to take the blame for your failure this time."

45

AFTER GALE AND Bryan left the house, Ekua immediately opened the windows to let the stink out and the frigid breeze in. I helped him by spraying the room with an air freshener I had gotten from Art Anthony. The Medical Examiner's Office uses it to contain the odors and the airborne germs in the autopsy rooms and right at that moment, I was glad I had a sampler of the stuff. When it all didn't seem to be enough to take away the problem, we decided to build a fire. As Ekua labored, I sat down in the chair next to Diane to call Walsh.

His responses were short, clipped, and grave-sounding, so before launching into my report about Sam Short's sighting, I asked him what he was so pissy about. This is what he told me: The channel nine weatherman was talking about a storm system starting to build in the Gulf of Mexico. If the computer models were anywhere near accurate, then we could expect a dumping of snow to hit D.C. in about three or four days. As always, it was a crapshoot, but the city was gearing up for the worst. So was Walsh: There would be another Winter Man murder, and if that happened, the Homicide Division was sure to lose the best lieutenant they ever had.

I put the conversation to bed by telling him that we might be one step closer to solving this blasted mystery. I would meet him at the intersection of Eighth and H Streets, NW, to explain about Sam. Twenty minutes later, we were communing beneath a burnt-out ghetto light, me hanging onto the car door to talk to him through the window just like one of the hookers we were trying to find.

Walsh appeared to be hovering on the limits of exhaustion. Reaching out with my hematoman radar, I sensed his blood pressure was low, but his heart rate was in overdrive. He had a wild-eyed look about him, but unfortunately, I couldn't tell if it was the result of caffeine or a couple of hits of Dr. Dixon's Weight Loss Miracle Pills. Studying him in the dim light cast by a second story window, I decided it was both.

"So, where's Chester?" I asked, trying to lighten his mood.

"Back at Headquarters, full, asleep, warm, and if necessary, with his very own cop standing by to show him where to pee." He smiled, but it was an effort. "Wish I could say that for me." Then, a quick change of subject: "Sam Short's afraid I'm going to call a shutdown on his operation, isn't he?"

"You know about that, huh?"

"Yeah. And Fang-Louey is no secret, either. They know we're on to them, but still they play the game and keep cautious. Can't blame them, but as far as Metro is concerned, they're considered incidental marketers. They both keep legit businesses and pay taxes. There's nothing illegal about practicing traditional medicine, as long as no drugs or hazardous materials are involved."

"But the health department officials feel differently."

He shrugged. "Ah, well, that's their job."

Walsh dropped his end of the dialogue, and I backed off to let him park the car. The only available spot was in front of a fire hydrant, but he took it anyway, throwing the Metro Police Officer on Duty sign onto the dash. He got out with a grunt to join me as I started down the street. He remained silent during our walk, his attention disintegrating into the human preoccupation of watching one's breath freeze upon hitting the cold air. He didn't say anything further until we entered Fang-Louey's Oriental Deli and Salad Bar Shop.

When you walk into a Chinese market anywhere in Asia, it smells like sesame oil and five-spice powder. When you walk into such a store in America, it smells like fermented cabbage kim chee, a scent that's not all that different from a decomposing body. Walsh gave off another grunt once we stepped inside, shaking his head against what could have only been the odor. It smelled as though Fang-Louey was curing something taken straight from one of Art Anthony's body bags.

Manning the cash register, we found a little old lady who appeared to be deaf to the fact that there were customers. She sat squeezed behind a counter loaded with racks of Japanese bubble gum and martial arts video cassettes, watching a thirteen-inch Sony that showed the replay of the Macy's Thanksgiving Day Parade. It was the part of the show where Santa Claus comes through to ho-ho-ho and throw candy to the kids, and from the look of it, there was no tearing her away from the jolly elf's yearly performance.

From down an aisle bolstered with sacks of Red Rose Rice, bottles of vinegar, and brine-soaked plums, a young woman appeared, brandishing a mop. She stepped around a display of plastic "mother-of-pearl" serving trays that were reduced for quick sale and peered at us for a long moment before speaking.

"We were just closing," she said, in perfect English.

Walsh flashed his badge, and then aimed it toward the cashier who was oblivious to it all as she counted the eight tiny reindeer crossing her TV screen. "We would like to speak to Fang-Louey, please."

She frowned, but nodded. Propping her mop against the wall, she called to the cashier in a Chinese dialect. I picked

up the word grandmother, but little else. The old lady
flapped a hand at her, and when she got that, the young
woman said: "Let me check to see if he's available," and
was gone into the back room.

I hadn't had the opportunity to meet this particular
Chinese medicine man, so I don't know exactly what I
expected when we arrived. He had a reputation for being a
chi master. Chi literally means, energy. Fang-Louey could
supposedly control the mount of chi flowing through a
person's body. He could heal using it, or he could fight
using it, and in the latter case, earn a couple of extra bucks
down at the local martial arts dojo.

I suppose I had the idea that he would be old and
venerable, and act like a character out of a kung fu movie.
He wasn't, and he didn't. Fang-Louey was an Oriental
James Dean.

He came out of the back, wiping his hands on his jeans.
I followed the direction of his fingers and saw that he wore
a pair of python skin cowboy boots. When he spoke, he had
a lazy southern drawl.

"I'm Fang-Louey," he said. "What can I do ya for?"

Walsh snapped open his ID again, and then piloted a look
straight into his eyes. "We're here concerning an ongoing
police investigation," he said. "Can we talk privately?"

"Sure. Come on into my office." He spun on his silver-
capped heels to lead the way down a short hall to the back
of the building.

The office was immaculate, trimmed in teak wood,
decorated with Indonesian batiks, a computer, and furniture
he must have paid full price for. Walsh immediately headed
for two lights flanking a nice stereo system. He stared for a
second at the deep blue globs floating in a clear plastic shell.
Then he glanced at Fang-Louey. "Are these things really
lava lamps?"

Fang-Louey smiled. "Yep. I'm into collecting stuff from the sixties and seventies."

Walsh angled a grin toward me. "I haven't seen one of these things in years."

"You guys want some coffee or tea?" Fang-Louey offered.

Walsh mimicked my no, disconnecting from the decorations to move right to the point. He jabbed a thumb at the sheet of paper I wrestled from my purse. "Did you write this prescription?"

Fang-Louey took the note and read it before he answered. "Yes."

"What's it for?"

He took on a suspicious expression. "Are you guys really cops, or are you from the AMA? I've been having trouble with them lately."

"We're really cops," Walsh said. "And right now, I've got a line on a woman who might be the next victim in a serial killing. I need to find her."

"The Winter Man, huh? I've been reading about that. He's got the Metro Police by the short-hairs, doesn't he?"

Walsh's patience was dribbling away. "Please. This woman is in grave danger," he said. "You're the only one we can find who can give us a name on her."

He stared at the note for a moment and sighed, moving to his desk to sit heavily upon the expensive leather chair. "The AMA is giving traditional healers a hard time," he answered. "Not to mention the health department and their rationale for interrupting the operations of local . . . pharmacists."

"They have a problem when the prescriptions call for rat tails and stir-fried roaches," Walsh said.

"Ridiculous. The government created that lie. It allows them to keep the people enslaved to the system." He paused to insert a snort for effect, and then, "We try to elevate the person's vigor, not destroy it with poison. Traditional treatments require the purest ingredients."

"We agree," I said, stepping into the argument. "We're not here to harass you." I held out the prescription for him to see again. "We just want to know her name and if you might know where she can be found."

"She's a prostitute," he answered. "I try to give back to the community, you know. I have an outreach program to help people down here in Chinatown. She was pretty sick and was referred to me. I don't know her name. I avoid names. Got no memory for them anyway."

"All right. Do you know who referred her to you?"

He thought a few seconds and shook his head. "She was one of Jow Lord's girls. Blond and skinny. Like I said, I don't have a good recall when it comes to names."

"Do you know where she lives?"

He shook his head. "After he was killed, I understand the house split up and the hookers went off to other pimps. I'm not sure who she's working for now, and I can't be certain where she's staying, what with the changes around here—"

"Yes?" I egged.

"I think she lives on Sixth Street, somewhere."

Walsh's expression flipped upward on the intensity scale and he blinked. He was thinking of Laura Roberts. "Sixth Street?"

"Yeah. Maybe you can find her there. Seems to me she works the Henley Park area, too, but I'm not sure, mind you."

It was definitely Laura Roberts.

"I'm curious," Walsh said. "In your opinion, what was the woman's medical problem?"

"Her chi is off. It's steadily evaporating."

"Chi?"

Fang-Louey displayed some of his own impatience. "Her body's energy is out of whack. In her case the yang has overtaken the yin. Her system has become highly acidic, when it should have a better ratio of alkalinity."

"Has she been suffering from this imbalance long?" I asked, getting a strange look from Walsh, when I did.

He nodded. "She instinctively knew her life force was damaged, but she sought out another practitioner before coming to me." He hesitated, flicking a look down to his hands. Looking back up, he said, "I don't usually talk about my colleagues working in this field, but once in a while even we get our quacks."

Walsh grunted for the third time and pulled at his hat.

I kept at Fang-Louey, despite my partner's obvious opinion. "What had this other healer prescribed for her?"

He shook his head, and then added a reflective tilt to it. "She allowed him to inject her a number of times with some substance in her groin area. I didn't see this for myself, you understand, but she said the places he had treated her became bruised and tender, and she was having pain while doing her . . . work."

"Why did she continue to allow him to inject her, do you think?"

"He told her that it was necessary to purify her soul." Fang-Louey shook his head sadly. "What some people will believe."

46

FANG-LOUEY'S MEMORY of the prostitute's body was much better than his supposed lapse where names were concerned, so Walsh was able to issue an APB on anyone answering the description of a Caucasian woman who was approximately five-five and weighed 110 pounds. She had black hair and a mole the size of a nickle on her right cheek.

After he got the word on the street, we took a ride over to Laura Roberts's apartment. The place was just as filthy as it was the last time. I could tell this just from the condition of her front door. There was cooking grease splattered all over it, and when she answered our knock, she wasn't too happy to see us, either. She stepped out into the hallway, dressed in her underwear and a blue crocheted shawl, hissing something about having holiday guests. It was poor timing on her part to become belligerent with Walsh. He grabbed her securely by the upper arm and proceeded to tell her the difference between entertaining johns and entertaining friends.

She stared at him defiantly. Worried his strung-out mood was going to make him blow her cooperation, I went ahead and put a Dracula Stare on her as I gently unclamped his hand. I had used this supernatural trick more in the last two weeks than I had in the whole year.

"Laura," I said, "we need to find a friend of yours. You sent her to see Fang-Louey for help." She hesitated in answering. It was partly my fault, because I noticed a huge roach crawling up the wall and it drew off my attention. In that second, she managed to spring loose of my hold.

"I don't know what you're talking about."

"Laura," I said, using my most motherly tone. "Do you remember how Gitana O'Quinn looked after the Winter Man killed her?"

"Yes. So?"

"So, the same thing is going to happen to your friend if we don't find her. We have good reason to believe that he's been slowly poisoning her."

"You're making this up."

I shot another Dracula Stare at her, undermining her resolve. "Your friend is a dead woman if you don't help us."

"Is there a reward for his arrest?" she asked.

Walsh lied with a smile on his lips. "Metro Police Crime Solvers Unit is offering a thousand dollars to anyone who can provide leads to his whereabouts. You interested?"

"Yeah. Let me get my clothes."

"Why don't you just tell us where she lives and save yourself the aggravation of going out on a night like to-night?" he demanded.

"She ain't got a real address, like me. You're going to need me to show you who she is."

"We have a description."

Laura pulled on my control like a stubborn child pulling on her mother's hand.

Finally, seeing that she wouldn't let us go off without her, Walsh gave in. "All right, get dressed."

"I'll only be a couple of minutes." She turned and started to slam the door shut, but Walsh's foot made it impossible. We came inside behind her in time to see two shadows scramble into the bedroom in front of her.

The place was dingy. The only light came from a small child's lamp that sported a base made to look like a clown holding a red balloon. Dim as it was, it was still bright enough to see the dog poop marking the floor.

Walsh fidgeted while we waited, though he tried to

appear nonchalant by leaning against the wall and digging out a breath mint to chew on. Seeing him do that, I realized the apartment harbored more bad smells than a crime scene.

Out of an old hunter's habit I developed years ago, I clicked on my radar to see who was in the vicinity. Not counting us, there were five people in the apartment, and from their dimensions, four were male; the guy hiding in the bathroom was by far the biggest. I glanced at Walsh. He was already unzipping his Redskins jacket while he crunched loudly on the mint. His left hand came to hover at chest level, and I knew right then that his own version of radar had switched on. From this posture, he could take a direct dive into his shoulder holster.

The best way to get out of an awkward situation is to back out; gracefully, if you can, or at a dead run, if you can't. "We stepped into a gang-bang, Joe."

"I was thinking that same thing. Let's go wait down at the end of the hall, near the stairs. What do you say?"

"I think that's smart."

"Hurry up, Laura," Walsh barked.

"I'm coming already," she called. "I've got to do my hair."

He pushed to the door, muttering, "Her hair. I wonder how many times she can get herself plugged while she tries to comb out that rat's nest?"

"I'd say she'll probably make about one hundred and fifty dollars on the whole deal."

He clucked a reply, breaking off another mint as we stepped into the hallway to wait.

Laura finished earning her wages for the evening and appeared ten minutes later. Before long, we were jumping on the subway at Rhode Island Avenue, leaving the car parked in the Metrorail garage reserved for riders, because as busy as Union Station is, there's never anyplace to park, even for cops who don't mind blocking fire hydrants.

The subway dumped us all off at Union Station after a short ride and we took the handicapped elevator topside, coming out into the refurbished train station.

Though it was once a thriving train depot where heads of state were greeted by past presidents, and where the servicemen of the region left to fight World War II, Union Station was closed for nearly a decade in the seventies and eighties, having fallen into disuse and disrepair. In 1988, taking the train became fashionable again, and the city, along with private donations, revamped the station. Now, while waiting for your train, you can shop in luxury stores or down a bagel or burger at one of the eateries.

We followed Laura Roberts through this mall as she headed toward the debarkation section. The place was busy, too, carrying a late-night holiday rush out of the city. As we passed a line of folks straining toward one of the boarding doors, I heard people talking about how good Miami would feel when they finally got there.

Laura led us farther down the concourse, her shoes making a slapping sound on the linoleum as she did. Toward the far end, sitting alone in an empty debarkation area, we found a dark-haired woman who looked to be in considerable difficulty. We all pulled up to her; Walsh bent down close to see what was wrong; Laura made some gurgling noises upon noticing her associate's predicament; and I was forced, to my dismay, into having to do the doctor thing. It was a night, then, for more action and suspense than I desired.

Don't get me wrong, it's not that I don't want to help humans. I wouldn't be tracking down one of their killers if I didn't. But I much prefer staying on the dead side of the equation. Live bodies squirming around in agony haven't got quite the same appeal as stone cold ones.

Besides, I wasn't real thrilled when the dean of my college decided that before any student could graduate with a medical degree, he had to first certify as an emergency medical technician. I didn't pay a great deal of attention, because to me, as a hematoman, it seemed stupid. We kill humans; we don't ordinarily save them. Yet, here I was, stuck helping a young woman who was having a hard time of it, and from all the pain she seemed to be in, it didn't take a genius to see she was in for the mother of all heart attacks.

I hunkered down with Walsh and told him to call 911 to report it. He was already pulling out his cellular.

The woman shivered and moaned. She had that gray, ashy look that comes with the first stages of a heart attack, but I wasn't sure how much of that was due to the overhead fluorescent. I felt for heat in her forehead, but she was clammy and cold. Taking her wrist, I pinched my finger down on her artery, checking for the pulse. It was thumping as fast as mine had after I'd gotten it jumpstarted with Duval's adrenaline mixture. I looked up to say something to Walsh and noticed we'd finally drawn a crowd.

Her voice pulled my attention back to her. "I've got a pain in my back," she slurred. She clawed at one of her breasts. "Can't breathe."

"Can you feel your hands?" I demanded. "Do they tingle?"

"Yes."

It was my guess that the hooker suffered from a form of bacterial endocarditis, but only a blood test would show for sure. Endocarditis is an infection in the lining of the heart and its valves. Usually, this illness will attack drug addicts, because they use dirty needles, introducing bacteria and fungi into the bloodstream. This dirt is trapped in the nooks and crannies, and when the blood flows into the heart, the microorganisms come in with it, but when the tide goes out, the junk stays behind to gunk up the low places. Each time there's a new delivery of fluid into the heart, the chances for getting a blood clot increases. If Richard Hanuman had truly been injecting her with gold, it could be the reason for her pain. Not only was poison settling into her joints, it had already started leeching into her organ tissue. Then again, it could have been something Fang-Louey had prescribed and Sam Short had cooked up. Either way, she was ready to check out to the dimension beyond. As cold as it sounds, we needed to get information before her pumper blew.

Walsh helped me get her to the floor and elevate her feet. I felt her fear rise with her blood pressure.

"What's her name, Laura?" I demanded.

"Toni. Toni Trent."

"Toni," I said in a low, commanding voice, "Look at me."

Her eyes rolled around and she squinted. "Help me," she whispered.

"The ambulance is on the way. Toni, the man who did this to you is Richard Hanuman. Where do you meet to get your injections?"

She groaned, giving a little shake to her head. "You're wrong," she whispered.

"What do you mean, Toni? Isn't he giving you shots to purify your soul?"

"No," she choked. "His name. His name is David. David Hanuman."

47

TONI TRENT COLLAPSED before I could get any more information. The medics came and took her away, clearing a space between the onlookers being herded by security guards back to their own debarking areas. Walsh let Laura Roberts go along for the ride to the hospital, telling her we would be right behind her with Toni's duffel bag. We waited until everyone was gone before he canceled the APB, and we sat down to go through the rucksack.

The pockets of this pack were an adventure. I had never been through a whore's personal baggage before, and the first thing my hand closed around was a unopened box of prophylactics. Digging further, I found a dirty bra, a torn, dog-eared issue of *The Washingtonian* magazine, and a blond wig. In the next pocket, I came across a pair of stiletto heels and her address book.

We both looked through the pages, Walsh peering over my shoulder as I did the thumb work. He grunted a couple of times when he recognized some names that came straight off the Senate floor. Then, knuckling his eyes, he sighed. "I don't know who or what I'm looking for anymore. David or Richard. I start going one way, and what happens? I get tossed into another blind alley."

I flapped the book at him. "Do you have to insert this as evidence right away?"

"I don't have to do shit, so long as no one but you and me knows about it. Why?"

"Here, listed under A: Ann Latrice. Isn't that David Hanuman's pretty partner?"

He blinked at me and pulled a heavy, slow breath. "God. What the hell is going on here?"

"Shall we make a late-night visit to Ms. Latrice and find out?"

"Yeah. Does she have an address written down in that mess?"

"She sure does. A nice Capitol Hill address. Not too far from here. Do you want to go back to the subway station and pick up the car, or do you want to walk?"

"Let's walk. Maybe it'll help me let off a little steam and clear my brain."

Capitol Hill is the area in the city that sits to the east of the Capitol Building. It's a posh section, where Senate staffers fresh in with the newly elected state officials, find residential accommodations befitting their elevated status in life. The streets are crisp, clean, and quaint and, some even say, safe enough for the President to take his morning jog. If there's a politician's neighborhood, Capitol Hill has got to be it.

From Toni Trent's book, we discovered that Ann Latrice had a nice little walk-up near Lincoln Park. She answered the door, dressed in filmy black lingerie. The sheer fabric showed her boobs pretty clearly, and caught staring at the set, Walsh had to clear his throat a couple of times before he could speak.

"I've been expecting you," she said, letting us inside.

"Why is that?" he asked.

"David, of course. The bastard."

She didn't say any more until we were seated in a living room, decorated with overstuffed furniture and expensive prints. Before she came to the point, though, she managed to overcome the businesslike demeanor Walsh had assumed by giving him a fast shot of her crotch as she crossed her legs. He recovered quickly, but he did start to sweat a little.

"Do you know where David Hanuman is?" he husked.

"He jumped bail, didn't he?"

"We don't know this yet. His court date isn't set for several days. What makes you think he did?"

"He withdrew fifty thousand dollars from the business account this afternoon. If he doesn't put it back in, we're screwed. I can't keep the company running on the line of credit we have left." She plastered her fingers against her temples and rubbed. "Is he the killer you're looking for?"

"We're not sure. Right now, he's a possible accessory before the fact."

A shiver went through her, but she didn't reply.

Walsh leaned toward her and pushed her button, right then. "Ms. Latrice, tell me why your name and number would be in an address book belonging to a known prostitute?"

She instantly went into a defense posture by pulling her negligee tighter and crossing her arms. Her response was snippy. "There's a reasonable explanation for that."

"What is it?"

"I'm helping David with his outreach program."

"Explain that in detail, please."

"David is active in the D.C. community. He helps prostitutes, runaways, and drug addicts to find a way out of their predicament by getting them free counseling, safe haven, and medical treatment. He's gotten commendations from the Mayor's Office for his work, too."

"What do you do for him?"

"David feels that street people need to hear a compassionate human voice instead of an answering machine. I have a live-in housekeeper who answers the phone here during the day and between the three of us, we manage his hot line. I pass the calls on to him, and when he's free, he calls them back. It's not a lot of work, understand. We don't get that many people bothering us."

"Do you have an opinion on why you don't?"

"David gives out our numbers to those he meets directly in the course of his community service. It's his life, don't you see? He wants to help a lot of people, but running an import business takes most of his time, and he rarely gets out. He's really a good man."

Walsh sat back in the plush chair and slowly took out his pad and pen. I was becoming used to the way he used this pause to make a transition in the interview.

"Do you know a hooker named Maggie Kahn?"

"I don't know her personally, but the name is familiar."

"What about a prostitute named Gitana O'Quinn?"

"No."

"A gentleman named, Edward Bunt?"

"No. I've never heard of him."

"You do know Toni Trent, though?"

She swallowed before answering. "Yes." Standing up, she swept toward the double French doors like a movie queen from the 1940s. "What's going on that I don't know about?"

"We're not sure," Walsh said. "That's the problem. If we did, we could discover our killer."

"David has always seemed like a generous man to me. That's why I went into business with him."

"Do you have reason to believe he's left the country?"

She shook her head. "No. He had his passport stolen about a month ago and he hasn't gone to have it replaced—at least, as far as I know. We've been busy. Getting away from the office in the daytime hours is difficult right now."

Walsh nodded. "Do you know Richard Hanuman?"

"No. I mean, I've never met him."

"But you do know him?"

"Only over the phone. He's David's cousin."

Walsh plowed ahead, despite his revelation. "Was he helping David with his community work?"

"Yes. He's a physician."

"Do you know where he lives?"

"No. David's never mentioned it, and I never thought to ask." She returned to the couch. "Don't you have his address? I thought the FBI had stuff like that."

Walsh shook off her question. "I ask you again: At this time, do you know the whereabouts of David Hanuman?"

She sighed. "No, but I may know someone who does."

48

ACCORDING TO THE sign greeting folks who take exit 153 off Interstate 95, Dumfries is Virginia's oldest town. It's one of those places that thrived in an era before the highway came along and made the cut down old Route 1 a waste of time until the first McDonald's was finally built at the cloverleaf. Dumfries is only thirty miles south of Washington and is practically in the middle of the urban sprawl from D.C. to Richmond, but at first look, it doesn't seem to move at such a frenetic pace as those cities surrounding it.

Dumfries was a major seaport in the eighteenth century, and today, it borders Quantico U.S. Marine Corps Base. It's a laid-back community, where the Season's Greetings banner goes up over Main Street in November and doesn't come down until the end of February. The citizens in this incorporated square mile have one claim to fame, which is known as the Weems-Botts House. George Washington's biographer, Parson Weems, lived here when he came up with the idea of the hatchet, the cherry tree, and George's inability to tell a lie.

Not only could we find history in Dumfries, but Ann Latrice had said we could find David's ex-wife, so after bidding Ann a good-bye, we hit the road.

Walsh pulled the Metro squad car into the town hall's small parking lot. We got out and he said he was sorry again about me having to share the front seat with a rifle, a lap-top computer, and a radio microphone that kept falling off its clip to bang me in the knee every time he took a bump. I flapped a hand at him and moved into step as we entered the double-wide trailer that served as the hall of justice.

You might wonder how I can safely travel out of a ten-mile radius of my home without worrying about being caught by the dawn. It's simple, really. Hematomans have spent centuries establishing a society within a society, and in every major city in the world one can find a night friend who'll offer the hospitality of a safe house. Before leaving the District with Walsh, I made a call to the hematoman locator for the D.C. area, who put me in touch with a gent living in Dumfries. I phoned him to make sure I wouldn't impact his unlifestyle if I needed a place to crash. He invited me instantly, saying there was fresh blood in the fridge and to please help myself. The key would be under the front porch mat.

We checked in with the local constable for directions and information. He told us to go past the car wash, make a left at the light, and then go straight until we came to a four-way stop. Hang another left and we would find ourselves in a neighborhood called Williamstown. He chuckled, then, adding that this part of town was referred to as Little New York, because any drug you might want could be found in the ten-block-long complex of town houses. After telling us to watch our asses, he went back to filling out a report of some kind.

Doing as we were told, we found ourselves on the front porch stoop of a rotten-looking corner unit. Iona Austin, David's former wife, answered the door, dressed in a pink robe and matching slippers. She was fat, too; in fact, she looked like an enormous roly-poly bug. She didn't do much to try to camouflage her corpulence and it gave Walsh a hard time. As she led us through a junked-up living room to a couple of broken-down chairs, he apologized for the lateness of the hour, but kept glancing at her huge butt, the outline of which was perfectly cast in the clingy fabric of her muu-muu. I know he dared not look at me. I could feel him locking a hold onto his laughter.

We each sat cautiously on the furniture. My chair wailed like a banshee.

"Did my lousy kid get into some kind of trouble?" she asked, after muting the TV.

"No ma'am," Walsh said. "Not that I know of, anyway."

"Good. He better not be, or I'm going to kill him when he gets home."

Walsh cleared his throat in an effort to interject a good starting point for the interview. "Mrs. Austin, we're here to ask you about David Hanuman."

Her face, which I imagined turned into a plain of mud masks and cold creams each night, fell like a cake. It was a moment before she could winch it up again. "What do you want to know about him for?" she murmured.

"He's a suspect in a murder investigation."

Her hand came up to cover her mouth, and then she dropped it away to reveal a hard expression. "Doesn't surprise me none. Good. I hope you catch the slimy SOB and then give him the death sentence—without a trial."

Walsh broke out his notebook and pen. "How long were you married to Hanuman?" he asked, putting on his innocent voice.

"We lived together for ten years. Ten years. I had two kids by him and lost my fortune and my figure."

"Your fortune?"

"Yeah. I had a trust fund given to me by my daddy. He couldn't wait to get his hands on it. Well, he did, and I didn't get a damned thing to show for it except a divorce and a measly little bit of child support that I don't see very often. Now, I'm working as a secretary and sitting outside of

Social Services trying to get food stamps, because the
second bastard I married ran out on me, too."

"Do you know what Hanuman did with the money?"

"Blew it. On one of his import deals. Only this one went
sour."

"How so?"

She squinted at Walsh and then at me. "My ex-husband
was a crook, detective. He did things illegally. He brought
stuff into this country he had no business bringing in."

"Like what?"

"Well, when I was married to him, he was bringing in
hides made from endangered species. He imported other
things, too. Plants, insects. When I would ask him why he
was buying this stuff, he would say he had a counterinsur-
gency deal with the CIA." She shook her head. "God, what
a bunch of bullshit."

"Do you know to whom he sold the goods once he had
them in the country?"

"He never did much with the junk as far as I could tell. He
had a legal business importing goods from Hong Kong and
Taiwan, but he was fond of saying how that just funded his
smuggling hobby. He called smuggling a hobby. Do you
believe it?"

Walsh scribbled a note, then said, "What can you tell me
about his family? Did he have any relatives he was fond
of?"

"Sure. Which ones do you want to know about?"

"What about a man named Richard. Is that a name you
recognize?"

"Of course. That's his good-for-nothing cousin."

Walsh glanced at me and I saw a mixture of curiosity and
satisfaction lurking in his expression. He quickly turned
back to Mrs. Austin. "Were David and Richard close?"

"Yes. They saw a lot of each other. David was always driving him someplace."

"Richard didn't have a driver's license?"

"I don't know if he did or not. All I know is, he wouldn't get behind the wheel of a car."

As Walsh was about to ask her another question, an animal that looked a lot like a weasel came flying into the room and squeezed underneath the couch. It startled me so, my heart almost took a beat.

I do not like any form of rodentia, and that goes for animals that even look like they came out of a sewer. I know that rats are supposed to be the allies of the undead, and all the myths say we can turn ourselves into such vermin, but the truth is, they aren't, and we can't. I make it a point to avoid contact with these beasties on a regular basis. I don't care what kind they are—cute little hamsters or cuddly white mice—as long as they have beady eyes and buckteeth, I don't want to have anything to do with them.

Mrs. Austin's screeching yell, though, gave me a worse scare than the animal had. "How many times have I told you kids to keep that ferret in the cage in your room? Mary, come out here and get this damned thing. We got company, for Christ's sake!"

A child appeared. She looked at us with a shy smile and a tiny "Sorry" at her lips. She fished under the sofa for the pet, found it, and grabbing it by the tail yanked it out into the open. She apologized again and hurried away, the polecat squealing at the viselike grip she had on it. A few moments passed before Walsh could collect himself to continue with the interview, but when he did, he got right to the point.

"Did you ever overhear David and Richard discussing murder?"

She scowled. "No."

"Did they ever, to your knowledge, associate with prostitutes?"

On that one, he got a nod. "You probably know that David had a run-in over beating up a whore." She looked sad for a second. "Why do men do that, anyway? Got a family and a wife, but still need to go out and pay for sex and a good time. I just don't understand. It wasn't like I was a nag or anything."

"After he was arrested for assault, did he continue to associate with prostitutes?"

"Sure. That's what eventually ended our marriage."

"What about Richard? Did he follow his cousin's lead?"

"That man was nuts. I don't know if he ever slept with any of those pigs, but he sure did talk about saving their souls."

"How?"

"Who knows. He was into that metaphysical crap, so I suppose it could be just about anything."

"When was the last time you saw David?"

"A couple of years ago. In court. I sued him for withholding child support."

"That was the last time?"

"I just told you it was."

"All right. What about Richard?"

She hesitated before answering. "Late this past year. I work for a company in D.C. and he came by to see me."

"What did he want?"

She shook her head. "He wanted to borrow my electric food dehydrator."

"Did you give it to him?"

"Yeah, and if you find out where he is, tell him I want it back. It was a professional one, made out of stainless steel."

"We'll do that. Mrs. Austin, can you tell us where we can find David and Richard?"

"Richard, no, but David? Isn't he home in his fancy house?"

"No, ma'am."

"Well, there's no telling, then."

"One of his associates claims that he has a house near a river in the tidewater area of Virginia. Do you know about this place?"

She considered the question for a moment before answering. "If it's the house I think it is, then that would be the house in Walkerton, Virginia. A huge old Victorian. It's his mother's home. She owned it before she married his daddy." She leveled a sigh at us. "She's a smart old woman for keeping the place in her name. That's where I made my mistake with David. He wanted everything I had and I gave it to him."

49

I was in a lethal mood by the time I said good night to Walsh. I don't know if it was because of Gale's increasing idiocy or whether it was the general confusion of the case. Whatever the reason, it made me want to kill something, so I paused on my return home to take down a victim, but the fresh infusion of blood did nothing to dispel my depression. Dawn drew swords with the night before I stepped across the threshold of my sanctuary. Though it didn't do much more to improve my perspective, at least the inside of the house smelled better than it had when I left it.

Diane was still zonked out on the couch, and Ekua peddled in the kitchen, making one of his blood casseroles that I am so fond of. I bypassed him with a quiet word and went right down to the lab to stare at Toni Trent's address book, but once in my hole, I couldn't bring myself to try to find that one piece of evidence that would lead us to the Winter Man. Walsh had put this chore on to me, relieved, I think, by his need to concern himself with extricating David Hanuman from his southern Virginia retreat. If he brought him back in the next few hours, perhaps it would make plowing through the pages of the hooker's compressed writing a moot point.

I turned instead to the computer floppy that Mrs. Pollack had given me on Richard Hanuman. When Iona Austin had mentioned loaning him her food dehydrator, something had clicked in the back of my hematoman brain. I was reminded of his discourse on the Aztec Indians, a race he thought was the reincarnation of the ancient Egyptians.

In his opinion, entire societies were reborn to work out their karmic debt of an eye for an eye. Just as life-after-life applies to individuals, he thought that whole races, geographically segregated, were up for rebirth, as well. In this case, Hanuman saw the similarities between these two divergent peoples.

He began by pointing out how both societies, though sequestered from each other by time, had shown remarkable similarities. Each had pyramids, and each had divinely mandated pharaohs. Egypt bowled over the Hebrews at one point in its history, making it necessary for Moses to cut a hasty path through the Red Sea. When the Egyptians returned as the Aztecs, they eventually got their just dues by being enslaved by the Spanish conquistadores. Hanuman felt that this retribution came about because of a simple error made by the Indians: They had served hot cocoa to Hernando Cortes during dinner one night. Chocolate was the gift of the sun god, intended for his people alone. When the Aztec leader dished up the drink to the Spaniard, he broke the sacred covenant between the natural and supernatural worlds.

I stopped for a moment to figure out what that had to do with anything, but I was at a loss to see any sensible connections in the dialogue. Moving on, I saw that Hanuman turned like a dervish, switching his discussion onto the Egyptian practice of mummification.

As though he'd actually been there, he launched into his theories on the existence of a kha. The ancients believed the kha was the soul of a person. Once the physical self died, it left, but similar to the reincarnation concept, it could reenter the body if it was correctly preserved.

According to Hanuman, the corpse of the honored dead was first washed with water and a substance known as natron. You can still find natron through chemical supply houses; it's nothing more than hydrated sodium carbonate. Once the brain was sucked out through the person's nostrils, the priest overseeing the whole burial ritual would then call in the sacrificer, a man who had great strength, both physically and mentally.

Hanuman openly expressed his identification with the sacrificer, saying that in recurring lifetimes, he had sought such employment. It was necessary for the completion of his soul's mission.

The members of this sect of Egyptian priests were considered to be unclean, but necessary, because their job was to cut through the body, sever the major organs, wrap them in linen soaked in resin, and stuff them into canopic jars, where they would dry out along with the body. Once this major chore was done, the burial process could continue; yet, before that could happen, the priest would have to be run out of the ancient funeral parlor by the other attending morticians.

In the midst of discussing the various methods to run off the sacrificer, Richard Hanuman switched gears again to bring in a thought about food dehydrators. His argument was this: The modern world holds the technology to greatly shorten such a long embalming process. By using technology wisely, namely adapting the principles of electricity and the flow of warm air over a body, one could make a person into beef jerky in no time at all. He said it was vitally important that the people of today not lose touch with their ancient traditions. They should be allowed to express their beliefs, because it was not so much the process as it was the ritual, itself.

Mild surprise flaked my perspective and I was forced to stop reading the passage. I jockeyed the computer into sleep mode, then got up to fill a glass with blood. While I sipped my drink, I realized that contained on the disk was a record of Richard Hanuman's fragmenting ego. It was easy to see that he was slowly losing his touch with reality.

The more reports I went through, the more ludicrous they became, but there was no evidence until Mrs. Pollack's intervention that the Smithsonian ever confronted him about his psychological instability. There were no memorandums to the record, no letters of concern, no simple reprimands.

They never even shouted down the hall to see what would answer.

50

Monday, November 30

At HALF PAST ten in the morning, Gale phoned home. His call roused me from a lethargy such as I haven't experienced in years, and though I was still mad, I talked to him.

"Where are you?" I asked.

"Over at Alan's."

I ruffled again at hearing his answer. "I pay through the nose to get you out of that place and what do you do? Go right back again."

"What did you want me to do? Go to a hotel?" Then, before I could jump in with a snide remark, he said, "I don't have any other friends here in Washington. At least, no one who would take me in on such short notice."

"That's part of your problem, isn't it? You've never had any friends—not here, not in Geneva, not in London. You've always played the part of the suffering artist. If it weren't for me, you'd still be sitting in that rotting garret in Paris, drinking pig's blood and talking to the world through the keyhole in the door."

I thought my words would provoke a fight, but he just sighed. "You're right. I'll admit it. You saved me from myself all those years ago, but you knew from the beginning that I was dysfunctional. I'm just not cut out to be a very successful vampire, and the longer I exist, the harder it becomes."

There was such defeat in his voice that I couldn't hold on

to my anger. "When you get through this illness, you'll feel better about yourself."

"Yes, but when will that be? I have no idea how to work through it."

"Do you remember any of your antics last night?"

"Yes."

"So you had control of the situation?"

"For the most part."

"Then you realize how bad that guy stank. Why didn't you consider the clan? Why did you play that little game with him in the kitchen?"

"I wonder, myself. It was different. It was what I felt like doing at the time."

"Because you're having a tough go of it doesn't give you unlimited license to disrupt this family. When you're in the midst of an episode, such as with the girl, I can understand better, but when you know what you're doing and blatantly disregard others . . ." I started to get worked up again and exasperation forced out my sentence with a hiss. "I can't condone it. I have to draw the line somewhere."

"I understand. May I return home this evening?"

"Of course."

On that, we hung up. He hadn't even apologized for his actions, yet he had given me a number-one guilt trip over having thrown him out.

I worried over it for another hour until Diane came tripping down the steps, looking like she was in the first phase of death—the part just before you go into the casket. She carried a tumbler of ice water with her and flopped heavily into the chair beside me.

"I have to admit that I looked better than you when I died," I said.

"OK, rub it in. I just came down to tell you that Justin

Lang is upstairs. He stopped by to see Gale, but since he's not around, he'd like to talk to you."

I let go of my own sigh, but before I could grouch about being interrupted, Diane spoke again. "You ought to stop being rude to him, Nicki. This guy is rich. He was highlighted in the *Washington Post* magazine last weekend and they talked about how he's a self-made man and all. He started out as a street artist with no formal education to speak of. Now he's one of the experts."

"Expert on what?"

"Don't be smart. He's got an eye for talent. His association with Gale could help this entire clan." She paused to slug her water. Then, "Besides, he's cute."

I dropped my attempt at whining when she said that, unable to contain a smile. "Cute compared to what?"

She got up and started back toward the steps. "For Christ's sake, just talk to him. He's concerned about Gale."

"Aren't we all?"

She left on the end of my comment and sent down Lang. He came into the lab with a frown creasing his forehead. "Hi."

"Hi, yourself. What's up?"

He sat down and started in immediately. "So, where's Gale? Sharing a coffin at someone else's house today?"

"He's out, if that's what you mean."

"Oh, then he can exist in the sunshine."

"I didn't say that. Is there a problem?"

"Yes. I need Gale to come by the gallery tomorrow morning and meet with a few people to finalize the opening, but he's refusing. This is important, Nicki, and I can't seem to convince him to stop playing vampire long enough to do it."

"He won't, Mr. Lang. You're going to have to work with him. Consider him an eccentric artist if you have to."

"Eccentricity is one thing, but this vampire stuff could impact the success of the show. I've got a lot of money riding on it."

I tried to veer the conversation toward a new subject, just to give me time to think of something soothing to say about the odd predicament encountered in the hematoman lifestyle. "I've been so busy, I haven't even had a chance to ask Gale what the theme of the show is."

This bucked up his expression a bit. "I've called it 'A Death in the Family.' It's a commentary on the passing of generations in a family. I've created dioramas of sorts, spicing up Gale's work with antiques from my adjoining shop. He's done some wonderful miniatures in the last couple of weeks, and my designers have used them all during the exhibit." He bent close to me and in a conspiratorial tone and said: "He copied that little figurine you showed me."

"He did?"

Nodding, he leaned back. "Yes. He's called them spirit catchers. I think they're going to be the most popular of all. They reflect his brilliance, that's for sure." His face brightened, but after an instant, his dejected look returned. "Unfortunately, he thinks the theme for the exhibit is innocuous. He feels it ought to show death in a harsher, more violent light. I keep trying to tell him that we've got to approach this thing with nostalgia. After all, it's the family season. We can sell an estimated thirty percent more using his angle. I can't seem to convince him that we'll go his way for the next opening."

"He's had a lot of promises made to him over the years, few of which have panned out in his favor. I can understand why he's leery."

"He needs to trust me. I've pulled out all the stops for this event. Can't you talk to him?"

I shook my head. "Gale and I aren't communicating too well right now. My interference might make things worse."

"You two really are having serious problems, aren't you?"

I was saved from telling him to mind his own business by the telephone. Diving for it, I beat Diane to the extension. It was Walsh.

"We found David Hanuman," he announced without a greeting, "right where his ex—old lady said he was going to be."

"Do you have him in custody?"

"Sort of. Apparently, he gave the locals a real fit when they tried to arrest him. Shot at them with a deer rifle. Hanuman blew a hole through the sheriff's hat and it pissed him off so bad he refused to transport him to D.C. He demanded that we get our butts down there if we wanted the prisoner. I suggested we go pick him up with a Park Police helicopter."

"And?"

"The chief gave us a car, but he told us we could go lights and sirens all the way."

It took a moment for his remark to register. "Joe, you are so full of bullshit."

"Lady Ice, you are so right."

Lang rose from the table and called a low-voiced, "I'll see you later," before taking the steps. Walsh was speaking again, and I had to ask him to repeat himself until my attention clicked in fully.

"I sent three officers to pick him up, but we've got an administrative check-out on the other end. They probably won't get back until eight or nine tonight, and then we have to process him on this side. Since we've got to wait, I'm going home to get some sleep, but I thought I'd drop by with a little goodie for you."

"What do you have?"

"Financial data on Hanuman Imports. Ann Latrice was very cooperative in handing over the accounts on the business." He stopped talking, and when he resumed, I imagined that he had put on a pitiful look. "Nicki, I'm swimming in numbers, here. I need a discerning eye to help me look over this stuff and compare it to the hooker's little black book."

I'm a sucker for a whiny story. "All right, let me give the info a peruse. I can't guarantee I'll find anything, but I'll give it a try."

"Thanks, I appreciate it," he said. "Oh, by the way, D.C. General called. Toni Trent died. She had a stroke following complications from acute endocarditis."

51

I KEPT AT the grunge work for as long as I could, dinking around in the information Walsh had brought over, but after the third hour, I finally begged Diane to help me. She agreed and went topside to use the computer in her bedroom, leaving me alone again in the lab with Fuzzy Nuts for my only company.

I had not made it over to the ME's Office to have a firsthand look at Jow Lord's body, but Art Anthony had sent over the autopsy protocol and photographs, so with nothing more to do than fight off a growing urge to call Stan, my bookie, I turned to the sheaf of papers drawn up on the pimp's remains.

The examination had been executed by Art, personally, and that meant I could trust it for accuracy. It was the only murder linked to the Winter Man series that had seen him break from his usual ritual. There was still the possibility that Jow Lord had been killed by someone else—such men often find themselves at odds with the more powerful and more corrupt purveyors in the city, but for my money, I was banking on the same murderer in all the cases.

Serial killers will, on occasion, change their routine to explore a different killing fantasy. From what we knew of Richard Hanuman's view of the way the universe worked, this murder was sure to fit nicely into his complicated cosmology. As far as the elusive David Hanuman, it was hard to say what might constitute the reason for such an action stemming from his hand. Since it was a good bet that both men knew Jow Lord intimately, it was necessary to figure out what he represented to each.

Jow Lord's tongue had been cut out prior to death. The incision took the muscle off at the halfway point and was cleanly done, suggesting a tool such as a scalpel had been used. Following this hideous torture, Art found a bullet hole at the base of the skull, which he marked as the entrance. There was a rim burn that usually comes from the weapon's flame upon firing, suggesting the killer held the pistol no more than an inch away for his execution. He found the usual mess inside the skull.

The handgun of choice was a twenty-two caliber model. A twenty-two doesn't have enough velocity to exit the head, so it bounces around in the brain to cause considerable damage. It was a successful, gangster-type execution, and had reduced the victim's gray matter to oozy pulp. The bullet itself was a twenty-two caliber short painted with gold leaf.

Art had confirmed the ulcer the pimp had, and going farther, he indicated that the cause of the condition was associated with type-one stomach cancer. His report included a toxicology workup, as well, but the results were pretty standard, showing no aggressive poisons.

The human body is a frail object when compared to the dangers existing in the world, so nature has given it the edge in survival by making it into what I like to term an organic counterinsurgent machine. Despite all the ages of plagues and diseases that have seen whole populations wiped out, the human species has, nonetheless, developed an immune system that's incredibly strong. It's adaptable, even after death. During decomposition, certain enzymes continue to break down substances present in the body. I tell you this, because in this day of designer drugs, it's always smart to look for evidence of crack use.

Cocaine disintegrates into benzoylecgonine, a substance that can't be found without high-powered instruments or a discerning tongue, so I turned off from the report long enough to go to the fridge. There, I found a Jow Lord blood sample and scraped a bit into a petri dish and waited for it to come to room temperature. When it was thawed, I sampled a little.

My tongue seemed to agree with the toxicology report in all respects. Nicotine filtered through the buttery taste of low-density lipoproteins, which meant Jow Lord smoked and consumed too many fatty, high-cholesterol foods. There was also the presence of THC, indicating the use of marijuana. It was still strong and gave a bitterness to the tenor of the blood. In recent years, pot has been used to relieve the pain of cancer victims, and I found myself wondering whether the good Dr. Hanuman had prescribed a couple of joints a day to keep Jow Lord's mind off the worsening ache in his belly. There was no sign beyond that of drug addiction: no cocaine, no heroin, no barbiturates or amphetamines.

I was about to move on when Diane came stomping down the steps. "Make room at the box," she said. "I found something in the accounts and the book."

She didn't wait for me to respond, instead going right to the computer and loading in the floppy information provided by Walsh. "Relics," she said, proudly.

"What's that?"

"It's listed here in Hanuman's accounts. It's a store specializing in reproductions of museum pieces." She glanced at me. "You know the place, Nicki. It's in the same building as Roy Riley's dentist office. I was there a few nights ago to get a cap replaced and Rog was up to his pointed ears in tooth extractions, so I had to wait. I took a stroll through the shop and ended up buying a pair of the gaudiest earrings you ever saw. Supposedly, they were modeled after those worn by Queen Nefertiti." She stopped her narration to flip to the R's in Toni Trent's book. "Here's the shop, spelled with a K instead of a C."

I leaned over her shoulder to stare at the book and noticed right below it, Laura Roberts's name and address.

"The numbers don't match," Diane said, "so I called Relics."

She pulled a smug look onto her face and waited for me to take the bait. "All right, what did you find out?" I asked.

"The one in Hanuman's account is the main number to the store. The one in the whore's book rings up their fax."

52

WHEN I SAW David Hanuman's lawyer, I was a bit surprised. He was a hematoman of my acquaintance by the name of Jacob Chauncy.

Chaunc, as everyone calls him, has been a fixture in Washington for forty years. He was in his late fifties at the time he crossed over. Luckily, he had a very fatherly look, which enabled him to combine it with a professional coiffure and Italian suits to create an image of softly mannered wealth. At some point in his long unlife, he had added a soothing Southern accent to his style. With that, a bogus law degree, and several human confidants, he went on to orchestrate his entire clan into one of the most popular legal firms in the District.

Chaunc glanced at me as I took the seat at David Hanuman's interrogation. He smiled, his apple-bright cheeks crinkling just under his eyes. I nodded, but gave no indication that we knew each other well enough to go betting on the ponies at Laurel Race Course; something we did on the second Saturday of every August.

Chaunc never appeared in court. He left that to the humans in his employ, but on those rare occasions when there was a great deal of money to be made from a client, he would come out of the shadows to make a preliminary assessment of the situation. I could tell he was already counting his ducats with this one.

Walsh flipped around one of the chairs and saddled up. He rested both arms across the top of it to better level an unsettling gaze at Hanuman. Before he began, he took the time to remove his Redskins cap and ran his hand through his hair. He brought the same hand down to support his chin.

"You do understand, Mr. Hanuman, that you've been charged with accessory before the fact in four murders?"

Chaunc started to say something, but Walsh cut him off. "Excuse me. I was speaking to the detainee. You're here as an observer only."

Chaunc nodded and directed his gaze toward his client, adding a little shrug.

Hanuman answered in a shaky voice. "I didn't do anything. Especially murder. I don't know what you're talking about."

"The Metropolitan Police Department currently has a woman in protective custody by the name of Toni Trent. You do know her, I assume?"

"No."

"Well, she identified you. She said you were giving her hypodermic injections needed, strangely enough, to purify her soul. She mentioned you by name."

Hanuman's head rocked like one of those little spring-loaded toys that people used to put in the back dashes of their cars during fifties and sixties. "It wasn't me. It had to be Richard, my cousin. Had to be. He's using my name."

"Ah, Richard Hanuman. You're related, are you? Why, then, didn't you say anything when I showed you the composite drawing of him?"

He scowled, and then, as if it mattered, he said, "He was adopted by my aunt and uncle. We're not related."

"The picture, Dave. I asked you about the picture."

"I didn't recognize him."

"You two were close, like brothers. This, I have according to a witness."

"My ex-wife, I suppose."

"It doesn't matter who it is." Walsh backed off the chair

to stand up. He began to pace the room. As he did, he brought a hand up to massage the back of his neck, accenting the movement with a sigh of impatience. Suddenly, like some panther going in for a strike, he banged his fist against the table. We all jumped. "You were like brothers, weren't you?" he husked.

Hanuman looked for assistance from Chaunc, but none came. "Yes," he murmured. "Once, a long time ago."

"What happened to sour your friendship?"

"Nothing. We just grew apart. We did different things."

"When you were buddies, you had some unusual hobbies, didn't you?"

"I don't know what you mean."

"You shared prostitutes." Walsh came back around the table and slid again onto his metal horse. "Maybe you shared these woman together; maybe apart, but you had your jollies, nonetheless."

He was noncommittal, and Walsh went on to bait the hook. "We know you started killing them. Maybe together; maybe apart. Doesn't matter." He shook his head for emphasis. "Doesn't matter, because like brothers, you're going to share the same murder conviction."

"I haven't killed anyone!" Hanuman screeched.

"Then tell me what's going on."

"Richard's crazy. He always has been, ever since—"

"Since his granny drove both his hands down into a pit of charcoal?"

He swallowed around a golf ball and nodded. "You found about that, huh?"

"We've found out an awful lot about the both of you. Do go on, please."

"I hadn't seen him for a couple of years. The business got going good; I got rid of the whale I was married to; and Richard was digging in over at the Smithsonian." He dropped his gaze to talk toward the table. "I took a trip to Hong Kong to buy some cheap goods for quick turnover to merchants in Los Angeles. While I was there, I bought a few pieces that were of questionable origin."

"They were stolen?" Walsh asked.

"I didn't know it when I bought them. I mean, I wasn't sure, and I didn't ask."

"Ah, you hoped to plead ignorance if the subject ever came up."

"Yes."

"What did you buy?"

"Serving ware. Ivory-handled scrimshaw. Like the one you saw at my house the other night."

"What makes you believe they were stolen?"

"Because I had been trying for years to purchase them outright from Ian Hunt. I was impressed by the fact that they were decorated with Hanuman, the monkey chief. That little obsession has cost me dearly."

"Ian Hunt. Wasn't he the Hong Kong industrialist?" I said.

"Yes. The same. It was rumored that he had them in his possession. The serving ware once belonged to a Mogul named Akbar. They were worth a quarter of a million dollars. I had scraped up the money and offered it all to him, but he refused to even acknowledge my bid. When he died, they came up for sale on the black market."

"The ivory ban was in effect at that time, wasn't it?"

"Yes. I could have lost everything just getting the goods into this country."

"All right, you managed to smuggle the load in; then what?"

"Then I tried to find a buyer."

"Why? Didn't you want to keep them for yourself?"

"No. I wanted to make a profit on them."

"So . . . ?"

"So I called Richard and asked him to help me find someone. He was active in the art community for a while when we were younger. I figured he still had some contacts who could get a couple of interested parties together for an auction.

"Richard said he would do it all. Set up everything. He called me about a week later and told me he had three buyers who would meet with me that night at the base of the statue in the Lincoln Memorial. I was supposed to come alone."

"Did you?"

"Yes. I had no reason not to trust him."

"What happened?"

He sighed and shook his head. "He was there by himself, and when I asked about the buyers, he told me they were late. He wanted to see the serving ware while we waited, so I unwrapped the utensils right there on the marble block next to Lincoln's foot. After I did, Richard pulled a handgun and demanded that I donate the ivory to the Smithsonian, saying he would expose me to the authorities if I didn't give it up. Smuggling can get you five to ten in the penitentiary."

"We have reason to believe he stole the scrimshaw from a Smithsonian warehouse. Why would he want you to donate them, just to steal them later?"

"Who knows? Richard's always fancied himself a thief. He had fantasies when we were kids about being a cat burglar. He got real good at picking pockets and doing sleight of hand. I guess the thought of ripping off the museum appealed to him."

"Don't stop with the story. What did he do next?"

"He started blackmailing me on a regular basis. Something started happening with his work at the museum, and he lost his job. He made me open several credit lines in my name. He threatened to kill me if I didn't do it."

"But blackmail wasn't enough, was it? There's still that little matter with Jow Lord and his associates."

"Richard loves to hear himself talk, and over the years, he's apparently gotten crazier and crazier. I think it had to do with his grandmother and being around a bunch of fundamentalist fanatics. He had gotten it into his head that some folks were evil, and it seemed he'd zoomed right in on whores. According to him, they and their allies corrupted the good people in the world, and they had to be ritually cleansed to avoid contaminating others in the present, as well as those in the future. He thought evil traveled through the generations right until the end of time. Don't ask me where he got that one from."

"Do you know how he was cleansing the prostitutes?" I asked.

"I figure he was burning incense and screwing them. I didn't want to know."

"That excuse of innocence, again," Walsh said. "I assumed he further involved you. How?"

"I had mentioned Jow Lord when we were spending time together a few years ago. He was already aware that I knew him. He wanted me to arrange an introduction, which I did."

"Is that all?"

His answer came too fast. "Yes."

"Then why would a hooker have Ann Latrice's telephone number?"

He swiped his tongue across his lips before answering. "It was one of the ways he communicated with them. He never does anything directly. He's hidden himself that way. They call in to Ann's house and she tells me. I then fax the word to different points in the city."

"How many places do you fax to?"

"Twenty. I never know where he picks the faxes up."

"Do these faxes contain information about where they want to meet?"

"Yes, I'm sure of it. I just can't read it."

"Why not?"

"Because he uses a code. Once he's made contact with the prostitute, he gives her special words to indicate where they can rendezvous. All the names are romantic-sounding, you know? Things like 'Meet me at Highcastle.' Now, you tell me. Where the fuck is that?"

"Hasn't Ann questioned this?"

"I told her David has a street ministry of sorts. He tends to the medical needs of the homeless at certain locations across the city, and they call these places by certain names. She's from upstate New York, and a kid at that, with no interest in anything but making money. She never asked anything more about it once I gave her this explanation."

Walsh dismounted the chair again and, loading himself with a stretch, he came to a stand. "I'm going to let you have a little rest, Dave," he said. "But before I do, I want to know this: What would Richard want with your ex-wife's food dehydrator?"

He took a moment to reply. "I can only imagine."

53

WALSH HAD A couple of uniforms roust Laura Roberts out of her cozy suite on Sixth Street to come down to Metro Police Headquarters for more conversation. She was waiting in the Homicide Division squad room for him to conclude his interview of David Hanuman, dressed to the nines in a fake fox fur and red vinyl boots. She looked like she had taken a dive into the British rock era of the 1960s and it made me wonder about the prospective john who would be enticed by such a fantasy.

Walsh was not fazed by the image she projected as he invited her to take Hanuman's vacated chair in the interrogation room. He slammed the door behind him, aimed his gaze at me, and said, "I'm going to have this place redone in blue chintz. I've been in this square so many times this week that I've figured out I'd be happier if it had curtains over the one-way glass."

He used his foot to push out a chair for Laura. He remained standing, starting right in on his questions. "Tell us about Jow Lord's relationship with Hanuman."

She squeezed her fingers together and formed a bony knot of oversized rings. "I'm . . . not sure what you mean."

"I want to know how they felt about each other. You knew Richard at one time, didn't you?" He pulled the composite picture from his jeans pocket and let it flap open. "This is Richard. I bet you recognize him, huh?"

She stared at the picture. "I recognize this guy, but he said his name was David. I never knew his last name. That kind of stuff wasn't important to Jow."

"David. That's interesting. Were they friends? Or maybe lovers?"

She blinked and unbolted her hands. "They liked each other, I guess."

"And not engaged in a homosexual relationship, as far as you know?"

"Jow was AC-DC. He could go either way; so maybe."

"Did Hanuman ever show open affection toward Jow Lord?"

She shrugged. "I don't know. He used to say he was sent to protect Jow's soul. I remember that."

"What do you think he meant?"

"He was sort of religious, I guess. He talked about how he had to strengthen Jow and purify his soul to keep it safe from evil."

"What kind of evil?"

"Sins of the flesh and that kind of thing."

"Did he consider Jow to have a good soul?"

"Yes, I suppose."

Walsh glanced at me before continuing. "Did you know that to build up his resistance to evil, he was feeding him herbal teas, meditations, and vitamins?"

"Yeah. The treatment. Jow talked about it a lot. He told me he had an ulcer that was getting better because of it."

"Did it seem to work to take away the evil influence?"

"How should I know?"

Walsh leaned toward her, resting his hands on the table. I sensed a sharp rise in the hooker's blood pressure and heart rate as she waited for him to ask the next question.

He lowered his voice to do it. "Did he act differently? Was he a better man; kinder, more patient?"

She answered immediately. "No. Not that I ever noticed.

Same guy. Maybe he was doing the whips and leathers less with the other girls. Not with me. I'm really not sure."

Walsh pointed to the picture. "Did you ever hear this man recommend that Jow fire Edward Bunt and get a new driver?"

"He said something once about getting a professional man for his limousine. Just for appearances, but Jow didn't do it. Until Eddie came up dead, that is."

"Would you say he was interested in wiping out the evil influences around Jow by having him change some of his friends and associates? Did he have some good people he wanted to bring on in their places?"

"He mentioned names of lots of people. Maybe that's what they were talking about."

"To your knowledge, did this man ever ask him to stop having sex with his girls?"

She relocked her hands. "I figure he probably did."

"Why?"

"Because the guy was always harping on the evils of the body. He reminded me of when I was a kid and the way my grandfather talked when he would come home from a church revival meeting."

Walsh angled back and clasped his hands behind him. I could smell mint on his breath when he said, "Did Jow Lord continue to have sex with his girls after this man came on the scene?"

Her mouth opened into an O before she answered. "Yes."

He leaned closer. "Did he ever have sex with you?"

She nodded.

"How often?"

"Once a week in the beginning. Less after Gitana joined us."

"Was he having intercourse with Ms. O'Quinn?"

"I think so."

"What about Maggie Kahn?"

"Yes. I know that for a fact."

A detective stuck his head into the room at the moment to hand him a note. Walsh's expression grew dark as he read it. "There's a storm system building up in the Gulf of Mexico. It looks like it's going to be heading this way. They're calling for snow again."

54

Tuesday, December 1

At 4:00 a.m., I left Walsh grilling the suspect and harassing Laura Roberts. I went out to find a suitable victim to quench my thirst, before going home. When I got there, I was satisfied to hear from Ekua that Gale had returned and was in the studio painting his unbeating heart out. I was determined for myself to take a couple hours off from the investigation to sit down at the kitchen table and go through the new bills collecting beneath the pile of Diane's entertainment and confession magazines.

Junk falls off my assistant like people slough skin. To round out her usual purchases of grocery store tabloids, she flavors the pile with the odd sale item or two. Sometimes it's a cassette tape featuring the mating calls of Minnesota loons; sometimes it's a Funk & Wagnalls encyclopedia offer. It doesn't matter that we don't have volumes one through twenty-seven; volume twenty-eight is the one being hawked for ninety-nine cents. There's always something you can learn, according to Diane, even if it is about zebras or zymosis.

In this case, she'd done it again, perhaps healing some of her angst over the killing done in the house by going to the local food store. She'd brought home book two of the F&W Medical Encyclopedia. It picked up in the *P*s.

I avoided the inevitable check-writing by pausing to scan the latest issue of her favorite gossip paper, turning after a bit to prolong my procrastination with a quick thumb through the encyclopedia. I couldn't help marveling at how she had thought such a purchase would get much more than a cursory inspection from anyone in the house. It was her den-mother ways, and even as upset with us as she was, she still maintained this indulgence. I smiled as I thought of how Ekua felt she was on a personal mission to help us live a more enlightened immortality through the study of esoterica that included information on UFOs and Elvis sightings.

Ten minutes later, I was busy squeezing money from my bank account when she stumbled into the kitchen wearing a blue robe and flip-flops. She stopped, blinked, and mumbled a good morning. From there, she clicked on the coffee maker and dug out a box of fat-free blintzes from the fridge, joining me at the table.

"You got an invitation to Gale's showing," she said. "If it's like mine, you can bring a guest."

"Did Ekua get one?"

"Yes. Are you going?"

"Of course. I wouldn't miss it."

She became silent and stared into her coffee.

"What's the matter?" I asked.

"Gale destroyed another canvas after he got home. God, he's frustrated."

"And I can't help him." Trying to lock a sigh inside me, I opened the medical encyclopedia and made an attempt to change the conversation. "Did you know that the crap you're eating is genetically engineered Styrofoam?"

She swallowed a bite. "Tastes like it, too."

I couldn't think of anything else to say, and I couldn't bring myself to write out the water bill at that moment, so I stalled again by flipping around in the encyclopedia, stopping when I reached the entry concerning the pineal gland. It was right there after Pimple and just before Pinkeye.

I started out skimming the passage, but at some point, my eye went back to the beginning and I read the section more carefully.

The paragraph navigated the reader through all the usual medical jargon. It talked about how the gland was a tiny, cone-shaped thistle of the brain's corpus callosum, and how it secreted a hormone that was thought to affect the body by regulating its natural circadian rhythm, those cycles occurring within humans on a twenty-four-hour basis.

Discovery of this gland led to new assumptions about the human condition, one being that we're all, while in life, subject to an internal clock that's literally twelve hours on and twelve hours off. The encyclopedia went further to discuss how the pineal gland was occasionally the site of tumors. From there, it started talking about the scientific and occult debate of whether it might actually be the seat of the human soul.

The hinges holding my lips together broke and there didn't seem to be much I could do to tighten the screws back up. I suddenly stood, stared at Diane just long enough until she stared back, then raced downstairs to the lab like I had an abrupt case of diarrhea.

Shuffling through the pictures and paraphernalia on the table, I searched for the baggie I had used to collect the scrapings from Catherine Forest's fetish. For just a second, I thought I had tossed it in the trash, but upon picking up Fuzzy Nuts, I found the pack wedged under his butt along with a missing hoop earring. He yowled at the indignity of having his rump hoisted, so I quickly slipped the plastic out from under him, giving the old boy a fast pat on the head. Satisfied, he stretched and readjusted his curl.

I placed the filings in the hopper of the computer

analyzer, and letting my fingers fly over the keyboard, I punched up the program I needed. In a moment, answers started meeting my hammering questions. What I had assumed was paint or clay was, in actuality, blood.

The analysis gave me all kinds of data, but to assure myself, I removed a little of the sample to a petri dish and then reconstituted it with a drop of water. I rubbed the tip of my pinky in the red oil and tasted it.

Type O-positive. Cigarette smoker. The nasty, tinny taste of metal.

It was Maggie Kahn.

55

IN THE END, Richard Hanuman did the only thing he could to save Jow Lord from unwittingly helping evil to win the day. He saw the pimp as a brother, a kindred soul hailing from the same reincarnational line as he did. He couldn't let the hookers influence him anymore with their bodies, or allow Edward Bunt to catch him up in his scams and street ways. He couldn't outright steal his soul like he had theirs, because he would need to be reborn to continue the fight for the good side.

I was out prowling along the Tidal Basin by the Jefferson Memorial, but the night was silent, and the few people out and about held no interest for me. I kept wondering what criteria had to be met before Richard Hanuman could decide to which faction a person belonged. I also wondered what he would do if he were to ever run up against a compliant hematoman.

It's true that we heal incredibly fast and there are many of us wandering around this earth who carry the treasures of old battles with humans: such things as silver bullets and the tips of daggers that have been broken off after an attempt at being plunged into a rigid breastbone.

But what if the pineal gland is the physical seat of the soul, the little piece of meat where the immortal self lounges during the current life? How would that affect a hematoman? If it were dug out and cast away, would we grow a new one along with a new spirit?

The wind played through the empty boughs of the Japanese cherry trees paralleling West Basin Drive. I paused to sit on

one of the benches and tried to get my mind off the killer for
a few minutes by fiddling with my imagination instead.

In late March or early April, D.C. holds the annual Cherry
Blossom Festival, and the whole basin right on up to the
Jefferson Memorial is a glorious profusion of pink blooms.
There are hundreds of trees, and when the weather cooper-
ates, the blossoms pop out precisely on the day the city
schedules a parade to kick off the spring celebration.

I've never seen the parade, of course. It's held in the
bright sunshine and the whole District seems to attend. No,
I visit in the evening, when the colors aren't so brilliant, but
the fragrance is magnificent.

My whole clan comes and we make a celebration of our
own. On those perfect nights, the moon is full and the
breeze is gentle. Gale and I stroll beneath this pink arbor,
hand in hand. Diane joins Ekua for his hematoman protection, and they find a soft spot on the bank of the Tidal Basin
where he can serenade us with his flute, choosing strains
that are inspired by the Oriental flavors of the walk.

Minutes dripped by as I pictured the scene, but after a
while, I let the fantasy drop. It was too cold for my
imagination to firmly root the scenes of spring in my mind's
eye.

The weatherman on channel nine news was still predicting a heavy snow to slice through the Mid-Atlantic states
beginning Thursday or Friday morning. The storm would
either cover the Winter Man's tracks or have us find the
fodder from his kill. It was the toss of the coin, and heads
and tails were both bad.

I smelled blood on the wind and rose from the bench
where I'd sat, plunging my hands into my jacket pocket just
to have a place to rest them. When I did, I remembered that
I carried the exhibit inventory of Gale's showing. He had
given me a copy as he bragged about the prices Lang was

going to get him if it panned out like he thought. Each piece was going for a good bit of money and there were over one hundred items for sale: everything from paintings to metal sculptures to the little clay figurines he called spirit catchers. I asked him about those, and he gave me a dark smile and said he was inspired by the Winter Man's fetish and Ekua's story of his grandmother.

I moved down toward the water and scraped along the bank of the Potomac River, following the scent of prey. While I walked, I mulled over an idea I had to catch the Winter Man, but if Gale ever found out what I was planning to do regarding this, he would more than likely never talk to me again.

56

WALSH WAS IN a bad mood when I arrived at Headquarters. He'd called a couple of detectives to the carpet, and as I walked into the Homicide Division, I could hear him yelling, even though his office door was closed. It was twenty minutes before he stopped his tirade. He let the boys loose to fly out of the squad room without a word passed to their comrades. He followed them out and grinned at me.

"Feel better now?" I asked.

"Great," he said. "You can't imagine the release you can get from practicing terror."

"Sure, I can. That's what makes you and me able to think like killers. We understand."

He choked his smile into a straight line, nodding as he did. "You said on the phone you might have a way to bring out the Winter Man."

"Can we go into the office? I want to discuss something sensitive with you."

He didn't answer, but instead, stalked away, whipping his hand up to invite me along with him. When the door was closed, I said: "I figure the odds on this shot are about fifty-fifty."

"I'll take fifty-fifty. It's better than batting zero."

"We can send him a bogus fax," I announced. "If we can secure cooperation from the owner of Relics, we can send it through them and cover ourselves in as many layers as Richard Hanuman has."

"All right, I'll bite. What's the scam?"

I winced a little when I heard him say, "I'll bite." It's a

hematoman thing and reminds me just how blurred the lines are between us and our human counterparts. Sitting down, I dismissed the notion and went on, suddenly a bit concerned that he might say no at the prospect I was about to offer.

"We invite him to Gale's gallery showing tomorrow night. Play on his interest in *art*."

He pointed to a chair and took one at the desk, glancing down before sitting. There was the sound of claws on linoleum and I knew Chester was with us. Situated, Walsh showed me a lip-puckered expression that meant he was considering it. "What would the fax say?"

"That the Lang Gallery is announcing its grand opening with an exhibit of the artwork of Gale Fabrice. The theme to the show is *A Death in the Family*."

He frowned. "This is a real event, isn't it? I remember you mentioning it."

"Yep."

"Is the theme really about death, or is that the lure?"

"I'm not making it up. It's really about death. And a convenient lure."

"Damn, hoping to cheer people up this holiday, season, huh?"

"It has a light tone, I believe."

"It would have to." He reached down and petted his dog before continuing. "Go on."

"According to David's confession, his cousin is deep into the art world. I asked Diane to look over the accounts for Hanuman's import business, and she found that a lot of the credit lines have charges from local galleries. If what he said is true, then Richard has been setting himself up with some nice stuff, lately."

Walsh snorted. "There's someplace out there that would appeal to Vincent Price: pineal gland fetishes tastefully offset by Pre-Columbian art and the occasional Hindu trephining saw. Ah, what a hideaway. It does it for me. What about you?"

"The image has a certain charm to it."

He shook his head. "OK, we call him with the bogus fax. Is this thing by invitation only?"

"As far as I know."

"It would be a perfect opportunity to pick him up just before he gets inside the gallery. We need to talk to the owner right away to get his cooperation."

"There's a problem with that."

He sighed. "There always is. What is it?"

"The guy who owns it is named Justin Lang. He's become Gale's art agent and plans to turn a bundle on his talent."

Walsh propped his feet on the desk, tugged on his cap, and rubbed his hand over his beard stubble. "You and Gale have been having problems lately. You said so yourself."

"It's true. If Lang tells Gale I had something to do with this operation, it'll piss him off so bad he'll make good on his threat to walk out on me. I couldn't really blame him if he did."

"So, if we capture the Winter Man, I should take all the credit here?"

"That's right. I want it to look like I'm an innocent in the whole thing. In fact, I'm going home tonight and mention that my part in the investigation is over and I'm moving on to the work I have to do for New York City."

"All right. I can do that for you. I don't need to share my medals."

I couldn't help a smile. "Is that why you have all those holes in your chest?"

He grinned, but talked business. "I'll admit, it's a good idea, but how do you suggest we get Hanuman interested enough to come to this particular opening? He probably scans the Style section of the *Post* all the time, looking for these events. What would interest him?"

"According to Lang, there's going to be an article about the show in the Wednesday edition. It's a perfect setup. Do you remember when Gale saw the fetish that Hanuman had given Catherine Forest?" After he nodded, I continued. "Well, he copied it. He then started turning out all these little whimsies for his show. He calls them spirit catchers. If that doesn't get Hanuman's attention, I don't know what will, and if he calls to confirm he's on the guest list, we can have Lang simply tell him the truth."

"What if this guy slips and mentions it to Gale? He'll know you had something to do with it. Even if he doesn't, he'll suspect you."

"The affair doesn't really start until seven o'clock in the evening, and knowing Gale, he'll be fashionably late and get there about eight or eight-thirty. We can probably have Lang ask him to come at nine o'clock to give the critics a chance to view the exhibit without him being around to influence their reviews one way or the other. We'll tell Hanuman that his invitation is from six to seven for interested buyers only. Have your snatch team ready at the door by five-forty-five, and we can take care of this piece of work before the actual event starts. Your mission shouldn't impact a thing."

"Unless we get blood all over the street."

"Then, it's just a coincidence. If Gale starts accusing me, I'll tell him you managed to track his movements into Georgetown. Lang's gallery isn't the only one there."

"You really do like to gamble, don't you?" he asked in a quiet voice.

I didn't answer, because his words had suddenly planted a rock in my throat.

He measured me off with his eyes for a long minute before glancing down at his wristwatch. With a flip of his hand, he picked up the phone.

57

Wednesday, December 2

IT TOOK MOST of the day to contact the owner of Relics Museum Pieces. During that time, Walsh and I both kept tabs on the cable weather channel as their reporters tracked the storm now over Pensacola, Florida, moving in a north by northwest direction. About five-thirty in the evening, Walsh called me at home and asked me to drop by Metro to discuss Operation Winter Man.

By the time I got downtown, Walsh had renamed the sting Operation Spirit Catcher and the word about the maneuver had spread through Headquarters like steam going through a vent. Walsh and his watch commander had selected five detectives and seven officers to help with the affair, keeping the snatch team relatively small and elite. I felt the vibrations of envy as I stepped into the unit squad room.

I hung out on the periphery of the whole setup, waiting for the part I would play in the affair. I wanted to do it, you see, because too much direct involvement was a gamble for me in more ways than one. If my name came up too often in the investigation, I could be subpoenaed for testimony, despite the information already provided to the district attorney by the Medical Examiner's Office. It's not that I wouldn't want to help, understand; it's just that a murder case is usually not tried in night court.

I make sure the District records state that officially, the only thing I do is determine the time of death. I've been working with Walsh and Art Anthony so long, they automatically erase my name from the rest of the investigation. They accept it as being one of my quirks, an aversion to courtrooms and lawyers and a need to keep my anonymity. I told them both a story once of how I was stalked by a killer who had been freed after a bungled investigation. He had gotten my name and tried to murder me in my own house. It was a bald lie, but like a poker game, I'm not above using my imagination to fold a bad hand before the ante is raised and I run out of playing chips.

I hung out in the interrogation room until the owner of Relics showed up for a meeting at Walsh's request. When he arrived, they joined me, and there, I met John Horn.

He looked like he would own some place called Relics. He was young, handsome, and refined. I could almost imagine him dressed in khaki and a pith helmet. He sat in the chair as though it were a canvas camp seat that needed the benefit of legs planted firmly and a torso tilted slightly inward to maintain balance.

Walsh handed him a cup of coffee and he sipped loudly at the liquid before asking: "What can I do to help the police, lieutenant?"

"We're trying to catch a killer, Mr. Horn," he answered. "You may have read about him in the *Post*—the Winter Man?"

He nodded.

"We have reason to believe he's been using your store as a receipt point to have faxes sent to him. Do you offer such a service, sir?"

"Yes. I'll accommodate good clients in that way. If they buy something expensive from me, I'll put their name on a preferred list. I keep my own computer bulletin board, and also serve as an intermediary forum for information regarding news in the arts and sciences. I get a lot of faxes concerning ongoing projects in several professional fields, so for these customers, I'll pick up part of the cost of transmission and notify them when they get a message or something interesting comes in. It's a sales ploy, but I've had good success with repeat business because of this idea. In fact, a lot of stores in the area are starting to copy me."

"Do you recall notifying a man about incoming faxes who goes by the name of Richard Hanuman? He may also use the alias David Hanuman."

"Yes, David. I've spoken with him a few times. He's an archaeological reporter for the *Smithsonian* magazine, I understand." His eyes grew wide. "He's not the Winter Man, is he?"

Walsh dug out the composite from his pocket. It was a tattered piece of paper by now, forever creased with folds. "We have reason to believe he is." He shook the picture open like it was a handkerchief and showed it to Horn. "Can you tell me if this is David Hanuman?"

"Yes. That's him. You say his real name is Richard?"

"Yes, sir."

"He's been in a few times. He has an interest in Peruvian art."

"What about faxes? Does he come in for them?"

"No. My assistant calls him and relays the message. They're usually pretty cryptic, and I haven't paid much attention to them. I thought it was information he needed for his job at the magazine, because most of the communications have mentioned names of archaeological sites."

Walsh laid the composite on the table and absently smoothed at the creases with the tips of his fingers while he spoke. "We need your help, Mr. Horn."

"Of course. Whatever I can do."

"We're going to call Mr. Hanuman to tell him about a bogus fax he received through your store. What we need you to do is to confirm it, should he call back with suspicions."

"No problem. Just tell me what to say."

Walsh launched into the explanation, and fifteen minutes later Horn was on his way out of Headquarters, confident that he was making the world a better place. After he was gone, my partner called up Justin Lang to try to convince him of the part he needed to play in the scam. Walsh's voice carried a note of weariness, and I could tell Lang was stonewalling him, just by the expressions that crossed his face.

"I assure you, Mr. Lang, that we don't intend to have the killer enter your establishment. We're going to pick him up on the street. All I'm asking for is your cooperation if he calls to verify an invitation to Gale Fabrice's showing. That ends the extent of your involvement."

He went silent and after several breaths said: "Nicki Chim knows nothing of this. She told me about the exhibit in passing. I'm sure she didn't think the Metro Police would do anything with the information. It was said in general conversation. Nicki and I are old friends and talk to each other about what goes on in our families."

His explanation wound down as he listened to Lang. A wince marshalled in the corner of his mouth before he again answered. "We spoke to other galleries about this idea, but to be honest, I couldn't secure permission. You're my last chance to catch this guy before he strikes again which, if his pattern remains consistent, will be with the next snowfall."

Another few words from Lang's side made Walsh sigh. "I realize you have your own agenda, but can't you see your way clear to take the chance that might save an innocent life?"

He glanced at me and rolled his eyes. "Yes, he kills hookers, but don't you agree they have a right to live? This perpetrator has also killed an old man who had grandkids. He's a violent psychopath, Mr. Lang. His focus could change instantly. He might start killing children or professionals or cab drivers. With his interest in the arts, he might decide to go after painters, too. We just can't be sure who'll be next."

He propped his feet on the desk as he listened, then: "I have a copy here of an article that appeared in today's *Washington Post* Style section. It talks about the show and the miniatures Gale calls spirit catchers. I'm going to let you in on a little secret. I was at Nicki's when he saw some evidence from this case, a small figurine used to symbolically store the soul. After reading that piece, I asked Nicki if he'd modeled his artwork after the thing. She said yes, that they were sitting all over his studio." He paused, adding a conspiratorial tone to his voice. "Now, Mr. Lang, from the profile the FBI and Metro Police have on the murderer, we feel that he's going to notice this information and become intrigued by it. His intention then may be to stalk Mr. Fabrice."

Another few sentences passed between them before Walsh gave me a grin and a thumbs up. "Mr. Lang, I'll send an officer over to your house to reiterate the extent of your involvement in this plan. He'll answer any questions you might have." He made his last sentence seem like an afterthought. "Oh, do me a favor. Don't mention this to Nicki. She would be furious with me for using Gale's professional opportunity for my own ends. These two are on wobbly ground right now, and while I've got to do what I can to catch this maniac before he kills again, I don't want to be responsible for destroying their relationship."

58

WALSH DROPPED THE receiver into its cradle, saying: "It's ten o'clock. Do you know where your killer is?"

I couldn't help a smile. "He finally agreed?"

"You were right about him. He's worried about his own ass."

He drew a hefty breath and, standing, motioned for me to follow him out of the Homicide Division and down the hall to a place intimately referred to as the computer cage. Entering, I saw tech types manning PCs and printers. Walsh squeezed through this maze of hardware, heading for the far corner where a petite, pretty black woman sat sequestered in a glass room. Shutting the door closed off the noise from the large room, turning the ten-by-ten-foot see-through box into an envelope of quiet.

Walsh introduced her as Sandy, and went on to say that she was Metro's electronic prima donna. She nodded her agreement and offered me a chair by her worktable where she had rigged a cellular to a computer that was, judging from the lines dropping down from the ceiling, hardwired to some bigger network. Satisfied that I was impressed, she threw me a lazy smile before looking at Walsh.

"So, we're a go, then?" she asked.

"I've got the number," he answered. "Did you finish writing up the copy for Nicki to read to the Winter Man?"

"Yeah. I just printed it out. It's ready to go in the form of a fax, if necessary." She patted the computer. "Good stuff, too, and all right here in the belly of the whale."

"Are you ready, Nicki?" Walsh asked, sitting down beside me.

I nodded, suddenly a little nervous as she handed me the paper I was to read from and dialed the phone through the PC.

There's an old joke about how one day the phone company will become so powerful that God will have to have a long distance calling card just to get through to us. It's true. We enjoy a seventy percent certainty that we can dial to any place on earth. Hinged to this technological fact are faxes, modems, and computers. A person can call up fantasies with recorded sex messages or electronically send fiber-optic prayers to be sung at the Wailing Wall in Jerusalem. With all that going on, we send out a constant busy signal. The joke ought to say: God is on call waiting.

If Richard Hanuman had a caller ID system on his phone, a cellular number wouldn't register.

The noise-dampening effect of the room made it possible to put the conversation on the speaker phone. The communication was also caught by the computer and checking the screen, I saw that it recorded everything on-line. As the dialing went through to Hanuman's end, it showed this fact on our side, indicating it with the words: ring, ring, ring. When he answered, it said: connect.

"Hello?"

It was time for me to go into my act. "Richard Hanuman, please."

"May I ask who's calling?"

"My name is Janine Craneman. I work at Relics in Washington, D.C. Are you Mr. Hanuman?"

There was a momentary hesitation, then: "Yes. Isn't it a bit late for you to be calling me?"

He had a silky tenor voice. It occurred to me that I thought he would speak in baritone syllables. "Yes," I answered. "I apologize, but I'm new here, and my manager is out of town, so please forgive me. We received a fax yesterday announcing an art exhibit to be held at the newly opened Lang Gallery in Georgetown. Relics received a block of reservations intended for the use of a few of our better customers. I was supposed to call you this morning, but one of our sales clerks messed up our computer database and it took me all afternoon and evening to recover the files. May I read you the fax?"

"Yes. Go ahead."

I glanced at the copy Sandy had prepared under Walsh's direction, and started reading it, verbatim. "The Lang Gallery proudly presents the art of Gale Fabrice. Mr. Fabrice has a unique way of looking at life and more importantly, death. In his upcoming exhibit this weekend, he will explore this theme in a show intended to highlight the passing of generations. *A Death in the Family* is a compilation of paintings and sculpture, antiques, and collectibles.

"The settings move through the gallery like the years move through the ages. In the first moment, the visitor is in Victorian England, surrounded by artifacts and treasures. Fabrice's paintings are hot: they give the illusion of steaming jungles, pith helmets and intrepid explorers. Perched upon tatted doilies turned the color of sand are his spirit catchers. Exquisite figurines, these little oddities contain a soul captured from a person at his death. Fabrice used the influence of ancient Peruvian and Egyptian art to create these mesmerizing pieces." I paused. "Shall I continue?"

"Yes," he said immediately.

"Turn the corner of a well-placed armoire and it becomes the India of Rudyard Kipling. For this section, Fabrice created a traditional sari, but instead of silk, he cut the robe from cotton and used a Malaysian technique of dye and wax to paint the cloth with the image of a bajang. The people of the Andeman Islands will tell you a bajang looks like a cat, but is really a vampire. Accenting this piece are scrimshaw ivories and Hindu prayer wheels." I stopped again. "Are you interested in attending, Mr. Hanuman?"

He lingered over the question for a moment before answering. "Yes. I would like to see this. What do I have to do to take advantage of the invitation?"

"All you need do is to show up. I'll fax the gallery your name so there will be an invitation waiting for you. The opening will be from six P.M. until eight, tomorrow night. If you want to read more about it, the fax goes on to say that an article will appear in today's edition of the *Post*."

"That's fine. Is there more I should know about the showing?"

"That's about it," I said. "I hope you enjoy yourself, Mr. Hanuman." I hung up and stared at Walsh. Through the whole conversation, I had watched his face draw up into a wild-eyed squint. When he spoke next, he practically hissed. "That sorry bastard is mine, Nicki."

59

Thursday, December 3

I ONCE VISITED an art gallery that featured paintings done by serial killers. I went because I wondered what kind of people would be interested in seeing the psychopathic pain of these murderers spilled across a canvas. To my surprise, I found a group of snooty art critics and Washingtonian blue bloods who would have been better placed judging the work of Monet or Piccaso rather than that of Gacy or Manson. They were all pretty unconcerned with the subject matter, as if seeing depictions of cannibalism and folks getting their balls whacked off was normal, day-to-day stuff. The reviewers made remarks about the intensity and childlike quality of the drawings while everyone else just wanted to know which artists had been executed. With anything, the demand goes up when the editions become limited.

Sometimes the ironies in my unlife surprise even me. Here I was, catching a killer-artist by luring him to look at the works done by a killer-artist. Both beings were cut from the same casket lining: one from the lace part and one from the silk part. I wandered through Georgetown thinking this, and each time I looked up from the sidewalk, my considerations were enhanced by a section of the city that both inspired the movie, *The Exorcist,* and celebrated the architecture of the early nineteenth century.

Stitching through the District, there's an expanse of city park called Rock Creek, named so for the tributary which

George Washington probably drank from. This woodland borders one side of the area, and with the university to support the other end, Georgetown has become the Soho of the nation's capital.

Trying to drive a car through this section of town is usually considered madness, especially on the weekends in the summertime. People come out at all hours to visit this place, looking for the most fashionable boutique, the trendiest restaurant, or the swankiest club. Wisconsin Avenue, NW, is the Rodeo Drive of the Washingtonian hobnobbery who are in search of notoriety as well as of the perfect salade niçoise and a light and fruity mountain blush. To have an address along this corridor speaks of wealth, and it made me wonder just how rich Justin Lang might be.

I entered his gallery right around six P.M., met by Diane and Ekua. The Metro Police had set up an observation post across the street above a busy French bistro, and Walsh lurked about at ground level. I noticed him when I walked by. He nodded my way but receded into the shadows of a doorway to conceal his identity from the others. I did see that he was ready for action, wearing running shoes, jeans, and a Gore-Tex jacket. The bulky coat hid his bulletproof vest.

Once inside the gallery, I was surprised by the reception; the place was packed. Gale obviously had more fans than I realized. True to his nature, he was at home, planning on being fashionably late. I could have killed Ekua, because during the day he had badgered him to come to the affair with us. In the end, I lucked out when Gale got snotty about the whole thing and told him he preferred to make a grand entrance by himself.

Justin Lang was schmoozing with the guests, but when he noticed me, he disconnected from a group of rapt listeners to greet us. Diane and Ekua didn't wait for his approach, instead wandering off to talk to a friend of ours whose name escaped me. Lang was the courteous gentleman, as usual, though from his narrowed look, I thought he was going to ask me what I knew about the stakeout.

"You look ravishing, tonight, Nicki," he said in a husky voice.

I had paid particular attention to my dress this evening, not wanting Gale to become suspicious, should he find out about the police operation. Taking the entire day to prepare, I first filled up on whole blood to give myself some color, and then chose a nice little black number from my closet, added pearls and stiletto heels.

"Did you bring an escort?"

"No. I expect Gale will be along shortly. Why would you ask?"

He loosened his squint and smiled. "There were two invitations. I thought you might bring a friend."

I played dumb to his probing about Walsh. "Most of my friends are coming tonight. I can't think of anyone to invite."

"Come now, the lady of the night? The vampira? You should know so many people. After all, doesn't eternity allow you the time to cultivate acquaintances?"

"It has," I said. "But my friends are all over the world. Since I was born to the undead side, I've lived other places besides Washington, D.C."

"When were you born, then?"

"Nineteen seventeen." My words made him take an involuntary step backward. I asked, "Does that surprise you?"

He stumbled on his words before he got out the answer. "No, no, of course not." Gently touching my shoulder, he started guiding me deeper into the gallery, stalling for time, I suspect, to work up his next pearlized line. Finally, he spoke it. "You were born originally into the Victorian era?"

"Yes, that's right."

"A very romantic choice for the birth of someone who professes to be a succubus."

"I never said I was. A succubus is a female demon." Then, putting on my coy look, I whispered, "I'm not that to you, Justin, am I?"

"You called me by my first name. We're making progress."

I have a hard time with people who are so sure of themselves. This belligerence annoys me so much that the older I get, the harder it is for me to ignore it. If I run up against someone I'm forced to work with who's got a case of the ass, I'll usually make it easy on myself and take hold of the situation by giving them the Dracula Stare. If they're really bad and I have to work with them for several hours a night, I'll simply convert them into a temporary feeder and get control through their blood.

I imagined locking my canines into Lang's beautifully defined jugular vein, but I didn't do anything, down to not even trying my Lugosi imitation on him. Why I didn't, I couldn't figure.

"What do you think of the show?"

"Impressive," I answered.

We passed through a section that featured one of Gale's tribal feather masks. It was because of me, you might say, that the piece was made at all. During one of the weekly poker games, I lost my bloodrights to Alan, and as usual, Gale was left to pay off the debt. The term of indenture was a lunar month spent house-sitting for Alan as he took his clan on an Amazonian expedition. He brought the plumage back to Gale as a gift.

Lang had used a wooden ironing board to present the brilliant blue mask. It was arranged atop a red sequined dress that looked like it was straight out of a Carmen

Miranda movie. The diorama was called *Mother's Dreams Died with Her.*

"You must have worked around the clock to put this show together," I said.

He chuckled. "I have five very good designers who did that for me."

My assumption about him was correct: He had bucks. Leave it to Gale to ferret out the money.

I was about to make a remark on this thought when applause from the guests drove the small talk back down my throat. We came around a corner, clearing a brass samovar to see that Gale had decided to arrive early. I couldn't help staring at my lover. What a beauty he was, wearing a pure white suit and the high color of a blood flush. The crowd gathered about him to kiss up and offer congratulations. His smile added a touch more radiance to his presence. I was feeling proud and excited for him until I noticed the man standing directly to his left. True, I had never seen Richard Hanuman face to face, but after two weeks of being intimately acquainted with this guy's cruel fantasies, I was sure it was him.

60

SOMETIMES I'M A damned fool. I know better than to try to hedge a bet and make it go my way. It always, always blows up in my face. My little scheme to catch this killer was no different.

Seeing the Winter Man, my first thought was how to get away from Lang and call Walsh. My partner was outside, freezing his ass off, thinking that he was going to be stood up by the killer with nothing to show for his effort except frostbitten fingers, and here, swinging in on the shadow of Gale, was Richard Hanuman wearing deep purple gloves and his long, gray hair pulled back in a ponytail. So, after a five-minute deliberation on what to do, I did a time-honored thing among women. I feigned sudden desperation.

Turning to look at Lang, I changed my expression to one of urgency. "Where is the ladies' room?" I asked.

He wigged his eyebrows and used his thumb to point over his shoulder. "Past the display featuring Gale's safety pin sculpture." I took a step in that direction, but his fingers scraped along my arm, stalling me for a second. "I didn't think vampires had to use the bathroom," he said.

"Most literature on us is wrong," I answered, starting up again.

I took off at a stiletto-heeled trot, looking just like I was ready to do some serious damage to my underwear if I didn't hurry. Rounding the corner at the appropriate point, I dashed into the potty and into one of the stalls. I locked the door and pulled out my cellular, lost for a moment because I couldn't remember the speed dial number that would ring up Walsh. Two failed tries, with one attempt being answered by Art Anthony, and the other a recorded message for the American Red Cross Blood Bank. Finally, I got through.

"It's Nicki," I snapped. "The bastard is inside the gallery."

There was a pause before Walsh answered. "What? He can't be. I've got four men posted around the entrance."

"I'm telling you, he slipped inside. He came in hanging on Gale wearing a black trench coat and carrying a fedora. Your guys didn't recognize him and Lang's own man probably didn't bother to check his name on the register."

"All right, I believe you," he answered. "We've got to get him out of there without storming the place."

"Stand by. I'll try to find a way to bring him to you. Put your hands in your pockets, Joe. I don't know how long this will take."

"I can send a man inside to help you. I've got one guy dressed in a tux, just in case something like this happened."

I panicked when he said that, thinking of Gale, and my voice cracked as I answered him. "No, don't send him in. I'll take care of it. Just be ready." I shut down the phone before he could protest further.

I unlocked the stall, went to the sink, washed my hands, and checked my makeup. It was an unnecessary action, true, but it gave me a moment to think. By the time I came out of the bathroom, I had an idea that involved Hanuman's fantasy of being a professional thief.

Before returning to the main gallery, I casually walked by the back entrance, where I found half of what I expected: Lang had a state-of-the-art security system. The surprise, though, came from reading the name on the monitor: Eltech. It was a baby version of the setup used at the Museum of Natural History.

Lang's voice drifted through the gallery and the sound of

his deep, rich baritone called me again toward the front. He and Gale stood before an antique table packed with high-priced potables and fancy snacks arranged on silver trays. They each held a glass of bubbly, as did several of the guests. Apparently, I had missed Gale's salute, but went immediately to him to offer my congratulations.

It was a twofold maneuver on my part, mostly done to cover my butt and to make me look innocent and unaware if Walsh got excited and blew down the gig by storming the joint. Yet, as I navigated the crowd, I purposely took a route that allowed me to scrape my body against Hanuman's.

He turned to see who had rubbed breasts up against his back. I lingered in his path for a three count, stalled by an opportune wall of people.

The Winter Man didn't have crazy eyes; in fact, they were deep-set, soft brown in color and, I'll admit, pretty, with long lashes that most females, human and hematoman, would have gladly killed to have. I guess I half-expected him to reveal his madness through a maniacal expression, something like Charles Manson or Jeffrey Dahmer, but to tell the truth, Walsh had a wilder squint than Richard Hanuman did.

He was a brawny, handsome man, and the energy coming off him was subtle, calm, and certain. His blood pressure pumped his heart easily. His smile was beguiling. I could see how he could easily attract someone into a trusting relationship.

When I snuggled past him, I felt the bulge of a weapon worn in a side holster. He came prepared to protect himself. It was probably the same one he'd threatened his cousin with and used to kill Jow Lord.

The group separated, allowing me to slip through to join Gale at the buffet table. As I did, I glanced back toward Hanuman. He moved farther into the gallery, halting to study one of the sculptures before disappearing among the people and the art.

"What do you think of all this, Nicki?" Gale asked.

I looked down at the nibbles before answering. "I think it's wonderful. Ritzy, too. There's not one bit of processed cheese or green olives in this whole pâté'd affair."

"I mean about the turnout," he said.

I grinned at him. "I know. I think that's great, too. You deserve it. Justin, here, will give you the chance you need. These parties will probably get fancier and bigger, and then you'll probably have to go traveling."

"He's going to be a superstar," Lang added. "My Palm Beach buyers are very impressed with him."

Gale nodded, but instead of smiling over the prospect, his expression remained bland. There was an uncomfortable silence between the three of us, until he saw Bryan and disconnected to greet him. Lang excused himself as well, going off to hone his sales pitch, which providentially left me free to court Richard Hanuman.

I didn't have to do much. A minute later, he approached me.

"You're a friend of Mr. Fabrice's?" he asked.

"No," I said. "I don't know him, and I can honestly say that I really don't belong here. This is my first time in an art gallery like this."

"What do you do for a living?"

I put on a droopy look, hanging my head just a little. "I'm a working girl, if you know what I mean."

He nodded. "How did you get here, then?"

"A client. He's around somewhere."

Hanuman copied Lang's approach and gently placed a gloved hand on my shoulder, offering to lead me off into the heat of the exhibit. I went along, but as we walked, I angled us toward the back of the place.

"What do you do for a living?" I asked.

"I'm a doctor of holistic medicine," he answered. "Do you know what that is?"

"Sure. Herbs and stuff."

He shot me another smile. "That's right."

"But you know about art, too?"

"Oh, yes, and to tell you the truth, in the brief time I've been here this evening, I'm not that impressed with what I've seen."

"You're not? Why? I think it's all beautiful." A short pause, then, "Some of it's strange, but still nice."

"Well, some of it is nice, but for the most part, the artistic execution is not that good. It looks like he hurried on some of these pieces. Perhaps he wanted extra things to add to the show and did them at the last minute."

That was an understatement if I ever heard one. "Ah, but you must admit his little spirit catchers are entrancing. Have you seen them?"

He shook his head. "Show me?"

As we talked, I weaved through the gallery, eventually landing us beyond the bulk of the crowd. Here was one of the sections that held several of Gale's figurines. They were situated on a red formica table and accented with a set of blue rubber place mats. The place mats were probably worth about three bucks apiece, but the table itself was pure junk. I knew for a fact, because from 1951 to 1959, I had parked my butt at it every day. Gale had rummaged our storage room for that piece.

"Aren't these little things pretty?" I asked, pointing to them.

He looked thoughtful and caressed his chin with the back of his hand. There was a moment there when he forgot me and focused entirely on the softness of the glove he wore. Finally, he spoke. "Yes. These are quite lovely."

"They're quite expensive, too, I understand."

"I don't doubt it." He picked up one shaped like a dragon. On its back was a basket with a lid that pulled off. Except for the creature doing the toting, it was the same design as the fetish Hanuman had given Catherine Forest. "This is exquisite. On these, he did a magnificent job."

"I believe so, too. It's a shame that I don't have the money to buy it." Pausing for a two-count, I continued in a conspiratorial tone of voice. "If I had the ability and the courage, I'd steal one."

A mischievous glint came into his eyes. It was the same look a gambler gets when he sees a good bet in the making. "Well, I have the ability and courage, so why don't we just take it?"

I grazed him with an interested expression and then turned an appraising squint on the piece. "How?"

"Out the back exit."

"They've got an alarm system. I saw it when I went to the bathroom."

"Doesn't matter. I'll put it in my pocket, and we'll head that way. They'll see us go out, but they won't know if we have anything on us. We can stash it somewhere and come back later for it. In fact, let's take two. I want this one. Which one do you favor?"

Two women walked up to the display and began discussing the merits of spirit catchers. I was afraid their lingering might give Hanuman an opportunity to reconsider his future actions. It was time to see how good a thief he was. I picked up a figurine of a bat with spread wings, carrying its own little basket. "This one," I mouthed.

He covered my hand with his and clipped up the piece. "I'll do it for you. For a price."

I frowned at him. "Of course. Now it comes. What?"

"A night spent with you," he said. "Do the men tell you how beautiful you are, and do you believe them?"

I released my frown and smiled. "Of course. And for that reason alone, one figurine is not going to be enough."

"Would you like another, then?"

The two women stopped their conversation to look at us, whispering something about a five hundred dollar price tag and how fortunate we must be to have the means to collect in such quantity.

I pointed to another spirit catcher; this one a monkey. He palmed it and drew close to whisper in my ear. "Move toward the front of the gallery," he whispered. "Count to ten, turn and follow me. It should draw off these two busybodies onto something else. I'll wait for you by the door."

Mrs. Pollack's thoughts on Hanuman's kleptomania had been right all along. He angled away from the two women and made it look like he was handing me the pieces, instead slipping them easily into his jacket's breast pocket. Seeing what looked like a juggling act between us, one of the ladies made a remark about how some people disregard manners when they have money. Her friend announced a little louder that there were assistants available to help interested buyers, and there was no need to disrupt the display before the show was over. We ignored them and drew their scorn, complete with a comment about how the nouveau riche think that the whole world works like a five and dime store and they can just walk up to a cash register and a gum-chewing check-out girl.

The women moved off, and we separated. I did as Hanuman asked and counted to ten, then turned back and followed him. He was at the door promptly, nodding when he saw me approach. In the instant he looked away, I collected up all my vibrations and cloaked my presence.

For all the sophisticated gadgetry Lang employed, I thought he would have ordered a silent alarm system, but the moment Hanuman pushed the bar on the door, the noise started. It was such a surprise that I almost lost hold of my invisibility.

He rushed outside, and I along with him. We found ourselves in a narrow alley, running behind the buildings. Hanuman dashed through the dark like he had hematoman night vision, missing trash cans and water puddles. Shouts sounded from the gallery and after that, we were being chased by Walsh's team. I stuck with the Winter Man the whole way down this narrow conduit, looking for just the right place to corner him.

I paused at the edge of a trash container to remove my heels and come back into human focus. Hanuman looked back and motioned for me to hurry. I obliged him by hiking my skirt to gain some leg room to run. Gaining on him, I passed him by a yard. Footsteps slapped down the bricks behind us and voices cut in on the breeze.

If anything, Georgetown has more alleys per square block than any other part of Washington. I think a person could hide for days in the little slices between the buildings without anyone ever knowing he was there; so seeing an opportunity to get Hanuman under my hematoman control, I shoved him into one of these dark sluices.

"In here," I hissed.

He didn't hesitate, instead, rushing up to the iron gate at the street entrance of this passageway. The barred door to freedom was ajar just a bit, but the rust had frozen up the hinges, and though he pushed on it, the gate never budged. I knocked him out of the way and, using my supernatural strength, moved it open a few inches, just enough to allow him to slip through behind me. Once on the other side, we fled across the street, ducking into another alley behind the bistro that exhausted smells of grilling steak into our refuge.

You might wonder why I didn't scream for the officers. I can't really explain it except that it was exciting: a human killer and a hematoman killer sharing a few seconds together. Caught close in the shadows, I heard him taking hard breaths, and with my acute senses, I felt the rise of his homicidal passion. He drew his weapon.

Hanuman was about to slip out of our hiding place when I grabbed him, yanking the gun from his grip as I did. My power surprised him. In the darkness, I could see his mouth and eyes open wide. I tossed the pistol away, and tracked it with my radar, pinpointing the spot where it came to rest.

He countered my attack quickly by aiming for my head with his fist. I blocked his punch and kicked him in the groin. He went down to his knees, crippled, and unable to breathe for the pain. I knelt beside him, placing my hand behind his neck to pull his head toward my face. As I did, I pinched his jugular up and thrust my fangs into the vein.

Type A-positive. Nonsmoker. The tinny taste of metal. He was injecting himself with gold.

He put up a weak struggle, but quickly gave way to the hematoman enzymes entering his system. I sucked down for a minute more until he stopped struggling altogether. Releasing him, I pushed him against the alley wall.

"What's your soul's mission, Richard?" I whispered.

His words came slowly, haltingly. When they did, he phrased them with a euphoric lisp. "To move throughout eternity fighting those who would align with evil."

"Did you kill the hookers and Edward Bunt for their souls?"

"Yes."

"How?"

"I took their pineal glands from their brains while they were still alive." He paused, and with my night vision, I could see he looked dreamily into the darkness. "When the soul is separated from the living body and then the body is allowed to die, it can't reincarnate because it needs to be released from the physical state by death."

"So, then, death is the vehicle the soul needs in order to be reborn, and it uses it like a booster from a rocket to propel it into another body and another incarnation?"

"That is what I believe."

In his cosmology, he had not only combined cultures, he had muddled spiritual concepts.

"What have you done with the pineal glands of your victims?"

"I took them home and put them in the little baskets of my soul fetishes. I've made some lovely figurines just for this purpose." He reached into his pocket and brought out one of the stolen pieces, fondling it as he spoke. "This man has copied me. I should sue him."

"You can do that later," I said. "Did you use a food dehydrator to dry out this brain matter?"

"Yes, but it was only after I started placing them raw into the fetishes."

"Tell me more about why you did that."

"Sometimes, in the act of reincarnating, a person forgets certain things, and I became worried that by putting the glands into the figurines without mummifying them first, I might be allowing the evil to escape. I couldn't be sure if I was neglecting something important in my ignorance." He tossed a serious expression my way. "I'm the universe's last survivor's policy, you know. They killed my father, you see, so I had to take over for him. Without me, evil will win and the world will be destroyed."

The detectives were backtracking and fanning out. It was time to get the killer in the pokey.

"Richard, you will do as I say. Do you understand?"

"Yes, of course," he answered.

"You will confess everything to the police. You will show them your scrimshaw-handled instruments, and you will show them your collection of stolen souls. You will go with the officers quietly and cooperate fully. You will remember nothing of me. I am a shadow in your mind. I have no reality."

"Yes. I'll do as you wish."

I stood up, stopping to consider him before flagging down the cops, realizing as I did, that between the two of us, I was the true killer. He was just a madman who had no understanding of what he did.

I walked to the end of the tunnel, but it was a moment before I could signal my comrades, because I couldn't dismiss an abrupt encounter with troubling thoughts.

The Winter Man was a murderer whose private agenda was guided by insanity. Gale, on the other hand, was a murderer who, in the midst of a nervous breakdown, was temporarily overcome by this same madness. He and Richard Hanuman shared a frenzy that was driven by a fantasy, which to them, seemed realer than real.

Thinking about it made me jealous.

61

Friday, December 4

THE WEATHERMEN HAD, as usual, overshot the mark in predicting the snowstorm due to wallop Washington, D.C. Diane went out early to go shopping, and returned to join Ekua and me with a report on how the sun was shining and the temperature felt like it had risen into the forties.

"Where's Gale?" she asked, as she put on a pot of coffee and broke open a new box of pretzels.

"Upstairs, sulking," I answered.

"Well, he has the right to, I guess. Last night started out so well and ended up so weird. And the fight you two had. God. What does the studio look like?"

"I don't know. I got the hell out of there when he started squeezing tubes of paint at me."

"Was it that rise of the beast thing?" she asked.

"I suppose."

I must have put on a forlorn face without realizing it, because Ekua took up my hand and squeezed it. "He'll make it through. Don't worry. I did some checking with a couple of my older friends. They all told me that the first time the breakdown occurs is the worst. After that, the fits don't last as long nor are they so violent. I guess a person just adjusts to living out eternity."

"I feel afraid for him," I said, and meant it.

The evening had turned sour after Metro cornered Richard Hanuman. Lang came rushing out into the alley, snarling

327

something about how the man had stolen a piece from the gallery. This brought out the curious, and among them was the sum total of the Palm Beach contingent. They all left shortly after the episode and the bundle of money that Lang thought they were going to drop left with them, still in their ermine-lined coat pockets.

It was a lucky thing for me that the guests gathered in a huge clutch at the back entrance. They shielded me as I snuck back into the gallery and into the bathroom. I came out after a few minutes with my lipstick and blush freshened and the best surprised expression I could muster. Just as I turned to face the commotion, Gale stepped up to me. I had the perfect alibi, but he was immediately suspicious and there was nothing I could say that would change it. After we came home, he went on a rampage, tearing up the studio.

"What about Lang?" Diane asked. "He seemed pretty bent out of shape."

"Yes," I answered. "He had five very good designers he's going to have to pay."

"How much sold?" Ekua said. "Any ideas?"

"No. I did notice some interest in a couple of his paintings, but I don't know if any money exchanged hands."

"Maybe nothing moved last night," Diane said. "That might be the reason he blew up like he did."

I nodded, and wished that it could be true, but down in my unbeating heart, I knew it was me who he railed against. It was all right; I understood. I've been taking the blame for years. In Gale's mind, the problem with his career couldn't come from the fact that his art wasn't good enough to sell big time. To him, he figured his failure always stemmed from an external source, and I was usually it. This time he was right, but I hadn't done it on purpose.

The phone rang then, cutting off a sour comment I was

about to make. Diane picked it up, and following a brief hello, she handed it to me. It was Walsh.

"It came off, Nicki, thanks to you," he said. "Is Gale pissed?"

"He'll get over it."

"He thinks you had something to do with it, doesn't he?"

"No. He's not sure. I was accused, though." I sought to change the subject. "Did Hanuman cooperate?"

"Oh, yes, indeed, to the fullest. The squad stenographer is having a field day with this guy. I was right about his house, too. Lon Chaney would have loved it. There was shit sitting everywhere and a food dehydrator stuffed with pieces of human brains. He had his very own lab of horrors down in the basement, where he was turning out all kinds of pills and pickling Jow Lord's tongue."

"You saw that?"

"Yep. He admitted that it belonged to the pimp. He waived counsel and spilled his guts to it all, including telling us about six other hookers who are currently taking his gold treatments. We're still trying to track down those ladies."

"Hedging his bet against D.C. having a lot of bad weather, this year, huh?"

He chuckled. "He said the Farmer's Almanac called for it to be the worst winter on record."

"It has been," I said in a low voice.

His humor evaporated when he answered, "I know."

There was a lull in our conversation until I thought of a new subject. "What about your job?"

"My job? I'll be able to keep Chester in dog food for a while longer. The mayor is one happy lady."

"As she should be."

I could almost hear him grinning again, and smell the mint I knew he was sucking on. He continued. "You know, Art Anthony wanted me to tell you that position in the

Medical Examiner's Office is still open. Pays thirty-five a year."

"That's not nearly enough to fund my lifestyle, Joe."

"Will you at least think about it?"

"I've already told you the answer."

He was quiet for a moment; then: "I understand. Thought I'd try, anyway. The real reason I called was to thank you for helping me out."

"No problem. You know my number if you need me."

Gale came downstairs at that second, still wearing his white suit, now stained with a rainbow of acrylic paint and blood. His expression was bland, but I braced myself anyway, knowing after all these years when I was in store for another yelling match.

I quickly cut the conversation with Walsh short and hung up so I could greet Gale, hoping a smile would help turn his brooding mood off. Ignoring Diane and Ekua, who remained defiantly in their places, he sat down at the table to stare straight at me. "I can't remember what the day looks like anymore, Nicki," he said in a quiet tone. "It's an awful feeling."

"You're not human, Gale. You gave up all the things of mortality when you crossed over."

"I had no choice in becoming undead. I didn't ask for it. Neither did you. We were attacked; the both of us. Sucked down into unlife before we knew what had happened."

"Do you miss the daytime, then?"

"Yes. As an artist, I feel so limited in my perspective. It seems to me that the night doesn't have much color left to it." I saw the tip of his right fang as he gnawed on his bottom lip. His next sentence made me wince, not because of the fire he put behind the words, but because of sadness I heard there. "I'm leaving, Nicki. I've made the decision. It's been too long, too many years."

I thought of trying to convince him to stay, but the sounds I needed to do that just couldn't scale the sides of my throat.

Gale stood up slowly and leaned over, kissing me deeply on the lips. Drawing back, he cupped my chin in his hand. "I love you, Nicki. I'll love you forever." He didn't wait for me to answer. Instead, he turned and walked out of the kitchen.

I thought he was heading upstairs to the studio to pack his things. It didn't dawn on me what he truly meant about leaving until I heard him open the front door.

P. N. ELROD